A QUESTION OF TRUST

She felt momentary panic as her mind jumped to what Jackson expected from her now. "I—I had a very nice time. Thank you, Jackson."

He reached up and gently cupped her face. She flinched at the sudden contact of his flesh on hers. As his long slender fingers trailed gently across her face to her chin, lifting it, her bones seemed to melt. She was actually trembling now.

As Jackson's warm mouth closed over hers, skillfully playing and coaxing, Brandeis lost all presence of mind. She melted into him, her arms twining about his broad shoulders. Jackson crushed her to him, molding their bodies tightly together.

Brandeis' mind began to send out warning signals. She struggled, and finally managed to tear her mouth away.

"What's wrong, Brandeis? What did I do?" He grabbed her slender hands in his. "I don't know what happened to you, but I know it has to be something terrible because I've never known you to react this way around me. I'm not going to hurt you."

"I'm so sorry Jackson. I really did have a good time with you tonight. Thank you." She walked into her apartment and closed the door.

Jackson stood outside her door perplexed. They were just beginning to find that closeness they once had. Was it gone now?

BOOK YOUR PLACE ON OUR WEBSITE AND MAKE THE ARABESQUE ROMANCE CONNECTION!

We've created a customized website just for our very special Arabesque readers, where you can get the inside scoop on everything that's going on with Arabesque romance novels.

When you come online, you'll have the exciting opportunity to:

- View covers of upcoming books

- Read sample chapters

- Learn about our future publishing schedule (listed by publication month *and author*)

- Find out when your favorite authors will be visiting a city near you

- Search for and order backlist books from our online catalog

- Check out author bios and background information

- Send e-mail to your favorite authors

- Meet the Kensington staff online

- Join us in weekly chats with authors, readers and other guests

- Get writing guidelines

- AND MUCH MORE!

**Visit our website at
http://www.arabesquebooks.com**

HIDDEN BLESSINGS

Jacquelin Thomas

Pinnacle Books
Kensington Publishing Corp.
http://www.arabesquebooks.com

PINNACLE BOOKS are published by

Kensington Publishing Corp.
850 Third Avenue
New York, NY 10022

First Printing: June, 1998
10 9 8 7 6 5 4 3 2 1

Printed in the United States of America

ACKNOWLEDGMENTS

For Bernard
You believed in this book from its inception. Like no one else could, you walked every step of the road with me, offering never-ending support and self-sacrifice. My best friend, my love, for all this book has required of you and what future books will require of you in the years to come, I am deeply grateful.

For Nicole, Lauren, and Jonathan
I am truly blessed to have the three of you in my life. Thank you for being so patient and understanding. It has been an honor to be your mother. I love you.

For my mother and my grandmother
Thank you both for being wonderful role models, and for encouraging me to share my stories with the world.

For Carmellia, Tammie, Anita, Lorna, and Johanna
I am so thankful that without reservation all of you offered your never-ending support, your time, and your many words of encouragement. I couldn't have done this without the five of you.

For Billy Williams, Cheryl Williams, Debbie Lee-Long, and Cheryl Joseph
Thank you for being who you are—true Friends.

To the significant other people not mentioned by name, including relatives, no matter how large or seemingly small a part you played, please accept my deepest gratitude.

DEDICATION

This book is dedicated to

Nicole, Lauren, Jonathan,
Terrell, Larika, Bryant,
Alyssa, Mahalia, and Angelica

our future

Chapter 1

"Mom! Where are you? Are you ready?" Brandeis called as she let herself into her childhood home. Once in the living room, she eyed the rows and rows of family photographs on the textured wallpapered walls. She paused in front of the brick fireplace and gazed at her college graduation picture. Tears stung her eyes and she caught her lower lip between her teeth to keep it from trembling. Her graduation. It seemed a lifetime ago. But in actuality, it had been only two years.

Memories of the dreams she'd had at that time besieged her. Brandeis had had her life planned from childhood. Her goals were to be a lawyer, marry a wonderful man, and raise a family. At the time, it seemed an easy enough dream to accomplish. *So, why did everything have to change? Why did it have to happen?* She stared intensely at the photograph, her mind plagued with memories. Brandeis didn't hear her mother enter the room.

"Hello, dear. I didn't know you were here." Mona Taylor walked over and kissed her daughter on the cheek. She carried a pitcher, and as she moved about the room, Mona watered her Boston ferns.

Brandeis pulled her eyes away from the graduation picture and watched her mother go from plant to plant, talking and watering. She recalled her mother once saying that talking to plants and flowers helped them grow. Mona's voice was soothing and caressing. She supposed that was why Mona's plants thrived.

Brandeis sank down on the arm of a leather recliner. She examined her nails and grimaced when she caught sight of her chipped nail polish. After a heavy sigh, she knitted her fingers together.

"Mom, when do you think you'll be ready? You're still planning to go to the mall, aren't you?"

"Yes, I'm still planning to go. I'll be ready in about forty-five minutes," Mona answered without looking up from her plants.

"Oh." Brandeis sighed again, running slender fingers across the top of the chair.

Mona glanced up. "Are you in a hurry? I didn't mean to keep you waiting," she said, turning toward Brandeis.

"Not really. I'm not in any hurry." Brandeis pressed her right hand to her forehead. "It's just that I'm not feeling very well." A sensation of intense sickness and desolation swept over her. Swirling images of a man and a woman entwined ran through her head.

"What's wrong, sweetheart?" Mona watched as a mixed display of emotions washed over her daughter's face.

Brandeis was about to answer in the negative, but Mona cut her off with a wave of her hand.

"Now, don't tell me it's nothing. I can look at you and tell something's bothering you. Don't you worry about taking me to the mall. I can go some other time."

"Mom, we can still go today," Brandeis said. "I just want to make it quick." She eased down into the green leather recliner and settled back, trying to muster what she hoped passed for a natural smile.

Mona stopped watering her plants and thoroughly surveyed her only child. "I declare, child, you don't look well at all. I'm worried about you, dear. Why don't you go on upstairs and lie down? As a matter of fact, just plan on staying here tonight."

"Thanks, Mom." Brandeis, having spent the last two nights at Mona's house, was secretly grateful not to have to go back to her apartment yet. "I'll go upstairs and take a nap. I'm sure I'll feel better after I get some rest." She stood up slowly.

"I hope so, dear. I hope so." Mona placed the pitcher of water on the fireplace mantel, then proceeded to fluff the overstuffed pillows on her sofa and love seat.

Brandeis hated having her mother so worried about her. She knew her mother remained unconvinced about her daughter's health and happiness, even though she tried to appear otherwise.

A heaviness centered in Brandeis' chest as she headed upstairs. Tears threatened to spill and she blinked several times to hold them back. Brandeis rushed into her old room. She stood with her back pressed against the closed door. Putting her hands to her face, she let her tears run free. Pain squeezed her heart as she thought of Martin St. Charles. *Damn you!* she thought angrily. *It's been a year and I'm still suffering. I hate you for having hurt me this way!*

Brandeis took a deep breath. Slowly, she made her way over to the full-size bed. She closed her eyes and fell into a troubled sleep.

An hour later, Brandeis awoke with a start and jolted upright. Was that the doorbell she'd heard? As she walked down the hallway to the bathroom, she heard voices. Her mother's and that of a man. *Who is here?* she wondered. Brandeis knew her mother didn't have many male friends.

After quickly washing her face, Brandeis pulled her shoulder-length, dark brown hair into a ponytail and rinsed her mouth. She headed downstairs.

She paused halfway down the stairs to sneak a peek at her

mother's guest. At first glance, Brandeis was momentarily taken aback by the handsome man sitting on the damask love seat. He looked very powerful, his chest broad and muscular, out of place against the rich, green and gold floral patterns. Gold eyeglasses framed his square face with its smooth, coffee-colored complexion. His firm mouth curled as if on the edge of laughter. He seemed familiar somehow, like an old friend. She struggled to place him in her mind.

Jackson Gray!

Why, she hadn't seen him in eight years, and he hadn't been wearing glasses back then. She had had such a huge crush on him. But that was a long time ago.

Brandeis smiled to herself when she heard her mother's girlish giggle. She walked quietly down the rest of the stairs and strolled into the living room to join them. "Hi. Am I interrupting?"

"Why no, dear. Come sit next to me." Mona motioned for her daughter to join her on the sofa. "You remember Jackson, don't you?"

"Of course, I remember him," Brandeis said softly before raising her eyes to look at him. She was mildly surprised to find him watching her. "How are you?"

Jackson stood up. "I'm fine. It's good seeing you again, Brandeis. The last time I saw you, you were wearing braids and braces." He couldn't seem to help smiling as he held out his hand to her.

By sheer force of willpower, Brandeis made herself breathe deeply and evenly, and then advanced to take his outstretched hand. "Ugh, please don't remind me about the braces," she said.

Despite the thrill she'd felt when he first spoke to her, she had not yet granted Jackson one single smile. It wasn't that she hadn't felt like smiling, but the habits of distance and reserve were hard to break. And perhaps, she told herself, it would be unwise to do so. You could never tell about men.

This was the first time a man had been so close to her

in a long time. She trembled slightly at the touch of his hand. After gently easing her hand from his, she picked up a hand-embroidered pillow, and hugging it to her, sat next to her mother. Brandeis hoped Jackson couldn't sense her nervousness.

They sat in uncomfortable silence until Mona took charge.

"Jackson was just telling me he's accepted a position here in Brunswick at the Davis, Kinard & Donaldson Law Offices. He's going to head their criminal defense department."

"Congratulations!" Brandeis was impressed. DKD was one of the top law firms in the state of Georgia. "It's a good law firm."

He smiled and asked, "How do you like working for Frank Matthews? Did you know that I almost clerked for him during my summers away from law school? I ended up clerking for a judge in D.C."

Brandeis let go of some of the tension in her body. "I didn't know that," she said. "He's been so wonderful to me. I've learned a lot from him."

"He's a good bankruptcy lawyer." The beginning of a smile tipped the corners of his mouth. "Are you still thinking about going to law school?"

"I was accepted at Temple University. I'd planned to go last fall, but . . ." Brandeis faltered.

"We were just about to have dinner. Will you join us?" Mona interrupted. She patted her daughter's hand and smiled.

Brandeis knew her mother could see the appreciation in her eyes. She didn't want to go into details as to why she had decided not to attend law school. It was still too painful for her to discuss.

"Are you sure you don't mind?" Jackson asked.

Mona nodded. "We would love to have you eat dinner with us."

"In that case, I'd love to stay. I really have missed your cooking, Mrs. Taylor. Thanks for including me."

"There's no need to thank me, Jackson. You're a part of this family."

As Mona stood, she smoothed her hand over her hair in an attempt to retrieve an errant curl. Still an attractive woman who looked years younger than she was, her caramel complexion contrasted nicely with her silver-gray hair. Mona had a genial mouth and sparkling brown eyes. She ran a slender hand down her skirt to remove invisible wrinkles. "Why don't we head to the table?"

Brandeis smiled at her mother's gestures. Mona was always well-groomed. Brandeis was proud of that quality in her mother. As a little girl, she'd wanted to grow up to be just like Mona.

Brandeis often wished she looked like her beautiful mother, but she didn't. She looked exactly like her father, a man who'd caused her mother nothing but grief. Brandeis often wondered if her mother saw her husband each time she looked into her daughter's face.

During their five years of marriage, Brandeis' father had hurt her mother deeply with his adultery and abusive ways. His final betrayal occurred when Brandeis was just four years old. He was killed in an automobile accident, but he didn't die alone. His lover and their child died with him. Although Mona never talked about it, Brandeis supposed she'd suffered greatly. Once, a few years back, she asked her mother why she'd stayed with him.

Mona had looked at Brandeis for what seemed a long time and then replied quietly, "I stood before the Lord and my church and I promised to stay with this man until death. I loved him and I tried to keep our marriage intact. I fought to keep my family together."

"Brandeis?" Mona's voice invaded her thoughts. "Are you coming?"

"I'll be right there, Mom." Brandeis took a deep breath and steeled her back. She prayed for strength to get through this evening. *Why did you have to invite Jackson to stay for dinner, Mom?* She immediately chided herself for thinking such a selfish thought. Jackson was a very old and dear friend. He had been the big brother she'd never had.

Jackson pushed his glasses up on the bridge of his nose as Brandeis eased off the sofa and followed Mona into the dining room. He stood to get a better look at the woman he hadn't seen since she was sixteen years old. She had grown into a very beautiful woman. Tall and graceful, her facial bones were delicately carved, her mouth full. Wisps of curling hair framed her honey-hued face. Almond-shaped eyes the color of amber contributed to her exotic appearance.

He was entranced by the silent sadness of her face. He'd felt the slight trembling when he'd held her hand, but put it out of his mind while he savored the feel of her soft flesh. Warm and soft. Just touching her reminded him he hadn't had a woman in a long time. Calling to mind the nervous expression on Brandeis' face, he wondered why his old friend seemed so nervous around him now. He supposed he should have done a better job of keeping in touch over the years, instead of sending only the occasional cards at Christmas and birthdays.

While they took seats at the oak dining table, Jackson studied her openly for a moment, noting again the signs of tension in her face and hands.

Brandeis sat next to Mona and across from Jackson. Dinner consisted of a caesar salad, succulent roast beef, baked potatoes, green beans, buttery rolls, and an ice-cold pitcher of lemonade. All heads bowed and Mona murmured a short prayer of thanks before they began their meal.

Brandeis helped herself to a thin slice of roast beef, a baked potato, and half a glass of lemonade.

Mona stopped eating. "Honey, aren't you going to eat more than that? I declare, that's not enough to feed a gnat."

"Mom, I don't have much of an appetite," Brandeis

said quietly. "I'd rather start with a little. If I want more, I'll take it."

Jackson quickly came to her rescue. "I like Bran's way of thinking. I hate to see food wasted while so many people are starving in the world."

Brandeis wrinkled her nose at her mother.

Mona laughed as Jackson murmured, "Some things never change, do they?"

In spite of herself, Brandeis chuckled.

Conversation was kept to a minimum while they ate their meal. After a second thin slice of roast beef, Brandeis turned to her mother. "Mom, dinner was delicious," she said. "I love your roast beef."

"I agree. Dinner was great," Jackson added. He glanced at Brandeis and smiled.

Brandeis returned a quick smile. Biting her bottom lip, she looked away. "Why don't the two of you go back into the living room. I'll clear the table and do the dishes."

"I'll help you," Jackson offered.

"N-no, Jackson. I can handle it." Brandeis cocked her head to the side. "Besides, when did you start doing dishes? The way I remember it, you used to disappear when it was time to do them at our family gatherings."

"I've had to wash dishes ever since I left home. I'm actually quite good at it. I can even cook," he added proudly.

"Yeah, right! I bet you have a dishwasher and a microwave, don't you?"

Jackson chuckled. "Yes, I have a dishwasher and a microwave."

Brandeis laughed. It was the first real laugh since she'd come downstairs. It sounded like music to his ears.

"Mom is still in the ice ages. I have to use my hands—"

"*Your hands,* Bran?" Mona shook her head. Turning to Jackson, she said, "That girl won't put her hands in dishwater unless she is wearing gloves. Doesn't want dishpan hands, I suppose."

"Mom! I think it's time for the two of you to go into the living room and let me get to work."

"Don't forget your gloves, dear," Mona called as she and Jackson headed into the living room.

"Mom!" Brandeis laughed.

Jackson stopped in midstride and turned. "You sure you don't want me to help you? I really don't mind."

Brandeis shook her head. "Just keep Mom company for me."

Brandeis stood by the kitchen door to observe Mona and Jackson as they retreated to the living room. She could feel the tension leaving her body. The strength of his personality came through his eyes. His gaze was compelling, sharply intelligent, and deeply unsettling to her.

She quickly cleared the dishes off the dining room table, then proceeded to run water in the stainless steel sink. The newly remodeled oak kitchen was the newest addition in a long line of renovations that had taken place in her childhood home over the years. All Mona needed now was a dishwasher and a microwave, she thought.

A half hour later, with the dishes washed and dried, Brandeis strolled into the living room and took a seat next to her mother on the sofa. Jackson had reclaimed his place on the love seat. As soon as there was a break in the conversation, Jackson directed his gaze to her.

"So, tell me, Bran, do you really enjoy being a bankruptcy paralegal?"

She nodded enthusiastically. "Yes. I love it. I love the researching portion most of all. You know, checking property records, verifying taxes owed and tax liens."

"I enjoy research, too," Jackson said. "Unfortunately, I don't always get to do my own. Do you primarily work with consumer BKs?"

"I work mostly with corporate bankruptcies. Chapter Elevens."

"Are you planning to attend law school this fall?" he asked.

"Er, no. I-I don't think I'll be going." Her senses, already heightened, quickened to an acute perception. Here was a man who would not easily be fooled. This man had the power to look within her and lay bare not only her secrets, but her most closely held hopes and desires.

"But wh—"

"I think Brandeis just wants to wait a while, to see if going to law school is what she really wants to do." Mona looked to her daughter as if seeking approval.

Brandeis nodded. "Law school puts you under a lot of pressure. I think it's best that I wait for a while. To make sure I can handle it. It's just too expensive to go and mess up." Brandeis wondered helplessly how much of her discomfort Jackson could now sense. *Anything, anything please, but not the truth. Not now.*

Turning toward Mona, she added, "Mom, I think I'd better go back upstairs and lie down. I'm still not feeling well." Brandeis looked at Jackson and said, "It was nice seeing you again. Oh, when you talk to your mother, please tell her that I said hello and that I miss her. It hasn't been the same since she moved to Texas."

Before Jackson could respond, Brandeis was gone.

Once upstairs, in the safety of her room, Brandeis looked in the mirror, intending to take down her ponytail. She gasped. Instead of her own reflection, the image of a man glared back at her. She shut her eyes. When she opened them again, the image was gone. Brandeis slumped weakly onto her bed, her heart thumping in her chest.

She fought to still her racing mind. The image had appeared so real. She began to wonder if she had any control over her own imagination. That, she told herself, was just foolishness. She wasn't crazy. Not yet. Brandeis slammed a mental door on the man's image and marched over to the mirror again, this time, in defiance of her fear. Maybe she couldn't control her dreams, but she could certainly control her mind while awake. She glared at her own reflection and made a vow not to let what had happened to her control the rest of her life. With studied deliberation she concentrated on preparations for bed.

After crawling in bed, Brandeis glanced around her room. It was a beautiful room and had always made her feel safe. Mona had such a flair for decorating. The room's mint-green walls and forest-green drapes were a perfect complement to the cherry wood Queen Anne furniture. A forest green-and-ivory floral border around the ceiling matched the colors in the English cabbage rose patterned comforter set and the rugs. The polished hardwood floors gleamed to perfection.

The boisterous ringing of the phone echoed through the room. From a distance, Brandeis heard her mother's voice calling her, telling her to pick up the bedside phone extension.

"H-hello," Brandeis said slowly, her voice, a lifeless monotone.

"Bran? Hi, this is Carol. I thought I'd find you at your mom's, so I took a chance and called. I've been worried about you."

"I'm okay, Carol. Really."

"Look, I know what today is and how it must be affecting you," Carol went on." If you want to be alone, I understand. But whenever you're ready to talk about it, just know that I'm here for you. Anytime."

"I know," Brandeis whispered. "I can't talk about it yet. I just can't." A hot tear rolled down her cheek.

"It will get easier. I promise you. It'll get easier. I hope and pray that Martin is rotting in hell for what he did to you!"

At the mention of his name, Brandeis finally yielded to convulsive sobs. She didn't tell her best friend that she had seen Martin's image in her mirror only minutes earlier. Instead, she mumbled, "I-I'm s-sorry. Now is just not a g-good time to t-talk."

"You have nothing to be sorry about, Bran. Just don't

try to keep all this stuff inside. You have to get it out," Carol advised.

"I know." Brandeis sniffed loudly. "I'll be fine. I'll call you t-tomorrow." She bit her lip to control the sobs. After placing the receiver back in the cradle, she rubbed the palms of both hands across her eyes.

Brandeis tried to fall asleep but couldn't. Every time she closed her eyes, she could see a man and woman entwined, groping, struggling. Frustrated, Brandeis turned on her bedside lamp and propped herself up in bed. Retrieving a copy of the latest *Legal Assistant Today* from the nightstand, she flipped slowly through the pages. Halfway through an article that had caught her eye, she drifted off to sleep.

She dreamt that Martin came into her room. He crept to her bed and knelt beside it, whispering soft words of love. The moonlight cast a golden glow about him. She felt his fingertips skim down her arm to rest lightly on her wrist. Her arm burned from his touch, and she winced. She pulled with all her might, but the harder she struggled, the more her strength was given over to him. He clutched her more tightly. Her scream was a muffled sigh, pathetically inaudible. A few moments later, Brandeis came completely awake. She choked back a cry, frightened, electrified. She huddled in her bed, her eyes searching her bedroom. Finding nothing out of the ordinary, she took a deep breath and put her head back on the pillow.

Jackson could not get over the changes in Brandeis. She was not the same girl he remembered. And in more ways than one. Brandeis was bright and self-assured. At least, that's the way he'd always remembered her. Not some fragile beauty who seemed afraid of her own shadow. Why such an extreme change? He had to admit he was completely baffled.

He was glad to be home, Jackson admitted. Life in the big city was too much for this small town boy. He missed the Sea Islands most. When most people discovered his Georgia origins, they immediately thought of Atlanta or Savannah. To Jackson's way of thinking, nothing compared to the beauty of his beloved Brunswick.

Surrounded by live oaks with stout, gnarled trunks, as well as with pine trees and other trees of foreign origin, Brunswick was a picturesque city. In the eighteen seventies, the poet Sidney Lanier fell in love with the small coastal community. Brunswick had inspired him to write a poem entitled, "The Marshes of Glynn." Jackson could certainly understand why.

The one thing he hadn't missed about this town was the way news traveled. Around Brunswick, gossip spread like wildfire. He'd only been back three weeks and his phone had never stopped ringing. Friends, old girlfriends, and the like. But there was only one person he'd wanted to hear from. Brandeis. When he hadn't, he decided to take matters into his own hands.

Jackson took his glasses off and laid them on the nightstand next to the bed. He rubbed his eyes and yawned. Jackson lay back on the pillow, his thoughts on Brandeis and her mysterious behavior earlier tonight. He wondered if she had been distant with him because he hadn't kept in better touch. But then again, neither had she. They were both at fault.

Before Jackson finally drifted off to sleep, he decided he would have to get to know Brandeis all over again. She was *not* the same girl he'd dreamed of all these years.

Chapter 2

Brandeis opened the door to her office with one hand. She carried her briefcase in the other, and her purse thrown over her shoulder. Dropping the briefcase and her purse onto a chair, she smoothed the silk blouse beneath her black pinstriped suit and headed down the narrow hallway on her way to the employee's lounge.

As she passed the secretarial bay, Brandeis almost collided with a strikingly beautiful woman, the firm's only legal secretary.

"Oh, good morning, Carrie."

"Good morning to you, too. My, don't you look nice today."

Carrie's perfect mouth was curved upward in a smile of feigned delight. "Thank you," Brandeis said.

Not wanting to carry on a long conversation, Brandeis hurried to the employee's lounge where she promptly fixed herself a cup of strong coffee. As she stirred the steaming liquid, she stifled a yawn. Goodness, she was so tired. Somehow, she'd have to put an end to her nightmares. *As if such a thing were possible,* she thought.

Back in her office, Brandeis frowned as she surveyed the

clutter on her desk. Folders, case files, and papers were strewn about. Open law books were scattered across the desk and on a chair standing in the far corner of her office. In two days, her boss, Mr. Matthews, had to argue an important motion. He was counting on her to do the necessary research and summarize her findings.

As Brandeis gathered documents, she wondered how long it would take her to complete her project. *Darn!* she thought, *I have so much work to do.* Finally, she had her sources organized. Brandeis glanced around, satisfied. She was now prepared to work.

Four hours later, she was finished. She stretched and stood up. Walking over to her window, Brandeis was stunned to see it had been raining. She had been too immersed in her project to notice anything. The raindrops on the leaves glittered, making them look as if they had been sprinkled with a million diamonds. Brandeis longed to take a stroll outside. She wanted to savor the sweet scent of magnolias and the rich smell of damp earth.

Her attention was drawn to a couple strolling along the sidewalk. They were holding hands, looking into each other's eyes and smiling. It was obvious they were very much in love. Brandeis watched as they passed, her eyes glued to them until they disappeared behind a huge oak tree. She leaned her head against the window pane. Brandeis knew she would never experience that wondrous feeling of loving and being loved. She knew she could never again take the chance of being hurt.

The weekend finally arrived, much to Brandeis' delight. She loved driving across the bridge from Brunswick to Jekyll Island. She enjoyed taking long walks along the sandy beach.

Brandeis stood looking out toward the ocean, brilliant with a thousand sparkling wavelets, but she noticed nothing. Her eyes were clouded with visions of the past, reliving the agony of that final scene. She shivered in spite of the hot, humid weather. The memories were painful and Brandeis wondered if the suffering would ever diminsh. If she would ever be able to trust another man again.

She walked down the long strip of beach, ignoring turning heads and admiring glances, searching out a vacant arca. Upon finding one, she sat down and hugged her knees to her chest. Brandeis closed her eyes, put her head down, and tried to shut out the picture of the couple, naked and writhing on a bed. Her stomach churned with nausea as she remembered vividly how everything had happened, like a horrible nightmare.

The tide rolled in slowly, sneaking like a thief in the night. Then it dashed away, taking the evidence of her footprints. The sky was clear. Brown pelicans flew in formation just inches above the water. Brandeis envied the fact that they could be so carefree. How she longed to feel that way again. Glancing down at her watch, she decided it was time to head back across the bridge to Brunswick.

Brandeis stood up and brushed the sand off her indigo-colored fleece shorts. She bent to retrieve her sandals and spotted a sand dollar covered with velvety, reddish-brown spines. As she reached to pick it up, she heard her name. Brandeis spied a young woman in a pair of red shorts and a bright white T-shirt running toward her.

"Brandeis! How . . . are you?" Carol Chaney stopped to catch her breath. Her chest heaved laboriously.

"I'm fine." Brandeis broke into an open, friendly smile. "But are you okay?" She watched her friend take slow, deep breaths. As tiny beads of perspiration formed on Carol's forehead, her skin glistened like dark chocolate.

"I . . . will be . . . as soon as I catch my breath." Carol paused for a minute to fan her face with her hand. "There. That's much better." She reached up and fingered through her short, curly hair. "Did you get my message? I called your apartment this morning. I wanted to know if you would sing a solo at church on Sunday?"

"I stayed at Mom's again last night and haven't checked my messages yet. Sure. I'll be glad to sing on Sunday. You know, I almost forgot that you're in charge of the Easter program."

Brandeis was thoughtful for a moment. "How did you know I was here?"

Carol shook her head. Her medium-sized gold hoops swung back and forth. "I didn't. I just came to Jekyll to collect shells."

"What on earth for?" Brandeis raised her perfectly arched eyebrows slightly.

"For lamps." Carol giggled at the bewildered expression on her friend's face. "You've seen the glass lamps with the shells inside, haven't you?" When Brandeis nodded, Carol continued. "Well, I realized it was cheaper for me to buy an empty base and put the shells in myself. I already have the shade and the base. I just need the shells. Since you're here, wanna help?"

Brandeis laughed. "No. I think I'll pass. Leave it to you to find a cheaper way of doing something."

"That's me—cheap!" With her hands on her ample hips, Carol looked Brandeis up and down. "You're looking well, girlfriend. I've really missed spending time with you. Seems like the only time I really see you anymore is at church. It's been a long time since we've done anything together."

"I know. I've been keeping really busy at work and by the time I make it home, I'm just too exhausted to do anything else."

"I understand. I just miss you."

Brandeis smiled. "I miss you too, Carol. I think it's been good for me to stay busy though."

Carol nodded. "Well, don't forget, we need to start shopping around for my wedding gown."

"But your wedding is still two years away. Why, I don't know," Brandeis added. "I've never met anybody who hardly could wait to become engaged, and then insisted on waiting two years to get married."

"I told you why," Carol said, speaking slowly, as if to a child. "I want this to be the biggest wedding this town has ever seen. I need time to save enough money to pay for my fancy wedding and reception. James and I don't want bills hanging over our heads after we're married."

Brandeis smiled at her best friend. "I think you're absolutely nuts."

Carol simply shrugged and grinned. "But you love me, don't you?"

"Yes, I love you, so I suppose I should question my sanity, huh?"

Carol threw back her head and laughed. "I would most definitely question it if you *didn't* love me. Look at me." She twirled around slowly. "What's not to love?"

Brandeis joined in the laughter. "I've got to go. I promised to take Mom to the mall this afternoon. Her car is back in the shop *again*."

"I don't know why Mrs. Taylor insists on keeping that car."

"I don't, either. It's not like she's keeping it for sentimental reasons. I think she just wants to be difficult."

The friends said goodbye. Brandeis began to walk away, but turned around when she heard Carol call her back.

"Oh, I know what I meant to tell you," Carol said. "Guess who's back in town?"

"Who?" Brandeis had a feeling she knew what was coming.

"Jackson Gray. I saw him at the mall last night. Girlfriend, he was looking good."

"For your information, *I've seen him already*." Brandeis laughed at the silly smirk on Carol's face. "He came by Mom's house the other night. The three of us had dinner together. Did he tell you he's heading the criminal defense department over at DKD?"

Carol shook her head, causing her earrings to swing back and forth. "No. Really? That's wonderful. I'm happy for him. He is one fine brother, don't you think?"

Brandeis shrugged. "He's okay. I didn't recognize him at first. I think it was the glasses that threw me off."

"I remember you used to have one serious crush on him." Carol's face wore a broad smile.

Brandeis frowned. "Now, why would you bring that up? That was a long time ago."

Carol stepped back with her hands on her hips. "Are you telling me that you're no longer attracted to Jackson?"

"That's right, I'm not," Brandeis lied. "And wipe that smug look off your face. I am not interested in Jackson Gray. That was a long time ago. Really." Brandeis tried to calm her swirling emotions. She wasn't sure *how* she felt about Jackson's return to Brunswick.

Carol watched her friend's face and grinned. "Okay. But I have one question."

"What is it?"

"Who are you trying to convince?"

"No one," Brandeis stated firmly, trying to avoid Carol's probing eyes. "Believe me when I say this, I'm not interested in Jackson. He's just an old friend and that's all he'll ever be. Even if I wanted more than that, it could never be. Not after what happened."

"But—"

Brandeis looked down at her watch. "Oh, Carol, I've really got to head back across the bridge. Mom is probably getting worried. I should have been there by now."

They hugged briefly and Brandeis left Carol walking the sandy beach in search of shells.

On Monday, Clayton Mintz came rushing into Jackson's office, out of breath. He placed his leather briefcase on a visitor's chair and sat down in another, facing Jackson's huge granite and black melamine desk. As he waited for Jackson to finish his notes, he admired the black leather sofa, positioned next to the door. Jackson's choices of African-American art were displayed proudly on the walls. The black lacquered bookshelves held African statues, as well as law books and journals. A matching conference table with twelve chairs stood in the corner of the huge, second-floor office.

The young man waited patiently for Jackson to complete his instructions to his secretary, Fran Bailey, whom he'd called into his office.

"I asked for a dismissal on the Browning matter. They're probably going to release him soon," Clayton said, when the woman had gone.

Jackson sat back in his chair and stretched. "So, she didn't show again, huh? This is the third time the District Attorney has asked for a continuance."

"Exactly. No one knows where she is, or how to reach her . . ."

"You did the right thing, Clay. I had a feeling it would end up like this. Our client was telling the truth, I knew it. After you add your notes regarding the dismissal, give me the file. I'll make my notes and return it to you."

Clay nodded in agreement.

Jackson smiled as the young man grabbed his briefcase and prepared to exit. "Clay. Good job. Keep it up."

Clay grinned and nodded. "Thank you. I really appreciate your giving me the chance to handle the case. To be honest with you, I thought I would spend my first year attending seminars or doing research. I didn't think I'd get the chance to handle a case like this, at least not for a while."

"I knew you were ready," Jackson told him. "You've worked very hard to prove yourself. You deserved a chance."

After Clay left his office, Jackson's mind drifted to Brandeis. She was extremely beautiful and very intelligent and had always known exactly what she wanted out of life. Brandeis was not weak, he thought. She was strong and proud and brave, a kindred spirit. So, why had she delayed going to law school? Had something happened? If so, what could it have been to keep her from obtaining her law degree? Becoming a lawyer had been Brandeis' dream, that and having a good marriage and raising a family.

Jackson was still pondering Brandeis' decision as he put papers into his worn briefcase. He'd have to stop thinking of Brandeis for a while. He needed to spend his evening at the library. He had to argue a complicated motion in a few days, and he still needed to complete his research.

Brandeis strolled down the library aisle looking for the various legal titles she'd need for the case she was researching. After finding the books she'd been looking for, she headed toward the copy machine. Her head was bowed down over the machine when she heard her name called in a whisper.

"Hi, Brandeis." Jackson touched her shoulder.

His strong grip sent a flood of warmth through her. "Oh, Jackson! You scared me half to death!" Brandeis placed a shaking hand to her chest.

Jackson chuckled as he pushed his glasses along his nose. "I'm sorry. I just wanted to say hello. I'm here researching a case."

"Me, too."

Jackson looked at his watch. "I'm almost done. If you'd like, we could grab a bite to eat when you're finished."

Brandeis cleared her throat and hoped her voice would come out right. "T-thanks for the offer, but I've already m-made plans. Some other time, maybe." The words were spoken in an unconvincing squeak. She cleared her throat again. She didn't dare meet his eyes for fear he could tell she was lying.

"No problem. Can I—"

She pretended to glance at her watch and said quickly, "I'm sorry, I've got to go, I should have been home an hour ago. See you later." She dropped the book she'd been holding on a nearby table and dashed off.

Brandeis felt like a first-class heel as she practically ran out of the library. Jackson was her longtime friend and didn't deserve to be treated so badly. Why couldn't she stop herself from behaving so rudely? She wondered. They had such a long history together and her behavior now was absolutely ridiculous.

But everything that had come before that dreadful night now seemed like a dream. Almost as if it had been some figment of her imagination, some fantasy. Yes, she had become herself—her new self—by leaving her old self behind. She had allowed the tragedy to devour the old in her, and thus, she had grown. Brandeis was now a different person. Jackson never again would see the pampered happy little girl he remembered.

Brandeis knew it would take more than just time before she would ever let Jackson inside her fortress. It would take a miracle.

Later, at home, Jackson wondered what was going on with Brandeis. It was obvious she had been hurt by someone. He assumed she'd recently been involved. The relationship must have ended badly because she seemed a little gun-shy when it came to men. He had hoped to learn more from Mona, but she was very evasive when he asked about Brandeis and her relationships. However, Mona had made it clear she thought it was in her daughter's best interest to start dating again. More specifically, to start dating *him*. Jackson admitted to himself that he wholeheartedly agreed with Mona.

His mind drifted to his first week back in Brunswick. After getting settled into his condo, Jackson had decided to drive around and reacquaint himself with the small, but delightful city. He had driven along Newcastle Street, past the shrimp boats and Victorian houses from when Brunswick was a busy nineteenth-century shipping center for lumber and naval stores.

Jackson drove by Lover's Oak, at Albany and Prince Streets. Local legend had it that an American Indian and his love met beneath its branches. Memories of when he and Brandeis were younger assailed him. She was the little sister he'd never had. At least, until she reached her teens.

That's when his brotherly feelings had started to change. He remembered the last time he'd seen her and how she'd set his blood to boil. He'd had to remind himself that she was only sixteen.

Mona had given him Brandeis' phone number, but he hadn't wanted to call before confirming it was fine with Brandeis. So far, she hadn't given him much of a chance to convey his interest in her. Perhaps she wouldn't choose to pursue a relationship with him. Maybe she still saw him as her big brother. He hoped not.

Her decision not to attend law school really puzzled him. He knew becoming a lawyer had always been her dream, just as it had always been his. Years ago, Brandeis had made him promise to come back to Brunswick after law school and open a practice. They would become partners, she'd said. *What made you change your mind?* Jackson wondered. *Who made you change your mind?* Jackson knew Brandeis well enough to know that he would have to be patient if he wanted answers to his questions.

Chapter 3

A tower of papers littered the left side of Brandeis' desk, and a copy of the *Bankruptcy Rules and Forms* handbook lay open on the right. Weariness enveloped her as she tried to concentrate on her research. She was exhausted. She'd finally fallen asleep around three in the morning. Then, she'd had to be up again at six o'clock, for work.

She looked up from her computer screen when she heard footsteps coming toward her. Through eyes narrowed with suspicion, Brandeis watched Carrie McNichols saunter into her office. Leaning back in her chair, she asked, "What is it now, Carrie?"

Carrie sat in one of the chairs facing Brandeis. She admired her long, perfectly polished fingernails, and complained in her soft southern drawl. "Since you're the senior paralegal around here, I think you should be the one to sit Kyla down and have a long talk with her. She's impossible to work with!"

Brandeis groaned inwardly. She wished she liked Carrie. Heaven knows, she'd tried! In her opinion, the woman was impossible. She wanted everything handed to her on a silver platter. "What's the problem this time?" Brandeis kept her voice even, noncommittal.

"This morning I told her to type the memorandum for the Desi matter. I just checked a few minutes ago and it hasn't been done. She refuses to do anything I tell her!"

"Have you considered what her priorities may be? Carrie, please try to get along with her. She is a temp and will be here for only a few days."

"Well!" Carrie huffed. "Marlena told me Kyla was here to help anyone who needed her. I swear! I don't know why I ever bother to come to you at all. I should know by now not to expect your support!"

"You'd have my support," Brandeis said coolly, ignoring the sarcasm in Carrie's voice, "if you'd start doing your job around here, instead of expecting other people to do it for you."

Anger flared in Carrie's eyes. "I'm the only legal secretary for four lawyers and five paralegals. I work very hard!"

"Not quite," Brandeis said quickly.

Carrie managed to look wounded, causing Brandeis to suffer a pang of remorse. She wished she hadn't lost her temper so easily with her. If only Carrie weren't so exasperating.

"I'm sorry I snapped at you," Brandeis said. "But you caught me at a bad time."

"Oh, I'm sorry." Carrie didn't look apologetic at all. In fact, she actually had perked up. "Are you having man trouble, honey chile?"

Brandeis smiled smoothly, betraying nothing of her annoyance. "Is that all, Carrie?"

She pouted, then sighed. "Um, sure . . . I guess I'd better get back to my desk."

Brandeis looked closely at the woman whose selfish and haughty manners were so irritating to her. "'Carrie, please try to get along with Kyla."

The bright rays from the afternoon sun fell across Carrie's light brown, tinted hair, making the tresses shine with honey-blonde highlights. She was an attractive woman, her body petite, feminine, and voluptuous, her tawny skin flaw-less.

Carrie rose from her chair as fluidly as a dancer and hastily left the office, slamming the door behind her.

Brandeis massaged her temples and wished she'd called in sick today. She hadn't slept well at all, and was in no mood to put up with Carrie and her hysterics. The clock on her wall told her that she still had another three hours before the official end of the day. Carrie would leave right at five o'clock, as she usually did, freeing Brandeis to work in solitude for a couple of hours before calling it a day.

Brandeis had no idea how long she stood in the shower scrubbing. After having put in long hours at the office, the hot soapy water felt wonderful on her bare skin. Finally, she turned the water off, then climbed out to put on a pair of silk pajamas and matching robe. After brushing her teeth, she made her way to her mother's room. Mona's door was open.

Brandeis thought her mother gentle, serenely wise, and beautiful. She watched as her mother lovingly applied small stitches as she hemmed a small dress, oblivious to the fact that she was being observed. Mona looked so fragile and delicate, but Brandeis knew her mother possessed a strength that only served to heighten her femininity. Right now, she needed her mother's strength. Smiling, she tapped on the open door.

"Mom, what are you working on? You've been sewing almost nonstop for the past two weeks." Brandeis walked into the room and sat down on Mona's bed. Remnants of navy and white fabric lay scattered on the bed and floor. Patterns were spread out on a chair that stood in one corner of the room.

"I'm making some dresses for Mt. Olive's junior choir." Mona glanced up briefly, then down again to examine her handiwork.

"Mt. Olive has such a good choir," Brandeis said.

"Those young kids can really sing." She reached down to retrieve the pieces of discarded fabric. She placed them neatly in one heap on the footstool, covered in a burgundy colored moiré. Brandeis noted how well it matched the curtains.

"You know, they're going to Atlanta in a couple of weeks."

Brandeis shook her head no. "I didn't know that. Why?"

"For the Southern Baptist Conference," Mona explained.

"That's great, Mom." Brandeis picked up one of the navy and white dresses. "These are so pretty." Her eyes darted to her mother. "You should have been a designer."

Mona smiled and shook her head. "I love sewing, but that's not where my heart is. I'm happy with the way things turned out."

"I can tell. I'm glad you're the way you are." Brandeis stifled a yawn. She noticed how exhausted her mother looked. She decided against involving her with her problems tonight. It would be selfish on her part. They could always talk tomorrow.

Brandeis stood up and yawned. "Oh, dear. I guess I should call it a night. How about you? You've been at this all evening."

Mona yawned, too. "I guess you're right, dear. I'm getting a little sleepy myself. Thanks for picking up the scraps of material."

"No problem. Good night, Mom. I'll see you in the morning." Brandeis wearily made her way to her room. She crawled into bed and settled back against the soft pillows. As she waited for sleep to overtake her, various memories ran through her head. Suddenly, she vividly recalled the afternoon she had met Martin St. Charles.

She'd gone to Barbara's Record Shop on Norwich Street. While browsing through the newest selection of music CDs, a tall, muscular man had suddenly appeared beside her.

"Excuse me, I'm new in this town and I'm looking for

a good church. I . . . um, noticed you going through the gospel CDs.''

Brandeis had looked up into eyes that reminded her of green ice. His smile was wide, his teeth strikingly white, and his face the color of café au lait. She'd tried to throttle the dizzying current racing through her. He was so good-looking. One could almost consider him beautiful.

"What are you looking for in a church?" she'd finally managed to ask.

"I'm looking for a good Bible teaching church," Martin had answered. "Do you attend church in this area?" He'd openly admired her as she stood before him.

"I attend Trinity Christian Church. It's located on Albany Street." She'd held out her hand. "My name is Brandeis Taylor."

"Please forgive my manners. My name is Martin. I'm here at FLETC." He'd pronounced it as 'fleet tec.' "You know, the Federal Law Enforcement Training Center. I've been here for a week. I'm still trying to get familiar with the area."

She offered a smile. "It's hard to live in Brunswick and not know about FLETC," Brandeis had said. "What agency are you with?"

"I'm with the U.S. Marshals." Martin had checked his watch. "I've got to head back, but I'd like to visit your church this Sunday."

Brandeis had smiled warmly. "We'd love to have you. I look forward to seeing you there."

"Have a good day." Martin had flashed his dazzling smile once more and was gone.

For the rest of the week, Brandeis found herself looking forward to seeing him again. After church that Sunday, Martin came up to her and asked if he could call her sometime. She'd quickly given him her phone number and they'd said their goodbyes. Carol rushed over to her as he walked away.

"How do you know him?" Carol smiled at her friend.

"He's from FLETC. I met him at Barbara's Record Shop a few days ago."

"He's very handsome. Is he single?"

"Yes, he is. At least that's what he said. I didn't see a ring or a tan line where a ring should be." Brandeis paused and looked at her friend. "You know, you're worse than Mom." She laughed.

Carol laughed, too. "Don't say that! I just love you dearly. I'm looking out for you, that's all. As a matter of fact, you'd react the very same way if the tables were turned, especially where FLETC is concerned. You know how those guys can be. They come in from all over the country for a few months of training. Some of the women in town go crazy over them. When the men leave, there's a trail of broken hearts."

"But we can't very well blame the men," Brandeis had pointed out. "They can do no more than we women let them. Let's face it. We sometimes allow relationships to get out of hand. You just have to exercise good judgment when dealing with any man."

"You're right," Carol had agreed. "I just don't think anything long term can come out of a relationship with a FLETC guy, but anything's possible."

Brandeis had raised her eyebrows. "I guess you have a point, but I'm really surprised to hear you say something like that. You have such a romantic nature! By the way, how is James?" At that time, Carol's boyfriend, James, was planning to ask her to marry him.

Brandeis shifted in her bed to a more comfortable position. She smiled at the memory of Carol's excitement when she and James had become engaged. They were a loving couple and each other's best friend. It seemed so long ago that Brandeis had dreamed of finding a relationship such as theirs. But she knew she'd never find that special someone. That dream had been destroyed a year ago.

How could she have been so wrong about Martin? On their dates, he'd always presented himself as a perfect gentleman. At least until that last night. She'd trusted and cared deeply for him and he had hurt her. She closed her eyes against the painful memory. Her heart was still as full of sorrow, shame, and disillusionment as it had been that summer, a year ago. Tears squeezed past her closed lids and she let them run freely.

A wave of nausea threatened to consume her. *No! I can't get sick. Not now and not here.* Brandeis closed her eyes and forced herself to relax. After a minute or so, her stomach quieted. *I've got to stop thinking about him. I'm making myself sick.* Brandeis was certain she would not be able to sleep that night. She wondered if she would ever recover from the nightmare.

For a moment, she thought about calling Carol but changed her mind. What would she say? What could she say?

A short rap sounded on the door. It opened, revealing Mona. She came in quickly. "Are you okay, Brandeis? When you were in my room earlier, I was under the impression you wanted to talk to me."

Brandeis sat up in bed and wiped tears from her face. She propped her pillows around her. "I just needed to be around you. You're such a strong person. I guess I was just hoping to absorb some of that strength. Silly, huh?"

"No, it's not silly, dear." Mona sat next to her daughter on the bed. Wordlessly, she brushed away a lone tear on her daughter's cheek. "Are you feeling any better?"

"I'm fine, Mom. I haven't been resting lately and I think it's finally catching up with me."

Mona didn't hesitate. The lines at the corners of her eyes and mouth deepened as she said sternly, "You are a very strong person, dear. Please don't let that one horrible night deter you from having a wonderful life. I know this has been a hard year for you, but don't you dare let him win. Look ahead, not behind. Put the past behind you and leave it there."

Mona's words gave Brandeis pause. She leaned back against the bed frame and tucked a tendril of hair behind her ear. With her eyes shut, she said, "I'm trying to, but every time someone asks me out, I start to panic. I know it's because I'm afraid I'll make another bad choice." Brandeis opened her eyes and shrugged in resignation. "I figure it's safer just to be alone. Although I admit that sometimes I feel like I'm a prisoner in my own apartment."

"I was afraid of something like this happening," Mona said. "We all make bad choices sometimes, but most of us don't punish ourselves the way you do."

"All I want to do is work and find ways to stay busy, Mom," Brandeis said "I hate the nights most of all."

"Why don't you move back in with me? You're over here most of the time anyway. Besides, I enjoy having you home."

Brandeis took her mother's hand. "Thanks, Mom, but like you just said, I can't let Martin win. I'm not going to let him run me out of my apartment. I'm just glad he left town."

"Me, too. Let's not dwell on Martin." Mona grinned. "Now tell me, what do you think of Jackson?"

"I guess he's okay," Brandeis said quickly. "Before the other night, I hadn't seen him in a long time."

Mona frowned.

Brandeis looked at her mother and laughed. "All right! He's very handsome."

Mona leaned toward her daughter as if to share a secret. "You know, he's been stopping by here almost daily."

Brandeis tried to hide her surprise. "Mom, can I ask you something?"

"Sure. You can ask me anything."

"Are you interested in him?" she said, trying to keep a straight face. "I mean, as a boyfriend?"

Mona pressed a hand to her breast. "Heavens no! What on earth gave you that idea? For goodness' sake, he's like a son to me!"

"Calm down, Mom. I didn't mean to give you a heart attack!" Brandeis tried to keep from laughing, but failed miserably. "I was only teasing you."

"He's been asking about you, Brandeis," Mona said. "I

believe he keeps coming by the house hoping to run into you. It would be nice if you kept decent working hours. The poor man's running out of excuses to stop by."

Brandeis held her hand up and shook her head. "That's very sweet, but I'm not ready to become involved with anyone, Mom. I'm not sure I'll *ever* be ready."

"You will, my darling daughter. When you least expect it, you'll be ready to take that next step."

Her mother seemed so confident, for a moment Brandeis dared to hope. "Thanks, Mom. I really needed to hear that."

The conversation soon turned to the upcoming Easter program at church and the song Brandeis would sing. After some time, Mona stifled a yawn and murmured, "I was up early this morning. I think I'll turn in now." She stood up and stretched. Heading to the door, she said, "I'll let you sleep late, dear. You need to rest."

"Thanks, Mom." Just as Mona was about to shut the door to her bedroom, Brandeis called out, "Mom!"

"Yes, dear."

"I love you. I just want you to know that . . . I really want you to be proud of me."

"I love you, too, baby. And I'm very proud of you already." Mona closed the door and was gone.

Brandeis wrapped her arms around her knees. "I'm gonna get through this," she whispered to the silent room. "I have to." Somehow, she would find the strength.

Brandeis rushed down the steps of the courthouse. She was in a bad mood and wanted to reach her car before she exploded. She was so damn tired of men making passes at her! Brandeis wondered if men thought she was flattered by their attention. Well, she had a newsflash for them. *She wasn't!*

She'd just had to tell off one lawyer who'd made a lewd comment about her to his friends as she was walking by. Then, she'd practically had to yell for security to stop another man from trying to force her into accepting his invitation for drinks. She was at the point where she'd had her fill of men. *Why can't they just take no for an answer?* she wondered angrily.

She had just reached the bottom step when she heard her name called. She whipped her head around. It was Jackson. *Great!* He was waving and grinning so much, he reminded her of an adolescent suitor coming to walk his girl home from school. Brandeis was so angry she wanted to slap that silly grin off his face. She closed her eyes for a minute, took a deep breath, and waited for him to catch up.

"Hello, Jackson." She forced a demure smile.

"Hello, Bran. You look very nice today."

She rolled her eyes and muttered, "Thanks."

Jackson walked beside her cheerfully, talking about how hectic his day had been. She hardly heard him. When Jackson led her to the parking lot, her emotional confusion and frustration got the best of her. She couldn't remember where she'd parked her car.

With her left hand shading her eyes, Brandeis scanned the huge parking lot. Her eyes found her car, and then, another one. A bright red Volvo. Even from a distance, Brandeis could clearly make out its light-skinned driver. Her face paled with shock. She broke into a sprint across the parking lot. When she reached her car, she leaned wearily against it. She felt dizzy. She thought she might fall.

Jackson caught up with her. "Bran, what is it?" he asked, grabbing her shoulders. "Tell me," he demanded, his face inches from hers. "What just happened back there? What is it?"

His concern finally penetrated her shock. She fought off his hold, and turning her head away from his, leaned against the car as if it could hide her.

"Go away, Jackson. I'm all right. Just go away!"

"I don't understand," he said, his voice revealing his concern.

"Of course. You have to know *everything* that's going on, don't you?" Brandeis cried. "You just can't take no for an answer, can you? Well, not this time. You'll have to settle for no. Now, just leave me alone!"

She felt him step back from her, and when she turned, she saw that his eyes became analytical, almost cold. She remembered too late that this man was her friend, and she forced herself to speak calmly. "I'm fine, Jackson. Thank you for your concern. I've had a very bad day and I didn't sleep well last night, but that's all it was. You don't need to worry."

They stood staring at each other, and she mustered every ounce of pride she had to quench his concern. She lifted her hand in a self-deprecating gesture and laughed. "You must think I'm crazy. But really, I'm fine."

Only a fool would have been deceived by her effort, and Jackson was no fool.

"All right. As you wish. I was only trying to help. I'll see you later," he finally agreed. Jackson turned and left her without another word.

Brandeis knew she had offended him, possibly even hurt him. Although that thought almost defeated her, she couldn't bear Jackson's knowing the truth. *Not that indignity. Anything but that!* she cried silently.

As she drove out of the parking lot, she discovered the driver of the Volvo was a Caucasian woman and not a light skinned, green-eyed man, as she'd first assumed. *Thank God!* She wondered what she would have done if it had been Martin.

Chapter 4

Jackson sat in his car watching Brandeis drive away. He was amazed by the way she'd carried on. This was certainly not the same girl he remembered from years ago. She seemed almost bitter now.

She must have had a helluva day, but Jackson felt the trouble ran much deeper than that. He had seen the fear in her eyes. Something had frightened her. At first he thought it had been his imagination, but the more he concentrated on what had taken place, the more convinced he was that fear had made her turn away from him. But what could have scared her so?

Jackson tried to convince himself not to take her outburst personally, but it was hard. Maybe he was rushing her. No, that certainly couldn't be it. Every time he tried to have a conversation with her, she was off and running. *Maybe I should change colognes,* he thought cynically. He decided to let a day or two pass before calling her.

He pulled out of the parking lot and turned in the direction of his condo. Then, he changed his mind. He decided he needed a night out on the town. He headed to Pier Seventeen, a popular nightspot. There were plenty of attractive women in Brunswick and right now, his bruised ego needed a boost.

Once seated at the bar, he ordered a beer. Just as he was about to take a sip, he heard a voice. Turning around, he looked into the face of a tall, beautiful woman. She was asking him something, but Jackson couldn't hear her over the band.

"Excuse me?"

She smiled and ran her fingers through her long wavy hair. "Hi, I was just asking if I could sit with you. It's crowded in here and I feel uncomfortable just standing around by myself in a bar. Do you mind?"

"No. No, I don't mind," Jackson said politely.

"Thanks." She sat down and held out her hand. "By the way, my name is Tracy."

He shook her hand. "Nice to meet you Tracy. I'm Jackson."

"Yes, I know who you are."

Jackson raised one brow incredulously. "Really?"

Tracy ran her fingers through her hair again and laughed. "You look surprised. Have you forgotten how small Brunswick is and how it suffers from a shortage of good men?"

"I, er, never knew there was a shortage of good men in Brunswick," Jackson said.

"Well, there is. There's a shortage of good men, period. I'm glad you're back, Jackson. I've always wanted to get to know you."

He could see desire in her eyes. She reached over and placed her hand on his. "Are you seeing anyone?"

Jackson was quiet for a moment. "No. I'm not seeing anyone at the moment."

"I'm glad to hear that. Jackson, I want to be very honest with you. I'm very attracted to you. I can tell you feel the same way. I don't see any need to beat around the bush. Why don't we leave? We can go back to your place."

"Tracy, look—"

"It's okay, Jackson. I know you don't remember me, but

you're all I've thought about throughout the years. I had a crush on you all through high school, but you never even noticed me. I've regretted never letting you know how I felt about you."

Tracy was very beautiful, with her green eyes and voluptuous body, but she did not interest him. Jackson's mind was on a certain, amber-eyed beauty. If only he could penetrate that hard shell Brandeis had wrapped around herself. He glanced at Tracy and wondered if he was crazy for what he was about to do.

"Tracy, I'm flattered," he began, "but I can't take advantage of you. I'm not involved with anyone at the moment. However, I *am* interested in someone. I care a lot for her. As a matter of fact, I plan to spend a lifetime with her." A thread of regret ran through him as he watched Tracy fight back tears.

"Whoever she is, she's a very lucky lady," Tracy said quietly. She started to rise.

Jackson put his hand on her arm. "Tracy, you don't have to leave. Actually, I would enjoy some company. Why don't you tell me how it is we went to school together and I don't recall ever having seen you. I'm sure I would have remembered someone so beautiful. Glynn Academy is a big school but I think I would've remembered you."

"I wasn't beautiful back then," Tracy said, settling on the barstool again "You wouldn't have given me a second look. What am I saying? You *didn't* give me a second look."

Jackson wasn't sure how to respond.

"Jackson," she went on, "I don't have green eyes. These are contacts. I've never had long hair. This is a weave." She peeked at Jackson, confused by the slow grin spreading across his face.

"I know who you are! You're Tracy Cannon. I remember you now."

"You *remember* me?"

"Yes. I always thought you were one of the prettiest girls in school." He laughed when he heard her shocked gasp. "What are you doing now?"

"I'm a pharmacist. You thought I was pretty? I never knew you noticed me."

"I thought you were *very* pretty," Jackson admitted. "Sweet and shy, too. I wanted to ask you out, but I didn't think you would give me the time of day."

"It wouldn't have been like that, Jackson," Tracy said.

About to tread on dangerous ground, Jackson decided to change the subject. "I remember that a lot of kids used to give you a hard time because you were so smart."

Tracy laughed. "Yeah. Those good ol' days, huh?" She ordered a round of drinks and they continued to talk about school, college, and their lives since then.

Suddenly, Jackson felt the skin on the back of his neck prickle. Scanning the bar, he came upon the face of an ex-girlfriend. Monique Allen. From her expression, he could tell she was seething mad. He started to wave, but she already had turned away from him and was storming off. Following his gaze, Tracy gave him a questioning look. Jackson shrugged in response.

When Tracy excused herself for a moment, Jackson flashed back to Monique. He wondered what her problem was. Surely, she couldn't be jealous. What they had once was over and done with. He knew he would never travel down that road again. He hoped Monique realized it, too.

Brandeis quickly dressed. The tantalizing aroma of bacon, sausages, pancakes, and scrambled eggs floated toward her as she walked down the stairs, and toward the dining room. Her mother was just finishing up her breakfast.

Mona slowly put her fork down and delicately dabbed her mouth with her napkin. "Good morning, dear. Do you want something for breakfast?"

Brandeis shook her head, too nauseous to speak.

Noting her daughter's pale complexion and the dark shadows under her eyes, Mona took Brandeis'hand. "You look as if you still don't feel well. Why don't you stay home today from work? You could try to get some rest."

"Mom, I'm okay. I've been doing a lot of thinking. I'm going to take your advice. I'm just going to take one day at a time. Nothing I can do or say will change what happ—" Brandeis stopped short. She hadn't meant to say so much. She poured herself a glass of juice and sat down across from her mother at the breakfast table. "Mom, I'm going back to my apartment. I've been here long enough. Let me know when you want to go shopping for a car."

"I don't need a new car. My old baby will get me where I need to go."

Brandeis shook her head. "No, it won't, Mom. It breaks down every other day." She quickly drank the tangy orange juice and abruptly pushed her chair back from the table. "I gotta go."

"Brandeis! You need to get some rest. You can't go on like this."

"Don't worry, Mom. I'm going to take a personal day today. See you later," she yelled as she rushed out of the house. It was time to go home, she'd decided. Sooner or later she would have to face her demons. And she still felt terrible about how she'd treated Jackson yesterday. Brandeis decided she would have to find a way to make it up to him. She thought about buying him a nice card. She knew it was the coward's way out but . . .

She drove into her garage and sat in the car for a while before summoning up strength to enter the building. Finally, she made it upstairs to her second-story apartment. Slowly opening the door, she walked in and placed her keys on a hook near the door.

Although sunlight was streaming in through the windows, Brandeis went from room to room and flipped on every light in the apartment. She checked the dead bolt on the door to make certain it was locked. Ever since that night a year ago, she went through the same ritual. She was just being safe, that's all. Before she could enter her bedroom, the telephone rang. Her answering machine came on. She paused to listen.

Jackson!

The sound of his voice affected her deeply, more than she cared to admit. Brandeis quickly turned down the sound.

She was too embarrassed to talk to him right now. She wondered if he would mention the disastrous scene at the courthouse to her mother. She hoped not. A rueful smile crossed her lips. Her mother would have a fit if she knew how badly Brandeis had treated their friend. Brandeis headed toward her bedroom, a room that would never be the same to her. She hadn't slept in that room in a year avoiding it in favor of her sofa bed. She quickly walked out and strolled into the second bedroom, which doubled as her office. Grabbing a book off the shelf, Brandeis settled on the sofa to read. She couldn't concentrate.

Her phone started to ring again. She closed her eyes in an attempt to block the ringing. Long after the phone stopped ringing, her eyes remained closed. Brandeis had fallen asleep, her breathing even. She slept through the entire afternoon.

When she finally woke up, Brandeis felt refreshed, better than she'd felt in weeks. She gave her hair a thorough shampooing. Then, she carefully combed the tangles out of her wet hair and dried it. She was about to curl it when once again, she heard the persistent ringing of her phone. This time, Brandeis decided to check her messages. Two from her mother and one from Jackson. Briefly, she wondered what he wanted. Her mother, of course was behind his call. She was sure of it. She made a mental note to call her mother later.

Hungry, Brandeis headed to her kitchen, decorated with cobalt blue and white accessories, all chosen by Mona. Her mother practically had had to drag Brandeis shopping for the floral wallpaper and matching dish cloths and towels. Brandeis had no love for decorating and had given her mother a budget and carte blanche to spend it any way she chose. Her mother knew her well, for Mona's selection of furnishings reflected Brandeis eclectic taste.

Browsing in her refrigerator, Brandeis decided on a dinner salad. As she ate alone at her glass dining table, she surveyed her home. It really was a cozy and lovely apartment.

The phone rang just as she finished cleaning her kitchen. Putting the mop aside, she walked to her answering machine and listened. After hearing Jackson's voice, she quickly picked up the phone. "Hello, please hold on, Jackson. I need to turn the machine off."

Her senses were charged with a sudden tension. Best to get this over with. Brandeis settled down on her plush love seat. "That's better."

"How are you doing?"

"I'm fine, thank you." She found that in spite of herself, she was relieved to the core to be speaking with him.

His voice sounded somewhat hesitant. "Your mother gave me your number and suggested I give you a call. I hope you don't mind?"

"No. Why would I mind? We are friends, aren't we?"

"Yes. But I must admit I was beginning to wonder, especially after the way you've been treating me."

"Jackson, I'm so sorry about everything. I—"

"Don't worry. I forgive you."

Brandeis heard the laughter in his voice and she relaxed. "I'm really sorry. We've always been friends but . . ." She wasn't sure if she could explain her behavior.

She was spared any explanations when Jackson spoke. Sensing her weariness, he asked, "Are you currently seeing someone?"

"No, I'm not seeing anyone. The last relationship took its toll on me. I don't know if I can handle another one right now," she mumbled wearily.

"I thought it might be something like that," Jackson said quietly. "I could tell that you were upset that night at your Mom's. You know, if you ever need a shoulder to cry on, I'm available. I happen to be a real good listener."

Brandeis smiled and murmured, "Thanks, I'll remember that. Right now, it's not something I can talk about."

"The reason I called was to ask you if you would like to attend a concert with me. Martha Wallace is going to perform on Jekyll next week. Would you like to go?"

"Martha is one of my favorite singers," Brandeis admitted. "I guess my mom told you that already?"

Jackson laughed. "Yes, she told me. So . . . will you go with me?"

Beads of perspiration popped on her forehead.

"Bran?" Jackson prompted her, gently.

She cleared her throat. "When is it?"

"Next Friday night. The concert starts at seven thirty. I thought maybe we could grab dinner around five thirty and head to the concert after that."

"Next Friday . . . Oh no, I-I already have p-plans. I'm s-sorry, Jackson. I would r-really love to go, but I can't. Maybe next time." Brandeis prayed he couldn't tell she was lying.

"Well, I admit I'm disappointed but I understand. Will you think about dinner one night soon?"

Brandeis knew Jackson didn't believe her excuse for a minute. She could hear it in his voice. Besides, she always stuttered when she lied and he knew that.

"Yes. We'll go out one night soon," she said. Anything to end the conversation.

"Well, remember what I've said. I'll let you go, but should you change your mind about Friday, give me a call." Jackson quickly gave her his number and hung up.

Brandeis felt terrible for lying to Jackson, but she wasn't ready to start dating again. The misery of that night still haunted her. She knew Jackson would never understand. Brandeis called her mother back and told her about Jackson's call.

"Why aren't you going with him to the concert?" Mona demanded.

"Because, I'd m-made other p-plans already."

Mona's voice was firm. "No you didn't."

"Mom! How do you know? I don't tell you everything."

"I know you don't have any plans. And you've never been a good liar. You always stutter. Now, why would you tell him a lie?"

"Because I'm not ready to go out on dates yet."

Mona didn't respond, but Brandeis knew her mother well. She was wondering how to get her daughter to change her mind.

"I hoped you would go. You've known Jackson all of your life. He used to baby-sit you, for goodness' sake. I thought that would make the transition easier."

"You just don't get it, do you, Mom?" Brandeis was frustrated. "He's still a man. I'm not ready to be alone with *any* man. I don't care if he is a friend or my old baby-sitter."

"I was only trying to help, dear." Mona sounded hurt. "I thought you'd at least give him a chance to take your mind off the past." She sighed. "Honey, there are some good men out there. Please don't retreat within yourself because you made a mistake in trusting one man. He hid his true nature well. There was no way you could have known. It's not your fault!"

Brandeis was not ready to accept that. "But *you* knew," she said. "You said you didn't trust Martin and I didn't listen to you. I don't understand why I didn't see it myself."

"Because he didn't let you see the truth, honey. He showed you exactly what he wanted you to see. Don't dwell on it, dear. Don't make all the other good men in the world pay for one man's crime."

Brandeis spoke with quiet, but desperate firmness. "I know you're trying to help, Mom. I really appreciate it but *please,* let me handle this in my own way."

Mona was quiet for a minute. "Sure, dear."

"Mom! Don't sound like that!"

"Sound like what?"

"Hurt. I didn't mean to hurt your feelings."

"Don't worry about me," Mona said. "You're right to be upset. I shouldn't put my nose where it doesn't belong. *Even if I do know what's best for you.* I know that it's selfish of me to want to see my daughter happy and living a normal life. I should just mind my own business and . . ."

Brandeis laughed until tears streamed down her face. "Mom!"

Mona laughed. "I'm okay. I've said all I have to say on the matter. I've got to run because tonight's Bible study. I'll talk to you later."

"I was thinking about coming by tomorrow. Are you going to be home around six?"

"Yes. I'll see you then. Bye."

"Bye."

Brandeis went to the balcony to sit quietly in the gathering darkness. The moon was barely out, and most of the stars were hidden behind clouds. She was too weary to think about much. Later, while getting ready for bed, she wondered if her private tragedy would forever keep her from opening her heart again to the world.

"I need you to fill out this questionnaire as thoroughly as possible, Mr. Stanton. Don't forget to attach copies of all outstanding debts to the back of these forms. It'll help us verify your balances on each account. Here's my card. Should you have any questions, please feel free to call me." Brandeis handed a copy of instructions for the bankruptcy questionnaire to the young man seated across from her. He shifted uncomfortably in his chair. It was obvious he was embarrassed about filing bankruptcy.

"I won't be able to buy a house after this . . . will I?"

"Mr. Matthews will also assist you in reestablishing yourself financially. He's a very good attorney. He's written a book on life after bankruptcy. People who file for bankruptcy now have several avenues available to them, such as secured credit cards. Some buy cars and some even buy homes."

"Miss Taylor is correct." Frank Matthews walked into the small office. "I'll assist you in every way possible in getting back on track. After your bankruptcy is discharged, you can apply for a major credit card. I'll give you a list of banks that offer secured cards . . .''

Brandeis listened as her boss explained the process of reestablishing credit after bankruptcy. She smiled when she heard him say he would throw in a copy of his book. Frank Matthews had already covered the cost of the book in the total fee for the bankruptcy. The book was well written and their clients found it very helpful.

After the young man had gone, Frank Matthews turned an appraising eye to Brandeis. "Are you feeling okay? You haven't seemed yourself in the last few weeks."

"I'm fine, sir. Staying home yesterday helped me a lot. I've been working long hours and not resting properly. I've also had a lot on my mind lately."

Frank looked carefully at Brandeis, "For the rest of the week, I don't want you to stay in this office past six o'clock. You need to rest. We have a light load this week so take advantage of it. If you're having any problems here in the office, you be sure and let me know. You're an asset to this company and I don't want to lose you. You remember that, now."

"I will." As he was navigating toward the door, she stopped him. "Mr. Matthews?"

He turned to face her. "Yes."

"Thank you. I really appreciate your telling me that."

"It's the truth." Frank Matthews smiled and walked briskly out of her office.

Chapter 5

Carrie lingered outside Brandeis' office while Frank Matthews was in with her, talking to a new client. When she heard someone turning the door knob, she rushed to her desk and practically fell into her chair.

"Mr. Matthews, you had a call from Mr. Reynolds," she said in a bubbly voice. "He said that it was urgent that he speak with you." She handed a copy of the message to her boss as he strolled slowly past her desk. Carrie was sure he had been admiring her. His gaze had traveled over her fleetingly, but with interest.

Carrie adopted her most glamorous smile. "I declare, Mr. Matthews, you're looking younger every day," she said in a provocative southern accent.

"Why, thank you, Carrie." Frank Matthews actually blushed before he continued on to his office.

Carrie believed that never in his life had a more beautiful and seductive woman showed him so much warmth. He *should* be flattered. Carrie smiled to herself. She enjoyed her job and would do whatever it took to secure her position there. *Except sleep with the boss!* Carrie wanted a man with money but not just any man. He had to be able to satisfy her sexual demands, too. Frank Matthews just didn't look up to standards.

Carrie wanted to believe all men found her irresistible. However, it seemed that the only men *she* found interesting, Brandeis snared first. After Brandeis was finished with them, they'd come running back to Carrie with their tails tucked between their legs. She was getting tired of Brandeis' castoffs.

Carrie grudgingly admitted that Brandeis was pretty, but not like Carrie. Brandeis was more of the girl-next-door type. Carrie was simply stunning. Men found her sexy and Brandeis an ice princess. At least, that's what they often told her.

Carrie refused to admit to herself that she felt insecure and inadequate around Brandeis. She couldn't help but wonder why all the good ones flocked to her co-worker first. Even so, they eventually came to their senses. At least, that's what Carrie wanted to believe.

Carrie was filing her nails when Marlena, Frank's daughter, and a part-time paralegal, stormed over to her desk.

Marlena's angry gaze swept over her. "What in hell are you up to? Are you trying to seduce my father?"

"Honestly, Marlena!" Carrie said testily. "I was simply giving him a compliment. But I suppose you're not familiar with those, are you?" She frowned as she looked at the plump young woman standing in front of her desk, hands on her hips.

Marlena reddened with rage, and her chubby hands doubled into fists. "I know what kind of woman you are. But you'd better not mess with my father. You're not good enough for him, tramp!"

Carrie refused to let Marlena see how much that remark had wounded her. "How dare you call me a tramp! For all your wealth, you look like a piece of poor white trash. You're just jealous that no man wants a woman like you." Carrie smirked. "You know, you've got such a pretty face and lots of money, but that body ... Girlfriend, haven't you ever heard of Jenny Craig?"

Marlena reached over the desk and jerked Carrie to her feet. "You little witch! I'm tired of your high and mighty ways. When I get through with you—"

They both turned at the sound of a door opening.

"What is going on out here?" Brandeis said angrily. "Marlena! Let her go! I want both of you in my office, *now!*" Brandeis was thankful none of the other employees were around. Or much worse, Mr. Matthews himself.

Minutes later, the two women sat in her office. Brandeis started. "I can't believe the two of you. What in the world is going on?"

Marlena, her head hanging, said, "I'm tired of this . . . this *slut* acting like a bitch in heat around all the men in this firm." She clenched her fists.

"Slut! Bitch in heat! You wish! Look, Brandeis," Carrie argued, "I didn't do anything wrong. All I did was compliment her daddy and she went crazy. She attacked me." Carrie was attempting a superb job of pretending embarrassment and fear. Turning tear-filled eyes to Brandeis, she said in a timorous voice, "I don't know why she hates me so much. *Everyone* hates me."

"I'm not going to sit here and listen to this crap!" Marlena cried. She clumsily maneuvered her ample body out of her chair and stalked out of the office.

"I'm sorry about all this. I just complimented him . . . I don't know what I did that was so wrong." Carrie covered her face with her hands, and feigned heartrending sobs.

Brandeis had seen and heard enough. "Carrie, enough of the acting. I'm not sure what happened out there, but I hope that the two of you will resolve your problems with each other. What if we'd had clients in the reception area? Your behavior was unprofessional."

"It won't h-happen again," Carrie promised. She sniffed loudly.

"If it does, I'm going to get Mr. Matthews involved. That may happen, anyway. Marlena tells her father everything that goes on behind his back."

"Mr. Matthews knows I'm not a troublemaker," Carrie protested. "He won't believe her."

Brandeis almost laughed. "Remember this. Marlena is his daughter. Blood is thicker than water."

Carrie shuddered. "Brandeis, I'm so upset. I can't possibly work the rest of the day. I need to leave." She brushed away invisible tears.

"Please go home, Carrie."

Carrie jumped up without a backward glance and left Brandeis' office.

As soon as Carrie had gone, Brandeis closed her office door and shook her head. She had been looking for a document in her file cabinet when she heard the commotion outside her office.

She was stunned when she'd heard the fury in Marlena's voice. She expected Carrie to fly off the handle every once and a while but Marlena? Had Carrie really been flirting with Mr. Matthews? Even if she had been, Marlena had overreacted. Brandeis knew that Carrie liked to put on airs and gossip, but for the most part, Carrie was harmless.

Carrie's bedroom was dark, relieved only by a ray of moonlight filtering through a small window. He stood still, just holding her, as if he also savored the moment. Unable to stop herself, made bold by her fear of losing him, Carrie placed a kiss on his cheek. Deep in his chest she heard a sensual moan. She laid a gentle hand on his cheek.

Angling his head, he pressed his lips to her palm. "I can't wait to make love to you. It's been on my mind a long time."

"Mine, too. I think I fell in love with you the first time I saw you," she said with a catch in her voice.

Slowly, he turned his head and gazed down at her. "You know, some people around here would try to cause problems if they knew you and I were involved. I think we should keep our relationship a secret."

"But why?"

"It could get nasty. I care too much for you. I don't want to see you get hurt."

Carrie's heart melted at his endearing words. "I won't tell anyone, if that's what you want. It'll be our little secret." Deep down, she wondered if he was ashamed to be with her.

As if sensing her insecurities, he said huskily, "You do understand that I'm just trying to protect you, baby."

"I know. No one's ever cared about me like this. You're not like any man I've ever met. You make me feel so special. Like I'm really the woman you want."

Moonlight fell across his face, sculpting hollows in his cheeks and lighting his extraordinary eyes. "When I saw you, I knew I'd never want another woman again."

"Aw, honey. You know exactly the right things to say."

He studied her leisurely for a moment, his ardent gaze raising gooseflesh all over her. He sat on the bed, settling her comfortably on his lap.

"Under all your little 'Miss Proper' ways, I know you're a passionate woman. And this dress . . . Girl, you definitely got it goin' on. You are one sexy lady."

Carrie stared at him with passion-filled eyes. Even her dreams hadn't done him justice. She wet her full lips. "Take me, honey. Make me yours." She stood, reaching up to undo her first button.

He gently pushed her hand away. "Let me take your clothes off."

Carrie closed her eyes as she felt the caress of his heated gaze on her body. He slowly unbuttoned her dress, then hesitated. She opened her eyes.

He lifted her hands to his lips and kissed her palms. He inflamed her with his kisses, embracing her with the hard strength of his need. Carrie couldn't wait much longer. She moaned as he ripped the dress off her. He swept her up into his arms and brought her to the king-size bed.

"I've waited so long for this, baby," Carrie murmured. "I've never wanted a man as much as I want you."

"I feel the same way, honey." He pulled away and quickly undressed.

He came to her and Carrie wrapped her arms around him. She called his name but was silenced by the commanding touch of his mouth on hers. She met the play of his tongue as her hips arched. He smiled as he finally gave in to the hunger that had brought him to her.

Later, as Carrie slept, he scanned her features. He took in her closed eyes and the slightly parted lips and felt an inkling of regret. She was not the woman for him. He closed his eyes and thought of another. A woman he wanted to hate. For the life of him, he could not. She was still under his skin. To him, most women were needy. But not her. It was as if she didn't need anybody. That was one of the traits that had attracted him to her. That, and her fiery spirit.

Sighing, he shook his head. He brooded. He was at a loss as to how to get her back. Patience, he thought, was the key. Somehow, he had to find it within himself. She was angry now and hurt over the way he had treated her. But given time, she would come around. He loved her and he believed with his whole being that she loved him, too.

Jackson stormed into his office, slamming the door behind him. He hurled his briefcase on the leather couch, sank down beside it, and slowly undid his gray and black silk tie. It was days like this that made him hate his job. For the last two weeks, he and another attorney had been in court, defending a young man accused of murder.

Jackson, the lead attorney, had offered no evidence, but argued that the homicide was not unlawful since his client lacked criminal intent. He had further argued that at most, the homicide was manslaughter rather than murder, since it had occurred in the heat of passion provoked by a homosexual assault.

He closed his eyes as he recalled the guilty verdict and his client's reaction. The young man had seemed to age right before his eyes. Jackson's ears were still ringing from the shrill wailing of his client's mother.

Jackson had fought hard to maintain control of his emotions. When the guards hauled his client away, the mother had cried even harder and his sister had spoken to Jackson of her brother's love for his family, his devotion to his fiancée, and the overall unfairness of the justice system. Long after the courtroom had cleared out, Jackson remained sitting there, feeling an overwhelming sadness.

He came out of his reverie when he heard his secretary lightly rapping on his door. After calling for her to come in, he stood and walked over to his desk.

Fran Bailey marched in with a stack of documents requiring his signature. In her crisp white blouse and black, straight skirt, she reminded him of a maiden school marm. The bun at the nape of her neck added a touch of authenticity.

Jackson glanced up after signing the court documents and gave a forced smile. "Thank you, Fran. Why don't you call it a day? You've worked very hard."

Fran took off her bifocals and grinned. "Why thank you, Mr. Gray. I would really appreciate that. I have some errands I do need to run. Thank you, sir."

Jackson watched her go. Her slim boyish frame actually had some bounce to it. Normally, she marched as if she were a member of the military. Fran Bailey rarely smiled, but today, she'd left his office grinning from ear to ear. Jackson shook his head and laughed softly. Perhaps the day had not been a total loss after all.

On Sunday, Brandeis could barely concentrate on the pastor's sermon. Sharp pains in her abdomen cut her like a knife. Her eyes clamped shut as she vainly tried to block out the discomfort. She wondered briefly what could be wrong with her. For the past few weeks, she'd been nauseous and at times, she'd experienced burning in her stomach. She was in so much anguish her body started trembling.

Mona felt her daughter's shivering. "What's wrong, dear?" she whispered. "You're not cold, are you?"

Brandeis shook her head. She prayed the pains would subside, at least long enough for her to get out of church and make it home. As soon as the service was over, she joined the crowd filing out of the pews.

Jackson's smiling face came into view. He was standing just outside of the doorway, talking to one of the choir members. Their eyes met and held. Smiling weakly, she waved. Her mother had joined him, and it was obvious they were discussing her.

She turned and headed out one of the side doors. Carol soon wandered over to her.

"Hi, Bran. You sounded great up there this morning. What's up for today?"

"I have nothing planned. Why?"

"Do you want to go to Ramada Inn for brunch with James and me?"

The thought of food made her stomach lurch. "N-no. I think I'd better pass."

Carol placed her hand on Brandeis' arm, as if to prevent her from falling. "What's wrong? You don't look as if you're feeling too hot."

"I'm not feeling well at all. It started right after I finished singing. I'm going to go home and get in bed. Tomorrow, I plan to call Dr. Myers."

"Do you want me to drive you? Your mom can take your car home for you. I'll cancel with James an—"

"No," Brandeis interrupted. "I'm sure I can make it home. You go on and have a good time with James."

"You sure? You know I don't mind. Besides, you and I haven't spent much time together lately."

Brandeis didn't want to tell her friend they hadn't spent much time together because she felt like a third wheel. It also pained her to see how much in love with each other Carol and James were when her life was in such turmoil.

"We'll all have brunch together on next Sunday, okay? By then I should be feeling better."

Carol smiled. They chatted for a few minutes more before Carol moved on.

Just as Carol was walking away, Jackson and Mona joined Brandeis. "Hello, Jackson." Brandeis was feeling worse by the minute. The last thing she wanted to do was stand around and chat.

"Hi. You look lovely, Brandeis." She wore a soft, slim fitting, violet silk dress. She certainly was beautiful, Jackson thought, but she was incredibly difficult, too.

Brandeis tried to smile. Her stomach was queasy. "Thank you. Especially since I'm not feeling well at the moment."

Mona was instantly concerned. "Have you seen a doctor, dear? You haven't felt well for weeks."

"No. I keep hoping that it'll pass, but it hasn't. Right now I think I'll just go home and rest. I'll call you later."

"I'll walk you to your car." Jackson offered her his arm for support.

Brandeis was too ill to do anything other than accept. She gripped his arm tightly.

"Why don't you let me drive you home?" His face showed his concern.

Mona, too, looked worried. Brandeis felt guilty. "Mom, I'll be fine. I'm going to go straight to my apartment and get into bed. Tomorrow, I'll call Dr. Myers."

"Sweetie, let me know if you need anything," Mona said as they arrived at Brandeis' car.

Jackson took her keys and unlocked the door to her black Toyota Camry. He opened the door and she almost fell into the driver's seat. She smiled up at Jackson and Mona weakly. "Thanks. I'll talk to you both later."

"Call me when you get home, dear."

"I will. Bye, Mom. Jackson."

"Take care of yourself, Bran." Jackson was concerned. He was surprised to hear Brandeis had been feeling ill for weeks. He recalled the night he had dinner with her at Mona's. He remembered her mentioning she wasn't feeling well, then. "How long has this been going on, Mrs. Taylor?"

"For the last month. She doesn't eat like she should and she works all those long hours . . . Jackson, could you do me a favor?"

"Anything, Mrs. Taylor." He leaned down as she spoke softly in his ear.

Chapter 6

Brandeis sat in her car for a few minutes with her eyes closed. *I've got to get home. Just give me the strength to make it home.* Although still queasy, she began to feel a little better. She was grateful the pain had gone away.

She drove a few miles before the motion of the car made Brandeis feel very nauseous. Suddenly, she pulled off the road. She opened her door, climbed out, and promptly vomited. She leaned against her car, praying the dizziness would pass soon. *What in the world is wrong with me?* She thought desperately. Pain gripped her once more and she doubled over.

In the distance, she heard a car pull up behind her and footsteps running. Trembling, her mind confused by pain, Brandeis tried to straighten up and run away. The heel of her shoe caught in the hem of her dress. She started to fall.

She felt arms pulling at her. Fear gripped her and she tried to scream, but no sound came out. Flailing her arms wildly, she fought her assailant. She heard a voice but couldn't understand what it was saying. The voice belonged to a man. *It was Martin!*

Hands balled into tight fists, kicking savagely, she fought as best she could. Then, she heard other voices. She glimpsed a few blurred faces. She didn't recognize anyone. *Why aren't they helping me?* They seemed to be trying to pin her down. The ground was spinning and coming up to meet her. Brandeis fainted dead away.

Bright lights sent stabs of pain to her head. Brandeis tried to sit up, but couldn't. The nausea was still there and blackness threaten to consume her once more.

"Brandeis, can you hear me? It's Jackson."

"W-where . . . am I?"

"You're in the emergency room."

"How did I g-get here?" Her throat was so dry. Brandeis opened her eyes and saw Jackson standing next to the bed. He looked so worried. "How . . . did you . . ."

"Your mother was really worried about you. She asked me to follow you. To make sure you made it home okay. I'm glad I did."

"It was you who found me on the side of the road?" Relief was evident in her voice. She'd thought it was Martin coming after her. "I'm glad it was you. I thought it was . . . someone else."

"Yes. You were . . . er, throwing up, and before I could say anything, you just started fighting me. You kept calling me Martin. Paramedics pulled up shortly after I did. Appar ently, they were right behind me. We tried to get you to calm down. The more we tried, the more I think we frightened you. You fainted and they rushed you here to the hospital. I followed in my car." He smiled and rubbed the right side of his face. "Did anyone ever tell you that you have a mean left hook?"

"I'm so sorry, Jackson," she said, quietly. "I didn't hurt you, did I?"

"Just my pride. And my glasses." Jackson laughed at the embarrassed expression on her face. "No, really I'm fine. I have a second set. Are you feeling better?"

"Some," Brandeis admitted. "I've been under a lot of pressure lately. So much I think I've been making myself sick." Brandeis silently prayed that's all it was.

"The doctor should be back soon. Why don't you lie back and rest. I've already called your mother. She's having car trouble, but she's going to try to get a lift here."

"Thank you, Jackson. Mom needs to get rid of that old car. It's always breaking down on her . . ."

The doctor came in and asked Jackson to leave the room for a minute. Dr. Gail Myers had known Brandeis since she was ten years old. She asked now about her eating habits, her sleeping patterns, and inquired as to her last period.

"I missed last month, but I've been under a lot of pressure, Dr. Myers."

Gail Myers looked up briefly from her note-taking. "Could you be pregnant, Brandeis?"

Brandeis felt as if she'd been slapped. Her response came out in a whisper. "No! There's no way I could be pregnant. *How could you even think that?* After all that happened last year."

"I didn't think so, but I had to ask. I've ordered a series of blood tests, a sonogram, and an upper GI series. After we get the results, I'll be back to talk to you. From what you've been telling me, I believe you may have developed an ulcer. If indeed you have an ulcer, you're going to have to change your diet and take it easy. You do know that stress can compound the problem?"

"Yes."

"The nurse will be back in a few minutes." Placing her hand over Brandeis', she said, "Relax, Bran. I know you've had a hard time of it." Gail Myers walked to the door and beckoned for Jackson to enter.

He came back into the room, just as Brandeis settled back on the cool sheets to watch TV. She glanced at him and smiled weakly. "I'll reimburse you for your glasses. I'm so sorry."

"Forget it. It was an accident." Jackson knew he would

never forget the stark fear he saw in her eyes earlier, on the side of the road.

"I hope there's nothing seriously wrong with me."

"What did your doctor say?" Jackson asked.

"She thinks I might have an ulcer."

"We'll know something very soon, Bran. So don't worry. I know it's easy for me to say, but try."

"You're right. It is easy for you to say," Brandeis snapped. "You haven't gone through what I have!" Worrying always made her irritable.

Jackson stared down at her, the silence lengthening between them as he searched her face. What was he looking for? She didn't know.

Finally, he spoke. "I'm here if you need me, Bran."

"You're very sweet, Jackson," she replied, in a breathy whisper, looking away from those eyes that probed too deeply into her soul.

An hour later, Gail Myers walked back into the room and banished Jackson to wait outside the room once again.

"I have the results of your sonogram. As I suspected, you have a peptic ulcer." Dr. Myers looked at the frightened young woman sitting in front of her. "Do you want to talk about what's bothering you?"

Her tears choked her. "No . . . I . . . he . . ." she began. "I-I keep thinking about that night . . . about Martin. I can't seem to get past it. I thought he was so nice, I cared for him. I really trusted him, Dr. Myers." She wiped at a lone tear. "I told him I was saving myself for my husband." Brandeis paused. "He-he t-told me that he l-loved me and wanted to marry me. He proposed to me and said he couldn't wait until our wedding night . . ."

With her hands clasped together, she looked down as if drawing her strength from them. "H-he tore my dress and he wouldn't listen to me. Wouldn't stop. I . . . I couldn't get away . . . He-he . . ." She lifted her head and her anguished eyes, filled with tears, pleaded with Dr. Myers.

"He raped you." Dr. Myers supplied quietly. "It's been

a year and you still haven't admitted to yourself what happened that night. Say it, Brandeis."

"He raped me! That bastard raped me and I hate him!" Brandeis sobbed.

Dr. Myers sat beside Brandeis on the bed. "It's okay, dear. Cry it all out," she said soothingly. She wrapped the young woman in her arms and said, "let it all out."

After a while, the sobs stopped. Brandeis accepted the tissue from her doctor and friend. "I'm so sorry. This is the first time I've really talked about what happened. I kept thinking that if I didn't *say* anything, I could just pretend it never happened."

"I take it then, you never reported the rape?" Dr. Myers asked.

"No. I didn't."

"Why?"

"Who's going to believe that someone I was dating could do something like this?" Brandeis said. "I'd been dating him for months. We talked about getting married. It h-happened in my own apartment. I kept wondering if I'd led him on or done something to cause it to happen. Besides, he left town a couple of days later. I don't know where he went."

"You've gone through a lot, Brandeis. Have you given any more thought to what I suggested months ago?"

"What? Oh, you mean about the counseling?"

"Yes. I really think it'll help. I would like for you to talk to a friend of mine. Her name is Helen Thayer and she's a rape counselor. She'll help you work through your feelings. I really wish you had pressed charges, Brandeis."

"At that time, I wasn't sure it was rape. He was my boyfriend and I cared a lot for him. Dr. Myers, I-I thought I l-loved him." She brushed a tear from her cheek. "I thought he loved me, too."

"Why do you question whether or not he raped you?" Dr. Myers pressed. "Did you say no?"

Brandeis nodded.

"You do understand that it's rape when a man compels

a woman to submit by force, threat of imminent death, serious bodily injury, or has substantially impaired her power?"

"Yes. But he really wasn't violent. He was persistent. He kept telling me that I wanted it, too."

"And what did you say?"

"I said no repeatedly."

"Then it was rape. You could have said yes in the beginning and then have changed your mind. It's still rape. Sweetie, I want you to do something for me. I want you to talk to your mother, and please consider going to see Helen," Dr. Myers suggested. "Don't carry this burden all by yourself. It's already affecting not only your mental health but your physical health, as well. Extreme anxiety, stress, and loss of sleep can cause you to become very ill. From now on, you're going to have to take better care of yourself. Watch your diet, too."

"I will. Thank you, Dr. Myers." She put her arms around the doctor and gave her a tight hug.

"Get plenty of rest. Before you leave, stop off at the pharmacy. You need to pick up a prescription of Tagamet. And give Mona my regards."

After Dr. Myers left her room, Brandeis dressed slowly.

As soon as she stepped out of the room, Jackson rushed to her side.

"How are you feeling?"

"I'm fine. Thank you so much for following me and trying to help me," Brandeis said. "I'm sorry about fighting you. I really appreciate what you did for me."

"Not a problem. By the way," Jackson said, "your mother called. She couldn't find a ride. She was going to call a taxi but I told her I would bring you to her house. I've also arranged for a tow truck to take your car to your mom's. I hope that's okay with you?"

"Sure. That's fine, but you don't have to go to all this trouble. I can take a taxi."

"You are not going to take a taxi. I'll drive you home," Jackson said, his voice allowing no argument.

During the ride home, Brandeis glared out the window, struggling to hide her panic. The silence lengthened until finally Jackson turned toward her in concern. "Everything okay?" To his own ears, the question sounded foolish. No! She was not okay. It was obvious, she'd had a terrible breakup with this person, Martin. But what had happened to make her so fearful of the man?

"Yes. Everything's fine. I just need to take it easy," Brandeis said. She sensed Jackson's concern was sincere. It was heartwarming. She knew he was confused about what had happened today. She felt she owed him an explanation, but wasn't sure she could explain. Brandeis' feelings were jumbled. Before Jackson had left for law school, she always wanted to be around him but now, his presence seemed to overwhelm her. She found his nearness both disturbing and exciting. Decidedly, she kept her eyes turned toward the window and pretended to be interested in the scenery. Would they ever get to her mother's house? The ride seemed to be taking forever.

Jackson wanted to reach out and touch Brandeis, but was hesitant to do so. He couldn't understood why she affected him the way she did. He had always been self-assured with women, and was never ill at ease either dating or simply carrying on a conversation with a woman friend or colleague.

Something about Brandeis made him unsure of himself. Was it because she seemed so uncomfortable around him? Another thought crept into his mind. Was he falling in love with her?

Finally, they arrived at the two-story red brick house. Mona was sitting on the porch in her white wicker rocker when they arrived. Brandeis could see the worry in her mother's face.

"Thank you again, for everything, Jackson," Brandeis said as she climbed out of the car. "I'll talk with you later." She ran past her mother and into the house as if the devil himself were on her heels.

Before Jackson could utter a response, she was gone.

He could only stare after her, baffled. He glanced at Mona and shook his head, perplexed by Brandeis' abrupt change in mood.

Once safe inside her room, Brandeis leaned weakly against the closed door. Long after Jackson had gone, Brandeis sat in her bed, reluctant to move, unable to read, longing most of all to escape the next few hours. Visions swept through her mind like a whirlpool, and try as she might, she couldn't slow them down. Visions of Jackson and dreams of the future drew her deeper and deeper until only Jackson's questioning gaze remained.

How often in the past she and Jackson had laughed together. How full their book of memories and how prominent his role! She recalled his helping her with her homework. He'd taught her how to drive. Jackson had always been a friend. To dream that his caring now could be the fruit of an emotion deeper than friendship, that he could know her so well and yet still want her, that he could do so forever . . . To dream this seemed indulgent, to believe it, impossible.

Between them stood the deep pool of her fear, doubts and inadequacies, yet there he stood, incredibly, all that she wanted, and she dared to imagine him beckoning.

In the end, no doubt, however demoralizing, could eclipse the power of his pull; no risk, however great, could diminish her wish to have Jackson love her. She loved him. Loved him! Where on earth had *that* come from? Brandeis couldn't love him. She wouldn't let herself. She was ashamed she'd so much as allowed the thought to cross her mind.

Brandeis was too frightened to think further, too anxious to sleep. Giving up, she impulsively threw back the covers and got out of bed. She needed to talk to her mother.

"Mom, are you busy?" Brandeis walked into the den where her mom sat sewing. She sat down slowly on the sectional sofa and ran her fingers across the southwestern pattern woven into the fabric.

"Hi, honey. No, I'm never too busy for you. What's the matter?" Mona looked up briefly from threading her needle. "Shouldn't you be in bed? You didn't have to come downstairs. I would've come up to your room. I stopped by to check on you earlier, but you were sleeping. I didn't want to disturb you."

"I'm actually feeling a lot better," Brandeis said. "I just need to talk to you. I saw Dr. Myers at the hospital today. She said to tell you hello, by the way." Brandeis lowered her eyes to look down at her hands folded neatly across her lap.

"I haven't talked to Gail in a couple of weeks," Mona said. "I should give her a call. And thank her for taking such good care of you." Mona looked at her daughter and frowned. Then, she walked over and sat beside her on the sofa. "What is it, Brandeis? I haven't asked you about what happened today because I knew you would come to me when you were ready, but I have to tell you that I've been worried sick. Now please don't shut me out, Bran. All your life you've been so private. It's as if you've tried to protect me from something. You don't have to do that. I'm fine."

Mona covered Brandeis' hand with hers. "I love you and I'll always love you."

"Mom, you know I never wanted to disappoint you." Brandeis' chin quivered. "Dad hurt you so much. I just wanted to make up for it by being the best daughter I could be. I didn't want to be like him."

Mona's eyes opened wide. "What do you mean, dear? Be like him in what way?"

"You know, making you cry all the time. I never want to remind you of him and all that pain."

Mona shook her head. "Brandeis, listen to me. You are the spitting image of your father. There's nothing you can do about that. When I look at you, yes, I'm reminded of him, but it's of the love that we shared. When you were conceived, it was out of love. I look at you to remind me of the good times I shared with him. He wasn't always a bad person. Don't put that kind of pressure on yourself."

"I used to hear you cry at night," Brandeis said softly. "Even though I was just a little girl, I made a promise that I'd never make you cry like Daddy."

Mona placed a loving hand under Brandeis' chin, forcing her to look into her eyes. "I will love you no matter what, Brandeis. Good or bad, you'll always be my child. Now please, stop trying to shield me and let me try to help you."

"Dr. Myers says that I have an ulcer. She also insisted that I talk to a rape counselor." A tear ran down her cheek. "I talked about it for the first time. About the rape."

Mona wrapped her arms around Brandeis. "I'm proud of you. And I think Gail is absolutely correct. You have to confront your past in order to live in the present. It's the only way to keep your sanity."

Brandeis had carried the nightmare with her for so long, suffering in silence. Now, she wanted to talk about that night. Mona realized how important it was for her to listen.

"Mom, I didn't want to have sex," Brandeis said. "I kept saying no, but Martin said I was just being coy so he wouldn't think I was easy. At the time, I thought maybe I'd led him on. But I know now that I didn't. When it happened, I was so afraid to tell you. To tell anyone. I kept thinking that if I didn't talk about it—I could just pretend it never happened."

Mona's expression changed to one of shock. "But why, dear? Why would you be afraid to tell me?"

"I was so afraid you would think badly of me. That's why I couldn't tell you. That's why I asked Carol to tell you. I was so humiliated."

"I would *never* think badly of you, dear," Mona said firmly. "You're my daughter and I know the kind of person you are. There's only one thing that's bothered me. I always wondered why you were so adamant about not pressing charges."

"I didn't want to put you through the embarrassment

of a trial." Brandeis gave a small laugh. "Actually, not just you but me, too. It was my fault for ever trusting Martin. Ever dating him. I couldn't stand everybody in Brunswick knowing what had happened to me. I just wanted to forget. I put my trust in the wrong person, and now, I can't even enjoy my life anymore."

"That bastard!"

"Mom!" Brandeis was shocked. She had never heard her mother utter such a word before. Her mother never had anything bad to say about anyone, including Brandeis' father.

"It makes me sick to see what that man has done to you," Mona went on. "I've watched you since that night. It makes me angry enough to kill! I hate not being able to do anything while you retreat within yourself. Brandeis, I hope you will consider talking to Gail's friend. I believe it'll help. One thing for sure, my darling. We're not going to let Martin ruin your life. Don't give him that power!"

"I thank God he didn't murder me," Brandeis said, "but he definitely messed things up for me. I was a virgin! I trusted him, Mom. I *trusted* him. Just like you trusted Dad. I thought he was a good person. Looking back, I realize that at times, he seemed too good to be true." Brandeis wiped away a tear.

Mona kissed Brandeis on the cheek. "I love you and we'll get through this. I promise you. I never trusted that Martin, but I hoped I was wrong about him. Sometimes, people can make us believe they're one way when they're not. But no matter how hard it is, you have to remember that there are still good people in this world."

"I know, Mom. I'm just afraid I won't be able to discern the good from the bad."

"Well, let's try to put Martin out of our minds, at least for a little while. There's a good movie on TV tonight. Why don't you watch it with me?"

"What's it about?" Brandeis settled back on the sofa, slowly releasing some of the tension in her body.

"About a woman whose face is scarred. She falls prey

to a smooth talker. She ends up going to prison for him. Eventually, she undergoes plastic surgery, changes her name, and sets out for revenge."

"Since when did you start watching movies like that?" Brandeis smiled. Her mother was just a bag of surprises.

"I think movies like this are interesting," Mona said, quirking an eyebrow. Running a hand through her hair, she said, "I think I'll go make some popcorn. Can I bring you something?"

"Mom. I'm not an invalid," Brandeis said. "You just stay here while I go make popcorn. I wouldn't want you to miss your *revenge* movie." Brandeis giggled as she stood and narrowly missed her mother's swat to her bottom.

"Who's sending you flowers? Why, they're lovely!" Carrie said, a wide smile plastered on her perfectly made-up face.

Brandeis grinned as she read the card that had come with the bouquet of yellow roses. "A friend."

"Oh, you must have a new man in your life. I can tell from that grin plastered all over your face. It has to be that Jackson Gray. I know he's been calling here for you a lot. Who is Jackson Gray, anyway?"

Brandeis stared for a long moment at the petite woman, then scowled at her. Despite her expression, she really wasn't angered by Carrie's words. Her eyes flashed with amusement when she finally said, "Carrie, have you prepared the inventory of Mr. Miller's assets and liabilities yet? I asked for them half an hour ago."

Carrie made a face and sashayed off to the copy machine.

Brandeis pulled the card that had come with the flowers out of her pocket and read it again. Jackson was asking her, once again, to have dinner with him. Reaching for the phone, she dialed his office. She was surprised when Jackson's secretary, Fran, put her straight through. According to Jackson, the woman guarded him like a watchdog. "Hello, Jackson."

"Hello, Brandeis. I take it you received the flowers."

"Yes, I did. They're lovely. Thank you so much for them, but I'm not going to be able to make dinner. I've got a lot of work to do to prepare for a case . . ."

"I understand," Jackson said, "but you still have to eat. Don't forget what Dr. Myers said. Are you taking your medicine?"

Brandeis smiled. "Yes, I'm being a good girl. I'm taking my medicine, eating right, and I'm trying not to work as hard."

"That's good to hear."

"Don't worry. I'll make a sandwich tonight and finish my work at home."

"Sure you don't want to take a break and have dinner?"

"I can't, Jackson," she said. "Please, try to understand."

"How *can* I understand when everything about you is such a mystery?" He sighed. "Okay. Time out. I want you to know something. I won't stop trying, Brandeis. Maybe not tonight, maybe not even next week, but one of these days, you'll have to say yes."

His voice, deep, sensual and exuding confidence sent a ripple of awareness through her.

"Will I? Why?"

"Because of the way you blush when I smile at you. I bet you're doing it now."

His observation was met with silence.

"I feel it, too, you know, Bran. This attraction. Someday, you'll let me prove it."

"I-I have to go. Thanks again for the flowers." Brandeis hung up. She took a deep breath and tried to relax. For goodness sake, he was only asking her out to dinner!

She put her hands to her face and closed her eyes. She told herself not to think, because if she did, she would realize just how foolish she was acting. If she'd been a little braver, she would have accepted his dinner invitation. He was a close and dear friend. And he'd already proved something to her; her emotions were like clay in his hands.

Brandeis hoped going into counseling would help her

overcome her fear of men. She didn't want to lose Jackson as a friend. She admitted to herself that she didn't want to lose the chance for something more. It was time to live again. But did she have the courage to allow herself to love him? *Remember what happened the last time,* her mind cautioned.

Jackson settled back into his chair, thinking about Brandeis. Who would have thought she would be so elusive? Why was she being so difficult? Even so, he would not back away, no matter how much she resisted him. He felt certain the fault lay not in himself, but in her, in the secrets she carried over her like a cloak, in the fears and guilt she wore like a covering on her soul. He wanted to battle her demons with her and help her uncover whatever bothered her.

Maybe she just wasn't interested in him. If that were the case, he would abide by her wishes, but it would be hard. Jackson was rapidly becoming painfully aware of how desirable she was. He wanted more than friendship with Brandeis. She possessed all the qualities he sought in a woman. She was intelligent, beautiful, and sophisticated.

Jackson hoped Brandeis would soon recover from her heartbreak and start to live again. She was too vibrant to become a hermit.

Jackson placed his hands to his face and rested his elbows on his desk. He thought briefly about going home early, but glancing down at the stack of papers on his desk, he quickly abandoned the idea.

"Mr. Gray." Fran stood in the doorway of his office. "Your next appointment is here."

Jackson sighed. "Give me a couple of minutes, then send him in."

Chapter 7

Brandeis and her mother sat in the rape counselor's outer office. After giving it more thought, Brandeis had called Helen Thayer and made an appointment. She had no idea what would come of it, but felt she had to try meeting with the counselor, at least once. After all, what did she have to lose?

Mona sat thumbing through a magazine while Brandeis reviewed some case notes she'd brought along.

A woman appeared in the door to the inner office and motioned for Brandeis to enter. She had soft brown eyes in a small, heart-shaped face, and short, tightly curled, auburn hair. She was dressed in a knee-length floral skirt and a green double-breasted jacket. "I'm Helen Thayer. You must be Brandeis."

"Yes . . . I am," she said uneasily.

Helen Thayer led her to a room with a sofa, coffee table, and two large, overstuffed chairs. Once they were seated, she began to quiz Brandeis on her childhood, parents, and her previous relationships with men.

"Can you tell me how you feel about the rape?" she asked at one point.

"How do you think I feel?" Brandeis stood up suddenly and walked over to the window. "I'm angry, hurt, embarrassed, humiliated . . . All of those things tied into one. I feel like it was my fault. You know, for ever going out with him, for trusting him. I've heard people say that sometimes in the heat of passion, things go too far. But I knew I wasn't ready for that next step. I kept telling him to stop. He acted as if he couldn't hear me."

"Why didn't you press charges? You can still do so," Helen said.

Brandeis turned around to face Helen. "Because I knew what they would do. I wasn't . . . I'm still not sure I could survive it. The police would make me relive the nightmare over and over again. It's too late for me to have a medical examination and without that a lawyer would advise me the rape would be hard to prove.

"His lawyer would treat me as if I were the criminal," Brandeis went on "especially after they found out Martin and I were dating at the time. Then, I would have to be further humiliated by testifying on the stand where Martin's lawyer would make mincemeat out of me. I don't think I could bear to sit on a witness stand and repeat the lurid details of that horrible night to a roomful of people. In a town as small as this one, everyone would know. I don't think I could bear it if everyone in town knew what had happened to me."

The woman didn't reply. Silence hung heavily in the room and Brandeis heard her own breath seeping in and out of her mouth. "I want my life back," she said quietly.

"Take each day one at a time . . ." Helen began.

Brandeis interrupted. "I've tried to do that. But in the process, I've completely shut out a lot of people. Especially men."

"You haven't dated since the rape?"

"No. I have a close friend who I've known all my life and I've treated him badly. Up until he moved back here a few weeks ago, I thought I had everything under control."

"You do, Brandeis," Helen said. "At least, on the sur-

face. Each person going through a crisis of any kind prog-
resses through stages of emotional adjustment. With sexual
violence, recovery may be defined in various ways. You are
experiencing what is called a rape-related, post-traumatic
stress disorder. Everything you're feeling is normal." She
placed her notes on the coffee table.

"Your greatest concern appears to be the fear that people will find out about the rape and blame you. From
what I can tell, you are a very strong young woman, very
controlled, very determined. With continued counseling,
you'll begin to realize that you are very much in control
of your emotions. You'll gradually begin to accept what
has happened to you and will stop punishing yourself. *It
was not your fault.* That's what we've got to get you to
understand. It's not by any means a overnight process.
Recovery takes time."

"I've been so afraid that I was going to continue to
suppress all these bad feelings and let them build inside
me for years," Brandeis admitted.

"Hopefully, you'll decide to accept counseling but it
really has to be your decision," Helen said. "If you do
decide to get counseling, in time, you'll no longer focus
on the rape. Eventually, the total rape experience will mesh
with all of the other experiences in your life."

Her hour was up before Brandeis realized it.

"I made another appointment with Helen," Brandeis
told her mother as they drove home. "I felt very comfortable with her so I'm going to start seeing her on a weekly
basis."

"I'm so glad, dear," Mona said. "She seems like a very
nice lady."

Brandeis nudged her mother's arm. "Thanks for coming
with me. I really appreciate it."

"I didn't mind at all."

"Did I tell you that Jackson sent me flowers yesterday?
They were at the office when I came back from lunch."
Brandeis smiled as she remembered. "They were the most

beautiful yellow roses I've ever seen. Everyone kept asking me who sent them, especially Carrie."

"Are you going to go out with him? He's asked you, what, three or four times already? You know he's going to give up on you," Mona warned. "He's a young, attractive man and any woman would love to have him. He could have his pick of any woman."

"I'll go out with him, eventually." Brandeis enjoyed teasing her mother. She knew how much her mother really liked Jackson and hoped they would get together. The truth was, Brandeis wanted it, too. "I'm hoping counseling will help me. I want to start dating again. I want to go out with Jackson."

Mona looked at her daughter and shook her head. "Providing he doesn't lose interest first. You would do well to remember that you're not getting any younger."

Brandeis threw back her head and laughed. "Mom! That's not very nice."

"Maybe not, dear, but it's very true."

Later that evening, Mona resumed her campaign to get Brandeis and Jackson together.

"I don't know why you keep turning Jackson down," Mona said again. "He's not asking you to marry him, for goodness sake. He just wants to have dinner with you."

Brandeis stood next to her mother's sewing table and graced her mother with a smile. "I know, Mom bu—"

"You two have always gotten along so well," Mona went on. "I just thought he'd be the one to help you get through this. You really shouldn't be so rude to an old friend."

Brandeis groaned and rolled her eyes heavenward. *Why are we still having this conversation?* Her mother was not going to give up on her crusade. "I'm *not* being rude to him."

"He really believes he's bothering you, but I've encouraged him not to give up on you."

"I actually enjoy talking to him on the phone," Brandeis admitted. "I'm just afraid to start going on dates with him. I'm afraid to be alone with him in any intimate setting."

"Him! You make it sound like *he's* bad somehow." A flash of humor crossed Mona's face. "I've got a solution! Tell him you'll go out with him if he promises to take you to McDonalds. Now, that's not quite so intimate."

"Mom!" Brandeis threw back her head and let out a great peal of laughter. "I can't believe you said that."

"Seriously, I have a better idea. Why don't you take Carol and James along? The four of you could go out to dinner together."

Brandeis thought for a moment. "Now, that's not a bad idea, Mom. Carol has been trying to get me to go out with her and James for a while now, but I didn't want to be a third wheel."

"If Jackson asks you again, please don't turn him down," Mona said. "Because if you refuse him this time, I don't think he'll ask you out anymore."

"You mean he gives up that easily? I didn't think you'd let him." There was laughter in her voice.

"Brandeis! I can't believe you. Why, you really think I'm a busybody," Mona said, trying to sound hurt.

"Mom! You know as well as I do that you and Jackson's mom have tried to play cupid for years. Come on, admit it."

"I'm not admitting any such silliness." Mona smirked. "Besides, I've always known about your crush on Jackson. My goodness, dear. What's wrong with a mother trying to make sure her daughter finds happiness?"

"My crush on Jackson was a long time ago and there's nothing wrong with what you're doing. I appreciate it."

Brandeis hadn't realized her feelings for Jackson had been so transparent. Was she still that easy to read? she wondered as she headed upstairs. Once there, she summoned up her nerve to call Jackson.

Carol fluffed her hair in the mirror, and then grabbed a piece of paper from Brandeis' desk to fan herself. "This is such a hot night!"

"It's the middle of July, Carol."

"I know. But usually it cools down some by evening, but not tonight. Maybe I should change my outfit and wear the blue one. What do you think, Bran?"

Brandeis fingered the strand of pearls around her neck. *I'm not ready for this. Oh, Lord, how am I going to get through this evening?*

"Bran? Earth to Brandeis."

"Oh, I'm sorry Carol. What did you say?"

"I asked if you thought I should wear the blue?"

"If you're going to be more comfortable, then wear the blue. I like the way it fits you."

Carol quickly undressed as Brandeis handed her the navy blue, two-piece dress. As soon as she was dressed, she followed Brandeis into the bathroom.

"Bran, are you okay about this? I mean, why on earth do you want me and James to tag along?" Carol asked as she applied a touch of clear lip gloss to her full lips. She handed a tube of ruby red lipstick to Brandeis. "I would think you'd want to be alone with that gorgeous man. Jackson looks good in his glasses, don't you think?"

"I'm not ready to be alone with him, but yes, he does look good in glasses." Brandeis dabbed some mascara on her lashes. She remembered how surprised Jackson had sounded when she'd called and invited him on the double date.

Carol looked at her friend and shook her head. "You're strange, girlfriend. Strange."

"It's what makes me so interesting, don't you think?"

They both laughed.

"Carol, it's hard to explain. I guess I'm nervous. It's been a year since . . . Martin, but I think it'll be easy if you all are there. I need the moral support," Brandeis said.

"If you say so. I know it's been hard on you. If it'll make this date easier for you, James and I are glad to go along. You know," Carol said, "I remember how you used to cry your eyes out every September when Jackson left for college."

Brandeis closed her eyes. "Oh, God, please don't remind me."

"You know, he graduated with Robyn. She said all the girls at school had the hots for him but that he was mostly into books and sports. He was still pretty popular, though."

"I didn't realize your sister was that old."

Carol laughed. "You'd better not ever let her hear you say that. She'll have your head on a platter." With long red fingernails, Carol picked through her curls to give her bangs a lift. Using the brush, she smoothed the tiny waves along the nape of her neck.

Standing next to the door, Brandeis straightened her shoulders and cleared her throat. "I really appreciate your coming tonight, Carol. I realize it was last minute and all." She took one last glance in her mirror. "Do I look okay?" she asked.

"You look fine. How about me?" Carol twirled around slowly.

"You are going to knock James off his feet. I really like that outfit. You look so good in navy."

Carol stood in front of the full-length oval mirror, straightening her ankle-length skirt. Brandeis moved behind her to adjust the straps on the back of Carol's sleeveless jacket.

"There, that looks better. It was too tight before."

Just as they reached the living room, they heard the shrill ringing of a doorbell. Brandeis took one last glance into her compact mirror before putting it in her purse. Carol opened the door to a smiling Jackson. The single-breasted suit he wore looked great on him. Brandeis could tell from the fabric and the style that it was expensive. As they were making polite conversation, Carol's fiancé, James, arrived. The four of them silently made their way to Jackson's car, a silver-gray Mercedes Benz.

Arriving at the restaurant, Brandeis quickly gave her attention to the dining room, which glittered beneath the lights of the dozen chandeliers. Each table had been set for four, except for three or four smaller tables for two, tucked in the corners of the room. The tables were draped with peach-colored cloths. In the center of each table was a pair of brass candlesticks and a brass vase holding fresh-cut flowers.

The maitre d'escorted them to their table. Brandeis sat facing Jackson; Carol sat next to her, facing James.

A few minutes after being seated, the waiter brought a bottle of champagne. Jackson tasted it, accepted it, and after the waiter had gone, offered a toast.

"To new beginnings and hidden blessings."

The rims of Brandeis' glass touched Jackson's as he spoke those words, and her hand trembled. The glasses clinked against each other, sending the tinkling sound of the fine crystal rippling through the air.

Jackson took in Brandeis' black lace dress, simple but elegant, the pearl earrings dangling from her ears, and her upswept hairstyle, which somehow managed to be proper and seductive at the same time. He could tell from the pulsating vein in her neck and the erratic swell of her breasts that she was struggling to breathe in a calm, normal fashion.

Brandeis was caught in Jackson's gaze. She wanted to look away, but could not. It was as though he held her by some invisible bond that reached from his eyes to her very soul.

The waiter came and served their salads.

Forcefully, Brandeis broke their stare, took a gulp of champagne and considered running from the table. With great effort she was able to remain in her seat. *Thank God for Carol and James!* She started to eat the caesar salad, mentally steadying her hand to keep her fork from shaking.

"So, has a date been set for the wedding?" Jackson asked as he spread butter on his roll.

Carol patted her mouth with her napkin. "We're thinking about June twenty-seventh of the year two thousand."

"Two thousand! That's two years away." Jackson glanced at James then back at Carol.

She laughed. "I need time to plan and organize the

wedding. James and I both want a big wedding. We're paying for it ourselves so right now, we're saving our money. Besides, I'm not good at doing things at the last minute."

Brandeis and James nodded and laughed. Brandeis glanced at Jackson and smiled. "Carol's telling the truth. She takes time to organize *everything*. She even makes lists of all the lists she has to make."

Jackson laughed. "James, you've got yourself quite a lady."

James pushed his gold wire-framed glasses back on his nose and grinned. "I think so."

The waiter brought over a tray of food. Moving from right to left, starting with Carol, he distributed steaming platters of flounder stuffed with crab meat, shrimp scampi, lobster, and steak.

"Everything smells delicious. I haven't been here in months." Brandeis found she was ravenous.

"Your scampi looks great! I started to order that, but changed my mind." Carol sliced off a bit of her flounder, pierced it with a fork, then put it in her mouth. "Mmmm, this is sooo good."

Jackson chuckled. "I'm glad you're enjoying your food. Bran, how's yours?"

"It's wonderful. This is one of my favorite places to eat, but then, I bet my mother told you that, too."

Jackson's smile was her answer.

"I thought so. Mom has a big mouth."

"She means well, Bran," Carol said, between bites of her fish. "My mother has always hated everyone I dated. She's just now getting used to James and we've been dating for the last three years."

"Amen, to that," James added. "For the first year, she wouldn't say anything to me other than hello and goodbye. Now, at least she'll ask me how I'm doing. I'm hoping after the wedding, we'll actually be able to sit down and have a conversation."

Jackson laughed as if sincerely amused. His laughter was

deep, warm, and rich. Brandeis loved his gentle camaraderie and his subtle wit. The timbre of his deep, rich voice sent tingles racing up her spine and put goose bumps on her skin. She found herself extremely conscious of his virile appeal.

After the waiter cleared the table, as they were waiting for coffee, Jackson said, "You've been awfully quiet this evening, Bran. Are you enjoying yourself?"

"Oh, yes. I've had a good time. It's been so long . . . I've had a wonderful time." The smoldering flame she saw in his eyes startled her. Her pulse skittered alarmingly.

"I'm glad." Jackson wanted to say more, but decided the time was not right. He wondered if Carol and James had noticed the interplay of emotions between them.

Jackson walked her to her door. "Where are your keys?"

"They're . . . right here." Brandeis reached into her purse and pulled out the keys to her door. She felt momentary panic as her mind jumped on to what Jackson expected from her now. "I-I had a very nice time. Thank you, Jackson."

He reached up and gently cupped her face. She flinched at the sudden contact of his flesh on her flesh. His touch seemed to burn. As his long, slender fingers trailed gently across her face to her chin, lifting it, her bones seemed to melt. She was actually trembling now.

As Jackson's warm mouth closed over hers, skillfully playing and coaxing, Brandeis lost all presence of mind. She melted into him, her arms twining about his broad shoulders. Jackson crushed her to him, molding their bodies tightly together.

Jackson was intoxicated by the sweet taste of her mouth, her exciting fragrance, her incredible softness against him. Feeling himself becoming aroused, his manhood hardening and rising, his kiss became strongly passionate.

Feeling that hard, throbbing part of him against her, enormous and frightening, so hot it seemed to scorch her right through their clothing, Brandeis' mind began to send out warning signals.

She struggled, and finally managed to tear her mouth away. "No! Stop it!"

Jackson released her. "What's wrong, Brandeis? What did I do?" He grabbed her slender hands in his. "I don't know what happened to you, but I know it has to be something terrible because I've never known you to react this way around me." She would not look at him, but kept her head down. He placed a gentle hand on her chin and lifted her face. "Look at me, it's Jackson. I'm not going to hurt you. I'm your friend, sweetheart."

"I'm so sorry, Jackson. I—I just don't want to rush things. I—" She was glad the dim lighting hid the extent of her embarrassment.

Jackson nodded. "Go on in. I'll call you later this week."

A look of tired sadness passed over her. "I really did have a good time with you tonight, Jackson. Thank you." She walked into her apartment and closed the door.

Jackson stood outside her door until he heard her propel the lock in place. *What in hell did you do to her, Martin?*

Brandeis slumped down on her sofa, her eyes bordered with tears. *How could I do that to him?* She didn't know how she would be able to face Jackson after tonight's episode. He probably never wanted to see her again. *It's just as well,* she decided. Tonight proved that she just wasn't ready for dating.

Twenty minutes later, as she readied herself for bed, the phone rang. Brandeis answered on the second ring, convinced it was her mother wanting a date report. She was surprised to hear Jackson's voice on the other end. "Hi, Jackson. I—"

"Bran, it's okay. I didn't mean to rush things. I care a lot for you and I'm prepared to take it slow. I would like to see you again. Is that okay with you?"

Brandeis couldn't control the wide grin that spread across her face. "Yes. Yes, it's okay with me. I'd really like that." Her decision to stop dating had just flown out the window.

She smiled on hearing Jackson's sigh of relief. She was touched by his obvious display of concern. Impulsively, she said, "I'm planning to go to the beach on Saturday. Would you care to join me?"

"Are you sure you want me to go?"

She knew he was a little more than astonished by her invitation. "Yes, Jackson. I want you to go." She was feeling bolder by the minute. "So, are you coming with me or not?"

There was laughter in her voice, but it didn't cover the nervousness he also heard. "Yes, I'd love to go to the beach with you."

After hanging up, Brandeis readied her sofa bed and went into the bathroom to take a shower. By the time her head touched her pillow, she was exhausted. Not so surprisingly, she found sleep elusive. She turned on her back and stared at the ceiling. Thoughts of Jackson flitted through her mind. His kiss had stirred feelings she believed long dead. Her newly awakened passions brought sensations with a bewildering intensity, as if every pore in her body was open, waiting to be filled.

She was frightened of this new awakening in her body and yet for the first time in a year, she felt totally alive. She couldn't stop thinking about what had happened between them and sleep was a long time in coming.

Brandeis walked to the water's edge and stood staring into the horizon. Her black-belted swimsuit, edged in white contrast, only served to enhance her natural sex appeal. She glanced back at Jackson and grinned. Brandeis loved the weekends because she could go to the beach and catch up with her reading. It was her time to just kick back and unwind. It was a wonderful, glorious day and there was no other place on earth she'd rather be than on the beach with Jackson.

Jackson's gaze moved slowly from her face to her body, taking in her bare legs, rounded thighs, and the feminine curves of her slender waist and firm breasts. He looked at her as if he were photographing her with his eyes. A minute or two later, he realized she was talking to him. "Er . . . huh?"

"Are you going to just stand there all day?" She placed both hands on her hips and stamped her foot impatiently.

"No. I'll be right there." He sat down on the sand and removed his Bass sandals.

Brandeis walked over and sat down next to him. "Where were you just then?"

Jackson was not about to admit he had been devouring her body with his eyes. "I just had something on my mind."

"Are you ready to have some fun?" Brandeis asked.

"Are you?"

"I'll race you to the water . . . hey!" She jumped up as Jackson suddenly rushed toward the ocean. His movements were swift, full of grace and virility. She ran behind him laughing and shouting, "That's not fair! You are still a cheater."

Brandeis found herself studying him as he waded knee-deep in the water. She took in his tempting, attractive male physique clothed only in swimming trunks. Just a glimpse of his strong, brown-skinned body made her heart beat more rapidly. An undeniable magnetism was building between them.

"Come on slowpoke," he called from the water.

The feel of the cold water sent a shock wave through her system. She shivered slightly, then relaxed as she became used to the ocean's temperature. "Why didn't you tell me the water was so cold?"

"It feels good to me. It's been so hot lately." Jackson didn't add that some of the heat he felt was due to her. He had raced out to the ocean in order to keep Brandeis from seeing his physical reaction to her.

Together they frolicked, splashing each other like children. Brandeis realized how much she had missed his company. After she and Jackson tired of swimming, they returned to the beach towels they abandoned earlier and sat down. Brandeis offered him a can of soda. She considered him as he methodically opened the can and took a sip. Every time his gaze met hers, her heart turned over in response.

Later that night, Brandeis lay on her sofa bed and remembered their first kiss, the way Jackson's mouth had molded to hers. She admitted to herself that she'd been disappointed when Jackson left her earlier this evening, after they'd been at the beach, without so much as a peck on her cheek. Brandeis longed to feel again the firm length of his body pressed against hers. She wondered why there was a deep emptiness inside her when he wasn't around? Why did she yearn to be normal again, to touch him, hear his voice, and feel rising goose bumps when he talked to her?

Her aching needs and longings scared her, but she knew she wanted to be in his embrace, to feel the tingling ecstasy of his lips and questing tongue.

But even as she dreamed and longed for him, reality brought tears swimming into Brandeis' eyes. She didn't know how to handle the emotional upheaval that now raged within her. Would he be able to scale the thick wall she had built between them? She closed her eyes. As the past receded, the future took her in its arms, cleansing her with a balm that soon became heavy slumber.

Chapter 8

Jackson turned restlessly in his king-size bed, sleepless, plagued by his nettled thoughts. He remembered the tantalizing fire of Brandeis' kiss after their first date. He also recalled how she'd reacted afterward. That was the reason he'd left without attempting a kiss tonight. It had not been easy to walk away without pulling her into his arms. Desire had sent his blood running hot from the first moment he'd seen her today. He tortured himself with fantasies of her passionate body under his, meeting his thrusts with a fiery passion of her own. The memory of each curve and plane of her body molded by the swimsuit taunted him.

He reached for the phone several times, intending to call her but thought better of it. She was probably sleeping. They'd spent all day together and planned to go bike riding tomorrow. He didn't want to make a nuisance of himself. Still, every time he closed his eyes, he saw her naked, smiling and beckoning to him. *Oh, hell!* He couldn't stand it any longer. He jumped up and headed for the shower.

The cold shower did him little good. Still frustrated, he climbed back into an empty bed, centering his thoughts on the preparations that had to be completed before his client's trial started next week.

"Hey! Wait up, Bran." Jackson pedaled his bicycle faster. He heard her soft giggle as she slowed her pace. Her hair, shimmering curls of dark brown, flew around her face like wild ribbons. She turned to him with a daring smile, laughter bubbling from her lips and whipping away on the breeze. Desire quickened his blood. He'd never seen anyone so beautiful, so desirable.

"What's the matter, old man? Can't catch up?" she teased.

Jackson was suddenly beside her. "Hey, who're you calling 'old man'?"

"Who do you think? I've had to slow down to a snail's pace three times because you couldn't keep up."

"Bran, it's been years since I've ridden a bike . . ."

"Excuses, excuses." Brandeis shook her head and laughed.

"You're a funny lady, today."

"Aw, don't get mad, Jackson."

"Now why would I get mad? I just get even." Jackson raced off on his bike, leaving Brandeis behind.

"Sore loser!" she shouted as she rode off in an attempt to catch up.

Jackson turned into the driveway of Brandeis apartment building. He was sitting on the front stairs when she arrived.

She was laughing as she dismounted. She approached him, shaking her head. "You, sir, are no gentleman. I could have been mugged, shot, anything." Brandeis pointed an accusing finger at him. "You just left me in the dust."

"I see you had no problem leaving *me* behind."

"Because you're a man."

"Oh, so you're not worried about my safety because I'm a man?"

Brandeis thought about this for a minute, then answered, "Well, no."

Jackson pretended to be hurt.

"Aw, I was only kidding. You know I would do all I could to protect you. Remember, I have a great left hook."

"Oh, yes, I remember it well." Jackson rubbed his cheek for emphasis. He stood up and walked over to Brandeis. "I'm glad you're my bodyguard." He stood extremely close to her and couldn't keep the grin on his face from spreading.

Brandeis laughed nervously and backed away. "I'm sure that body of yours does need guarding. I heard those girls honking at you."

"What about the guys that were honking at you?"

"They were honking at *you*, too. One guy even yelled out your name. Remember?"

"That was a man?"

"Yes." The look on Jackson's face made her double over with laughter.

"That's not funny, Bran."

"Oh, but it is."

Jackson started to walk away, but she reached out for him. "I'm sorry, Jackson. I won't tease you anymore." Despite her efforts, she couldn't stop giggling. "I forgot how much you hated to be teased."

Leaning over, he stole a quick kiss. This time he laughed at her expression. "I thought you'd straighten up."

"No fair, Jackson." She felt herself blushing. Brandeis gently pulled away from him and fought to control her trembling body.

"I guess we'd better take the bikes upstairs. It looks like rain."

Brandeis glanced upward. "It does look like rain. If you want, you can leave your bike over here. If it's still raining, when you leave, that is."

"Thanks."

Together they carried the bikes upstairs to her apartment. Jackson carried them from the front door to the balcony while Brandeis went into her bathroom to freshen up.

She soon returned wearing a pair of purple leggings and an oversized purple and white T-shirt.

"Are you hungry, Jackson?"

"Yes, I am. I'd planned to take you to dinner, but the weather looks bad."

"I don't mind cooking." She peered into her pantry. "Hmm, let's see . . ." She looked back at him. "I can make spaghetti, crab alfredo over linguini, or hot wings. Which would you prefer?"

"Surprise me," Jackson said as he carried his duffle bag into the bathroom.

Brandeis watched him until he closed the bathroom door. She walked into the kitchen. Opening her pantry door, she selected a can of crab meat, alfredo sauce, and linguini noodles. From the freezer she pulled out a loaf of garlic bread. When Jackson returned, she was preparing a salad. He had changed into a pair of navy sweats and a red T-shirt.

"Dinner is almost ready."

"Everything smells delicious. How did you prepare all this so quickly?"

"That's the cook's secret." She handed him two plates, forks, knives, and spoons. "You get to set the table."

"No problem."

Brandeis placed her hands on her hips. "You sure you know how to set a table?"

Jackson snorted. "Yes, I most certainly know how to set a table. You just wait and see."

Brandeis buttered the garlic bread and placed it on a tray. After draining the linguini, she carried the pasta out into the dining room. She looked around the table, smiling. "It looks beautiful, Jackson. Where in the world did you find the flowers?" He didn't look as if he'd been out in the rain. His clothes were dry.

"I stole a few off your neighbor's balcony."

"Jackson!"

"Well, she has plenty," he argued. "I don't think she'll miss these."

She shook her head. "I don't believe you."

"Are we going to discuss my morals or can we sit down and have dinner?"

He pulled out a chair for Brandeis. After she was seated, he sat down across from her. She watched quietly as he took a bite and chewed slowly. She waited for a response. When none was forthcoming, she asked, "Well?"

Jackson grinned. "Hmmm, this is good."

"Thank you. I'm glad you like it."

Jackson took another bite. "When did you learn to cook?"

"I've been cooking since I was sixteen. I still don't know if *you* can cook."

"I can cook." He saw the look of skepticism on her face. "I'll prove it to you."

"How?"

"Come to my house next Saturday night for dinner." When he saw a faint glimmer of fear in her eyes, he added, "Bring Carol and James. We'll make it a double date."

Relief flowed through her body. "Are you sure you want to do this?"

"Yes. I really like them."

"Should we eat before we come?"

"Ha-ha. I have to warn you, when you taste my shrimp scampi, you're going to want to marry me."

Her amber, almond-shaped eyes crinkled up in laughter. "Then perhaps you should cook something else. It would be a shame if James wants to marry you, too. I think Carol would probably kill you."

"Believe me, it'll be James who'll want to kill me. My cooking only has an amazing effect on women."

Brandeis raised her eyebrows and grinned. "You're that sure of your cooking?"

Jackson winked. "I'll let you find out for yourself."

* * *

"Lily, have you seen that fine piece of a man over at Davis, Kinard & Donaldson?" Carrie and one of the paralegals were in the employee's lounge, standing next to the coffee station. They both were so busy sharing tidbits of gossip, neither one of them heard Brandeis come in.

"Oh, yeah. I saw him at the courthouse about a month ago. He sure looks good, girlfriend. But you'd better keep your hands off him. *Someone else* already has her hooks in him." Lily brushed her knuckles across her blouse, as if to smooth out the stitched down pleats adorning the front.

"Who?" Carrie hated gossiping with Lily. Lily always seemed to delight in delivering bad news to her. The buck-toothed girl was probably just jealous of her.

"You know who." Lily pushed her nose upward with her finger.

Carrie stepped back and put her hands on her ample hips. "You can't mean—"

"Yep. I saw him at the beach with Brandeis about three weeks ago. They looked pretty cozy." Lily smirked, as if she was enjoying herself at Carrie's expense.

Carrie's mouth dropped open. "What? You mean that fine man is Jackson Gray?" She wanted to slap the grin off Lily's face. She knew she should just walk away but she couldn't, not yet.

"The one and only. He's heading the criminal defense department over at DKD."

"Are you sure he's dating Brandeis? Maybe they're related or something." *Oh Lord, please let them be related,* she prayed.

Carrie was so tired of being alone. She wanted to find a man whom others would envy and who would provide her with the affluence and class she desperately sought.

She'd had discreet affairs with two of the firm's attorneys. They'd sought her out after being turned down flat by the high and mighty Brandeis Taylor. Deep down, Carrie really couldn't blame Brandeis. The guys had turned out to be jerks. They only called when they wanted sex. Carrie wanted more than just a romp in the bedroom. More than anything in the whole world, she wanted to be married and raise a family.

"I don't think so," Lily went on. "They seemed lovey-dovey to me." She looked down at Carrie with an expression of mock pity. "Sorry, girlfriend. Brandeis beat you to him."

Carrie was livid. She'd intended on making herself known to Jackson Gray. A raging jealousy was brewing in her heart. Damn Brandeis! How dare she take Jackson away from her before she'd even had a chance at him. If he'd known he could have had Carrie instead, he wouldn't even have looked at Brandeis. What did he see in the ice princess, anyway? "I don't think—"

Brandeis cleared her throat and walked up to the two women. "I'm sure the two of you have plenty of work to do besides standing around the coffee pot gossiping." She briefly wondered what Carrie had been about to say. Probably something mean.

Carrie and Lily glanced at each other. Without another word, they paraded out of the room.

Brandeis smiled archly. She knew they wondered how much she'd overheard. She quickly fixed a cup of coffee for herself and returned to her office.

Carrie was on her heels. "Brandeis. I need to talk to you."

"Yes, Carrie?" she asked wearily. Brandeis was tired, and she was anxious for the workday to end.

"I want to apologize for gossiping about you and Jackson. I really didn't know you two were involved. Actually, I didn't know that the lawyer over at Davis, Kinard & Donaldson and Jackson Gray were the same person. I didn't even know the person calling you was a lawyer."

"It doesn't matter, Carrie." Brandeis bit back a smile. So, they thought she'd overheard their entire discussion.

Carrie, hands on hips, and eyes flashing, remarked, "I

just don't want you thinking I'm after your man, Brandeis. I have enough problems around here with the other women. I don't want you angry with me, too."

"First of all, Jackson Gray is not my man. Second, he is not a possession. Third, he has the power to choose for himself the person he wants to be with."

"I think *any* man should be able to choose who he wants to be with, Brandeis," Carrie said, enigmatically.

"What?" she had no idea what Carrie was talking about. "Never mind. I don't go around discussing my personal life with anyone, and most certainly not with you. I suggest we end this discussion right now."

Carrie's eyes were tear bright. "Why are you always attacking me? I know you've never liked me. But given the circumstances, we have no choice but to try to tolerate each other. I have tried to be friends with yo—"

Brandeis was getting impatient. "Please! Carrie, you have tried to do nothing but cause problems. You talk too much, for one. I think you thrive on making trouble and I don't want any part of it."

"That's not true!"

"I've seen you in action enough times," Brandeis argued. "You never have anything nice to say about anybody, Carrie. It's enough reason for me to keep you at a distance."

"Anyway! I just came in to make it clear that I'm not after Jackson. I saw him for the first time when I went to visit a friend of mine who works at DKD. Oh, by the way, did you know Jackson's representing Marc Wiley? You remember Marc, don't you? He graduated from Glynn Academy the same year you did."

"I remember Marc," Brandeis said. "He's a friend of yours?"

"Yes, he and two of my brothers are very close. Marc Wiley is like family to me."

"Why is Jackson defending him? What kind of trouble is he in?" Brandeis asked.

Carrie's eyes grew enormous. "Haven't you heard? It's been all over the newspaper!"

"What's been in the paper, Carrie?"

"Honey chile, Marc's been arrested for rape. They think he raped Peggy. He didn't though. She's lying—"

"Peggy Roberts?"

Carrie nodded. "Didn't she graduate a year behind you and Marc?"

"Marc raped Peggy?" Brandeis felt her face tighten with shock. And Jackson was representing him? *He couldn't.* She made a conscious effort to show no further reaction.

Brandeis was aware of Carrie's watching her intently. It was as if she were waiting to see some show of emotion. But Carrie didn't know. How could she?

"Honey chile, he didn't do it," Carrie said. "Peggy is nothing but a vindictive liar. You know, a lot of women are spiteful that way. They get dumped or something and they think that's the way to get even. Marc and Peggy were having a fling and he refused to leave his wife—"

Brandeis had heard enough. Her head was spinning. "I don't want to hear it! Please, could you just leave my office . . . I don't want to hear any more."

Carrie sensed that Brandeis had said all she intended to say on the matter. She left the room and closed the door loudly.

Brandeis put her face in her hands and squeezed her eyes shut. Her head was throbbing. She couldn't believe he could do such a thing! Jackson, defending a man guilty of rape! After a few minutes, the pain disappeared. *How could he do this?* It didn't matter to Brandeis that Jackson had no idea what had happened to her.

She reached for the phone, intending to call him, but suddenly, changed her mind. "I'd better talk to you face to face," she whispered to the empty office. "Marc's guilty and you can't get him off!" She grabbed her purse and left her office in a hurry.

Carrie, sitting at her desk, smiled as Brandeis rushed past and out of the building. As soon as she thought enough time had gone by, she pulled out her electronic phone book and scanned for a phone number. After finding the number, she picked up the phone and started to dial.

Jackson glanced up to find Brandeis in the doorway to his office. Standing up behind his desk, he removed his glasses and smiled warmly. "Hello Bran," he said. "I didn't expect to see you. Let's sit over here." He waved to the sofa.

Brandeis took a few brisk steps toward him. "I don't want to sit down, Jackson. I don't plan to be here that long. Tell me something. How can you, with a clear conscience, defend a rapist? Marc Wiley should go to jail for what he's done. How can you do this to me?" Hostility flashed in her eyes.

Jackson responded in sudden anger. Who did Brandeis think she was, storming in here without so much as a hello and attacking him? "What the hell are you talking about?" he said. "It's my job. In case you've forgotten, I'm a criminal defense attorney. That's what I get paid to do! Besides, I happen to believe my client is telling the truth. He didn't rape Peggy Roberts. Would you mind telling me why you're so upset about this? Is Peggy a friend of yours? I know you went to high school with her."

"No, we've never been friends," Brandeis said.

Jackson had had enough of unexplained outbursts. "What's going on with you, Bran?"

Brandeis said nothing. She was so furious, she found herself clenching her teeth.

"Why are you so upset about this particular case? Bran, please answer me."

Jackson was getting too close. He couldn't learn her secret. She wouldn't be able to bear it if he knew her shame. In a lightning-fast motion, Brandeis reached for her purse, preparing to flee.

Jackson was ready. He leaned across his desk to take her

hand. "Don't, Brandeis, don't pull away from me. Tell me what's going on with you? Why are you reacting this wa—" Realization hit him full force in the face. *She was raped! It all made sense. Martin raped her!*

"He raped you, didn't he? Martin raped you!" His face was a glowering mask of rage. He forced himself to speak calmly. "Answer me, Bran. Did he rape you?"

Brandeis was speechless. *He knows.* Defeated, she sat down in one of the visitor's chairs with her head bowed, silent, tense, stricken. She covered her face with trembling hands and gave way to despair. Among other emotions was a deep sense of shame and humiliation. Brandeis wanted so badly to tell him everything, but she couldn't speak without crying. She didn't want to break down in front of him. Besides, Jackson could never understand. *He's a man.* The thought of him defending a rapist paralyzed her with feelings of anger and betrayal.

"Are you going to answer me? *Damn!*" Jackson balled his hand into a fist, and slammed it on his desk with a thud.

Brandeis jumped, but said nothing.

"Why won't you talk to me? Can't you see I care about you and I want to help you get past this? But I need to know what happened to you. To make you this way. *Did he rape you?*"

When she still didn't answer, Jackson slumped down in his chair and swiveled around to face the picturesque window that was situated behind him.

The silence in the room was deafening to them both.

She never saw the hurt in his eyes. When she found the strength to stand, she slipped out of his office without as much as a goodbye.

He never saw the tears that fell.

Back within the safe confines of her office, Brandeis fell into her chair and put her head on her desk. Her mind was just not on her work. Since leaving Jackson's office, all she could think about was him. Why did she feel so betrayed by him? How could he defend a man who was guilty of raping a woman? Didn't he understand how that made her feel? Raising her head and pushing back from the desk, Brandeis rose to her feet. She walked over to the window and gazed outside. Her thoughts were in turmoil.

Brandeis wasn't sure how she felt about Jackson. She was so afraid of trusting him, of trusting anyone. Deep down inside, she had a feeling she could very easily fall in love with him. But now that he knew the truth, she cautioned herself to hold her expectations in check and carefully guard her emotions. Otherwise, she could end up with a broken heart. She wondered if he could still care about her after knowing she'd been raped. Would he even believe she was raped? He seemed so sure of Marc's innocence. Marc, Brandeis recalled, had been nothing but a troublemaker when they were in high school.

Brandeis slid gracefully into her chair and once again rested her head on her arms. She was drifting off when she heard a soft rap on her door. Mona opened the door slightly and peeked in.

Brandeis sat up and beckoned for her mother to enter. "Come on in, Mom. I'm so glad to see you."

"What's wrong, dear. You look so sad." Mona closed the door and settled into one of the chairs facing Brandeis.

"It's Jackson, well Jackson and me. I found out he's defending Marc Wiley on a rape charge and I lost it. Mom, I rushed over to his office today and I made a complete fool of myself. I was so angry. Then, Jackson somehow put two and two together. He figured out that I had been raped by Martin."

"Did he say that?"

Brandeis nodded. "Yes, he came straight out and asked me if Martin raped me."

"And did you confirm his suspicions?"

"No, I just sat there, not saying anything. I was afraid to admit it, Mom. I didn't want Jackson to think badly of me. I was never so embarrassed. I know he thinks it's my fault."

Mona frowned. "But why would you think that?"

"Because everyone is saying that Marc is innocent of rape. They're saying that he and Peggy Roberts were having an affair. That doesn't mean he didn't rape her, though. You see, it's what people believe when you're raped by someone you're dating."

"Brandeis, honey?"

"Yes."

"What does all this have to do with you and Jackson?" Mona studied her daughter's face for the answer.

Brandeis was bewildered. "What do you mean, Mom?"

"Just what I've said. What does Jackson's defending Marc have to do with you and Jackson? Why are you so angry at the man for doing his job?"

"Jackson's defending a man guilty of rape," Brandeis stated. "I thought you of all people would understand what that does to me. How it makes me feel."

"I'm trying, dear, but I think you need to understand a few things. First of all, Jackson's a defense lawyer. That's his job." Mona pressed on. "Second, you don't know if Marc raped Peggy."

"But—" She glared at her mother. "He's guilty!"

Mona held her hand up, silencing her daughter. "Now, you listen to me, Bran. You were not there so you have no idea what happened between the Marc and that girl, Peggy. I admit there are rotten men in this world, but there are some good men, too. Just because one man is guilty of a crime does not make the next one guilty. Seems to me you're looking to crucify someone for a crime he may not be guilty of commiting. You shouldn't want to make this man pay for what Martin did to you. And you know you shouldn't make Jackson pay for defending him, either. He deserves better."

Brandeis' mouth sagged a little. She was more than a little ashamed of herself. "You're absolutely right, Mom.

He does deserve better. Jackson didn't even know what I'd been through. I've treated him unfairly."

"I think the two of you should really sit down and talk. It's all right to tell him you're uncomfortable with his defending Marc, *but understand, it's his job.* Regardless of how he feels about you, he has a duty to give his client the best representation he can."

Brandeis knew what her mother was saying was right. She needed to sit down with Jackson and tell him the truth. She owed him that much. "I wonder if he'll want to see me again?" Brandeis wondered aloud.

It was Mona's turn to be thunderstruck. "Why wouldn't he?"

"Because of the way I've acted. I really can't blame him if he doesn't." Her fingers knitted together. "Mom, I can't believe I acted so stupidly. I don't think I can ever face him again. Oh, what have I done?"

Mona shook her head emphatically. "Don't fret so, dear. Jackson knows you almost as well as you know yourself. However, you two really need to talk about this, before your relationship goes any further."

"You're right, Mom." Brandeis smiled as she tapped her fingers in her desk. "I think I'll stop by his condo this evening, to talk to him. I owe him an apology and an explanation. Maybe we can start over. What do you think?"

Mona ran her fingers through her curls and murmured, "I think that's a superb idea. Now that we have that settled, this is the reason I came by . . ."

Chapter 9

Martin should have been strung up and left out to die.

The thought repeated itself again and again in Jackson's mind. Every time he thought back on his conversation with Brandeis, his hand curled into a fist. The more he thought about Martin, the more he was tempted to hunt the bastard down. An expression of distaste lined his face.

He thought of Brandeis and smiled. There was no denying she was a remarkable young woman. Her life had changed dramatically over the course of a year, yet it seemed as if she'd adapted as best she could. He admired that kind of fortitude, especially so in a woman.

Brandeis had an arousing effect on him he seemed helpless to control. Instantly, his mind recalled their first date, the feel of her in his arms as he had held her securely; the smoothness of her skin beneath his fingers; the gentle curves of her breasts against his forearms. That night he had wanted nothing more than to continue to hold her and absorb her body's trembling with his own. He'd wanted her more than he'd ever desired any woman.

Jackson swore beneath his breath, and his thoughts took

a chiding bend. *For the love of God, Brandeis had been raped.* His mind understood that but his body did not. Even now, the mere memory of their kiss made his blood begin to pound. He understood that she had been left with a fear of physical intimacy with any man and the last thing he wanted was to add to that fear. She needed time to forget. And time was going to be a problem. He didn't know how he was going to survive not being able to touch her. It was going to be sheer hell.

He poured himself a shot of cognac and lounged in a dark blue wing chair facing one of the windows in the living room. It was the first time since dawn that he had stopped to rest, and he took several seconds simply to absorb the sensation of relaxation.

The long lines of his body eased as he slipped lower into the comfortable cushions. Setting his snifter on the table close at hand, he removed his shoes and socks and crossed his legs at the ankles. A sigh of pleasure stole past his lips as he reached for his drink.

The brandy worked its way down his throat, spreading its warming essence over his chest and lower, to his stomach. Damn, he had worked hard today. Then to top it off, Brandeis had stormed clear across town and into his office, angry. They were just beginning to find that closeness they once had. Was it gone, now?

"Damn," Jackson muttered, his dark eyes narrowing. Just thinking about the sweetness of kissing her robbed him of a good portion of the contentment he had been seeking.

In search of relief, he took a healthy swallow of the cognac. The gesture was futile. Brandeis invaded his mind with a strength as undeniable as she was herself. Knowing it was useless to do otherwise, Jackson gave himself up to his thoughts of Brandeis Taylor. There was no denying the truth. He was in love with her.

After his shower, Jackson felt better. He had just started his dinner when he heard the doorbell ring. Quickly wiping his hands on a towel, he strolled out of the kitchen and into the living room.

Jackson opened the door, only mildly surprised at seeing a young woman standing there. She was wearing a sensual perfume. Her clinging dress showed off the gentle curves of her hips and breasts. Her waist was slim, her thighs long and lithe. It was obvious at a glance that she watched her diet carefully and kept herself in fine physical shape. Her dark hair fell luxuriantly to her chin. "I wondered how long it would take before you showed up on my door step. Please come in and have a seat. How have you been, Monique?"

"I've been fine," the woman said, following him into the apartment. "When I heard you were back in town, I didn't believe it. Not until I saw you that night in the bar, with what's-her-face. After your mom up and married that man from Texas, I figured you wouldn't be returning to Brunswick, Georgia. How's your mom doing, by the way?"

"She's doing fine, and very happy. But then, she truly deserves to be. My dad has been dead a long time. By the way, what's-her-face has a name. It's Tracy."

"Whatever." Monique made herself at home in one of the navy wing chairs, her gaze went over the room. She was immediately impressed by the condo's opulence, cleanliness, and neatness. The plush carpet, the chairs, and the couch all appeared inviting. The decor was elegant, and the furnishings obviously expensive. "Nice place you have here."

"Thank you. Would you like something to drink? I have juice, cognac, wine, or water."

Monique smiled. "I'll take a glass of wine. Thank you, sugar."

Jackson poured the drink and handed it to her. Then, explaining that he needed to check on his dinner, he left the room and headed to the kitchen.

As he stirred the spaghetti sauce, he was unaware of being observed.

Monique, standing in the open portal, scrutinized

Jackson with hungry eyes. His denim jeans were a good fit, as though they had been tailor-made especially for him. The white chambray shirt emphasized his lean, muscled frame, and the wide width of his shoulders. As Monique's eyes continued their devouring perusal, she couldn't recall ever seeing a man who aroused her lustful desires so flagrantly. He was the only man for her.

Jackson, suddenly sensing another's presence, turned toward the doorway. "I didn't realize you were standing there," he said, feigning a warm smile. Her seductive manner was far from subtle, and avoiding her sensual overtures was not going to be easy. He had to admit that she was an exceptionally attractive woman. They had dated briefly while he was in college.

She came to his side, her steps light, but with enough hip-sway to cause her calf-length dress to flow gracefully. Jackson watched her closely and for a moment, his body involuntarily responded to her provocative beauty. But as he recalled her less than admirable qualities, his desire quickly slipped away. She wasn't his kind of woman, not even as a meaningless fling.

"I've thought of you often over the years, Jackson. I don't know what happened to us."

"We er . . . had different goals, and things just fizzled out. We enjoyed each other's compa—"

"Among other things," she cut in, favoring him with a radiant smile. "We used to have some good times. We can have good times again. Any time, any place," she whispered throatily. Moving quickly, yet subtly, she laced her arms about his neck and leaned into his embrace. She kissed him on the lips. Her kiss was urgent, persuasive, but Jackson didn't respond. What he had felt was . . . Jackson gulped at the bleak thought. He felt *repulsed* by Monique's kiss. It was Brandeis' kiss he wanted. He yearned to have Brandeis' arms around winding his neck to draw him close.

He managed to gently release himself from her clinging hold. Stepping back and feigning a warm smile, he murmured, "Your invitation is very tempting, but my sauce is about to burn." He turned to stir his sauce once again.

Rolling her eyes and sucking her teeth, Monique cocked her head to the side. "What is it, Jackson, I'm not good enough for you now? I remember when you couldn't get enough of me. I guess Tracy satisfies you, then. Personally, I think the bitch is too skinny!"

"Monique, don't start! *Not* that it's any of your business, but Tracy and I are friends." Jackson turned away from her to cut off the burner.

She moved closer to him. "I know how to satisfy you. Remember?" As if to prove her point, she stepped back from him, unbuttoned her dress and stripped slowly. Her dress fell to the floor in a heap.

Jackson heard the soft whisper as her clothing fell. He turned. His eyes, jumping nervously from her large, jutting breasts to her flat stomach, were already angry. Cursing to himself, he wondered why he hadn't seen this coming. She was an aggressive woman and stopped at nothing to get what she wanted.

"Put your clothes back on, Monique." Jackson turned his back to her once again. "Look, I'm involved with someone and I care a lot for her. I don't want to hurt your feelings, but I have no interest in resuming a relationship with you."

Monique bent and picked up her dress. As she put it on, she gave him a hostile glare. "Oh, yeah. I heard something about you and that church girl, Brandeis. She don't know how to appreciate a man like you. She won't be enough for you." She smiled an insincere smile. "But then, I guess you figured that out already, cause you were with Tracy that night. It's only a matter of time before you'll come crawling to me. Begging for a good fu—"

Jackson reached out and grasped one of her arms tightly and escorted her toward the door.

"Jackson, what're you doing?" she asked.

"You have overstayed your welcome. Please leave." He spoke in a tense, clipped voice that forbade any comment.

She pulled away from him. "I'm not completely dressed. Jackson, don't you care if your neighbors see me naked?"

"Most of Brunswick and half of Florida has already seen you naked. What difference would it make now?"

Monique glowered at him. "Whatever!" She pulled the pieces of her dress together and stomped down the stairs.

Brandeis walked up the stairs to Jackson's condo. When she reached the top step she gasped. Through his large, picture window, she could see clear into the kitchen. She watched in disbelief as Monique Allen began to disrobe. Brandeis felt as if her heart was being torn out of her body as Jackson turned around and looked at Monique from head to toe.

It was a moment or so before she could will herself to leave. Jackson and Monique Allen! She was not only hurt, but outraged as well! How could he? Didn't he know what she was? He had to. In a town as small as this one, he had to know. Apparently, Jackson didn't care. It was all Brandeis could do to keep from knocking on the door and tearing into him. Hot, searing pain tore into her stomach. When she reached her car, she leaned against it for a few minutes before getting in. Sorrow crippled her heart, wounding her more deeply that she would have ever thought possible.

Conflicting emotions assailed her from every direction. She tried to tell herself that she had no business feeling hurt by what Jackson was doing with Monique. He was free to do whatever he pleased and with whomever. He and Brandeis had no commitment to each other. After all, they were just friends. Reminding herself of all this and accepting it were two different things entirely.

Brandeis didn't even have the satisfaction of being able to hate Jackson. A trickle of resentment did worm its way into her brain. A torrent of tears came and she cried until her throat was raw.

In the end, she filled her lungs with a cleansing breath and looked about, feeling as if everything in her life had changed. The world hadn't changed. Only her heart's perceptions had been altered. Brandeis prayed they would stand her in good stead. She was going to need all the courage and strength she had to go on from here.

During the rest of the drive home, she became angrier until, finally, her anger overcame her. Obviously, Jackson Gray was a womanizer! Well, he wasn't going to toy with her affections! Not anymore. Jackson Gray would not make a fool of her!

Despite the early hour, the temperature was rising quickly. It was going to be another scorching August day. Brandeis glanced up at the sky, hoping to find a sign of possible rain, but there wasn't a cloud in sight. Driving down Altama, on her way to work, she turned her air-conditioning up as high as it would go. She stared disconsolately ahead. Seeing Jackson with Monique last night had filled her with a deep sense of betrayal. Jackson hadn't even tried to call her since she'd rushed out of his office, she acknowledged sadly.

Her thoughts were interrupted by the ringing of her cellular phone.

"Hello."

"Good morning. How's my best friend?"

"Hello, Carol. I don't know how, but only you can be so bubbly early in the morning."

"I got your message last night, but I got home late. You said you needed to talk to me. Why don't we meet somewhere for lunch?"

"I would rather talk to you at my place," Brandeis said.

"Sure. Are you okay, Bran? You sound sad."

"I'm okay. I just really need to talk to someone. Mom's still in New York visiting with Aunt Kate, and I don't want to bother her with this. She doesn't get to see her sister very often."

"It's no problem, girlfriend. I'll be there around noon."

"I'll see you then. Thanks, Carol." Brandeis clicked off.

Late morning, Brandeis left her office early in order to prepare a nice lunch for Carol. The more she thought of how messed up her life had become since the rape, the angrier she became. She knew from her counseling sessions with Helen that what she was feeling now was completely normal. Brandeis picked up a glass vase and threw it against the wall. *I'm taking back my life, damn it! I'm not going to let Martin destroy me. The bastard!* Next, Brandeis went into her bedroom and tossed all the bedcoverings off the bed and on the floor. She ripped the curtains off the wall and tore down pictures. She placed the comforter, sheets, pillows, drapes, and pictures in several large heavy-duty garbage bags.

After throwing the bags in her car, she drove to the nearest trash site and dumped them. From there, she headed to the mall.

Two hours later, Brandeis returned to her apartment, just as Carol was leaving a note. "Hi, Carol. Sorry I'm late. I went to the mall to pick up a few things. I'm redecorating my bedroom." Brandeis pointed to the huge packages on the sidewalk.

"Why? I liked the way you had it."

"I need a change."

"I see." Carol glanced down at the shopping bags, Brandeis carried. "Why don't I help you with these."

"Actually, you can get the rest of the packages out of my car."

"Brandeis! I can't imagine you decorating," Carol said as she struggled to lift the heavy bag from Belk Hudson's department store. "Is Belk's having a big sale I don't know about?"

Brandeis shook her head. "No, I told you, I just needed a change. I have a salad prepared. Do you want a sandwich to go with it?"

"No. The salad's fine. Remember, I'm trying to lose thirty pounds before the wedding. That reminds me, we have to look over some designs for the bridesmaid dresses."

Together, they brought in all the shopping bags and set

them in her bedroom. Carol looked at the bedroom and its bleakness but said nothing.

"That's one of the things I wanted to talk about. Mom called me last night. She said she found the perfect fabric for your gown in New York. She's going to buy a sample of the material to show you."

"That's great! Oh, I can't wait to get married! I waited for three years for that man to ask me."

"You knew James wanted to have his own business up and running before the two of you got married," Brandeis said. "Besides, it was your idea to be engaged for two-and-a-half years," Brandeis pointed out.

"I know. But I've explained my reasons. I'm only going to do this once. This is my only chance to have the kind of wedding I want and that takes money. I have to admit, I love James so much I'm tempted to move the wedding date up. I want very much to be his wife."

Brandeis took a bite out of her ham and cheese sandwich. "And you will. I'm so happy for you, Carol."

"Bran?"

"Yes."

"Do you still think about . . . what happened? Martin was such as asshole!"

Brandeis was quiet for a moment. "No. Not so much, lately. Not since I've been going to counseling. I want to get on with my life and not keep dwelling on the past. That's why I trashed my bedroom. That's where it happened and I haven't slept in there since." Carol gasped. "Helen made me realize that I was still giving Martin control over my life. I needed to change that. I have a new bed being delivered on Saturday. The old bed is going to the Salvation Army."

"That bed will be a blessing to someone who needs it," Carol said softly.

"Mom is always saying that out of every tragedy comes a hidden blessing. I guess my hidden blessing is somewhere in my future."

"Is Jackson going to be a part of that future?" Carol grinned. "The two of you make such a cute couple."

Brandeis didn't respond immediately. "I-I don't know. I don't think so. He's part of the reason I wanted to talk to you today. I really need to get this off my chest."

Carol put down her fork. "He really cares for you, you know. By the way, are we still having dinner at his place on Saturday?"

"He *used* to care about me." Brandeis swallowed the despair in her throat. "And I think we can forget dinner."

"Why do you say that?" Carol asked. "Has something happened? Of course it has, I can see it in your face."

Brandeis shrugged in resignation. "We kind of had a fight. But after giving it some thought, and getting a good talking to from Mom, I realized I was wrong. Anyway, I went to see him a few days ago and he had . . . company. He's seeing someone. Monique Allen."

"I don't believe that," Carol cried. "She's a . . . a prostitute! Everybody in town knows that. Are you sure they're seeing each other? Maybe Jackson's her lawyer."

"No." Brandeis shook her head. "I saw them, Carol, through his window. They were standing in his kitchen and she took her clothes off. Right there, in the middle of the kitchen. I imagine they did it on the dining room table." Brandeis swallowed hard, trying to suppress her anger.

It was Carol's turn to shake her head. "Naw! Are you sure about what you saw? Did you knock?"

Brandeis scowled. "No. What was I going to say when he came to the door? Hi, Jackson. I just stopped by to make it a threesome." She ignored Carol's hoot of laughter. "I just turned around and left." She slammed her fist on the table.

"Hey, Bran. Don't take it out on me. I didn't do anything!" Carol held her hands up as if to ward off a blow.

"I'm sorry. It just pisses me off when I think of him with that tramp!"

"You're beginning to care deeply for him aren't you?"

Brandeis shrugged. "To be honest, I'm not sure what I'm feeling, Carol. I know I don't have any right to be upset, but I am. I hate the fact that he's seeing someone else. I have to admit, even if it weren't Monique, I'd still feel the same way."

"Does Jackson know about this? That you're falling in love with him?"

"No. And I'm not going to tell him. As a matter of fact, I won't be talking to him at all! He's not going to add me to his list of conquests. The dog!"

"Amen to that, girlfriend!" Carol then asked, "Bran, why did you two have a fight in the first place?"

"I found out from Carrie that he's defending Marc Wiley."

"Really?" Carol arched a brow. "I'd heard that Marc had been arrested for raping Peggy, but I didn't know Jackson had taken the case."

"It was quite a surprise to me, I can tell you that," Brandeis said.

"How does that make you feel? After everything that's happened?"

"It bothers me, but as Mom said, we don't know whether or not Marc's guilty. Either way, he deserves to be represented in a court of law."

Carol finished up her salad before she spoke again. "Marc told my sister that he never raped Peggy. He said after he wouldn't leave his wife for her, it was Peggy's way of getting even."

Brandeis quirked an eyebrow. "You believe that?"

Carol shrugged. "I wasn't there, so I don't know what happened. I'd heard rumors that he and Peggy were having an affair. I've even seen them together."

"I heard the same rumors and I've seen them, too. But it doesn't matter, he still could have raped her."

Carol said nothing further. She knew Brandeis well enough not to argue with her over something like the issue of rape. Her dear friend would have to come to terms with this by herself.

* * *

Jackson sat in his office, trying to concentrate on the notes on his legal pad. It was hard. As he removed his glasses to clean them, he thought of Brandeis. He couldn't get her out of his mind. A small, wry smile touched his lips as he brought her image to mind. It had been two weeks since he'd talked to her. Since leaving his office that day, she had refused all of his calls. Was she still upset about his defending Marc?

He supposed Brandeis had every right to feel the way she did, especially given the fact that she'd been raped. It was a sensitive issue and he hoped they would be able to get past it. He hadn't attempted to reach her right away. He'd given her a few days to think things out. Today, he decided he'd send flowers and a note of apology. Maybe invite her—

Fran buzzed him to let him know he had a call.

"A Mrs. Mona Taylor is on the line."

"Thank you, Fran. I'll take the call."

"Hello, Jackson. I hope I haven't caught you at a bad time."

"No, ma'am. I'm not busy. I didn't know you were back in town."

"I got in late last night. How are things going?"

"Brandeis and I had a misunderstanding, and now she won't return any of my calls." He heard Mona's gasp of surprise.

"That's very strange, Jackson."

"Why do you say that."

"Because she and I talked about your misunderstanding. More accurately, the episode at your office. She planned to go by your place that very evening. Bran said she wanted to sit down with you, to tell you everything."

"When was this? I haven't seen Bran since that day at my office. Maybe she just can't get past the pain." In a quiet voice, Jackson added, "I know she was raped by Martin."

"How do you feel about Brandeis now?" Mona asked.

"I care a great deal about her still. That'll never change."

"How did you find out? Brandeis is very close-mouthed about what happened."

"I sort of figured it out," Jackson admitted. "How is she doing? I can only imagine the hell she's been through. I understand why she's been acting as she has been." Jackson knew that in a case of rape, victims often were made to feel as if they should have known better. Had Brandeis been murdered by Martin, no doubt people would have been shocked but no one would have expected her to know ahead of time that Martin was a murderer.

"She doesn't talk much about it," Mona said. "She feels people will think she's being vindictive and making it up. That it really wasn't rape. She's been in counseling for the last three months, though, once a week. It seems to be helping."

"I had no idea," Jackson admitted. "But I really hope it is helping. Mrs. Taylor, I want you to know I care deeply for your daughter. I wish she wouldn't keep me so far at bay. I want to be a part of her life."

"I would like to see that happen also. I believe you two could make each other very happy."

"I was just about to order her some flowers and invite her to dinner. What do you think?" Jackson asked.

"Oh, I think that's a splendid idea. I'll let you go now, Jackson. Tell your mother 'hi' for me . Bye."

"Bye, Mrs. Taylor." Jackson hung up and smiled.

Chapter 10

Brandeis reached for the envelope partially hidden in the enormous arrangement of exotic blooms including hibiscus, anthurium, wild orchids, and bird-of-paradise. She read the card that was tucked inside.

> *Please accept this attempt to apologize for my actions. In an effort to amend things between us, may I take you to dinner?*
>
> *Jackson*

An apology from Jackson Gray? She smiled. He had already called her numerous times, both at home and here, at work. For one brief instant her reservations about him vanished beneath the romantic nature of his apology. As a child, she'd been acutely aware of Jackson's good looks; now that she was a woman, she was still very impressed. But it was more than looks that attracted her to the man. She had a deep admiration for him. He was patient, compassionate, warm, and the kind of man a woman would find dependable. Too bad he wasn't through sowing his wild oats.

She pulled a flower from the arrangement and held it to her nose. Closing her eyes, she savored its fragrance. If only . . .

Brandeis shook her head. Now was not the time to daydream. Laying the rose on her desk, she stood up and brushed the wrinkles from her skirt. She dug through her file cabinet in search of a prospectus she needed to review.

As much as she tried to concentrate, Jackson kept creeping back to mind. She missed him terribly. She knew what he wanted and she couldn't give it to him. Brandeis supposed it was unfair of her to expect him to be celibate.

It saddened her to admit that it would be best that they not see each other again. Jackson deserved to have a woman who could fully return his feelings. At this time, she was not entirely sure what those feelings were and what they entailed.

Impulsively she picked up the phone and dialed his office. She was able to reach Jackson quickly. After thanking him for the flowers, she went straight to the reason for her call.

"I think we need to have a serious talk. Can you please come by my apartment tonight?" she asked.

"Sure. Do you want to have dinner before . . . or after?"

"Why don't we just see how it goes, Jackson," Brandeis said. "I have a lot on my mind that needs to be said. As a matter of fact, let's not plan on dinner at all. You should eat dinner first."

Brandeis didn't know how best to tell him. Tears filled her eyes. Tonight, she was going to put an end to their relationship.

Jackson sighed. "Bran, I hope we can work this—"

"We'll talk tonight, Jackson. I mean, really talk."

"I guess I'll see you then."

She could hear the edge in his voice. She said quietly, "Bye, Jackson."

* * *

With one last glance in her mirror, Brandeis wandered into her living room. She was there less than one minute when her doorbell rang. Opening the door, she stepped back to admit Jackson.

Brandeis looked stunning in a black linen pantsuit with a double-breasted blazer. Her dark brown hair was gleamed to perfection and rolled to her nape in a chignon. Soft, curling tendrils framed her face. She wore lipstick with just a hint of color.

"Come in," she said. Her breath caught in her throat as she checked him out. Jackson looked so handsome in his blue jeans and white button-down shirt.

"Hello." Jackson paused to look her over. "You look exquisite!"

"Thank you for the compliment. You look as well, yourself. Please have a seat." Brandeis tried to keep her tone formal.

He sat in the armchair. "I'm sorry, Brandeis. I—"

"It wasn't your fault. You have nothing to be sorry about. I should be the one apologizing, Jackson," she said quietly, before turning away in uncomfortable silence. She didn't begin speaking again immediately. In fact, she waited for longer than Jackson thought he could bear. She sat there on the sofa, afraid to move, afraid to look at him, but when she finally spoke she told him everything, the whole unhappy story.

"You were right. I was raped by Martin, last summer. I didn't tell you because I was afraid you'd judge me." Brandeis glanced at Jackson and noted his look of surprise. She took another deep breath, then continued, "I couldn't even say the word 'rape' until recently. It's been a trying and emotional year for me. I kept all of this inside me for so long, it made me sick. It's why I developed the ulcer in the first place. This situation has made me realize a few truths about myself. It's why I agreed to see you. I . . . don't . . . think . . ." Each word came out separately, as if one had nothing to do with the other. Her voice was filled with regret and anguish.

"You don't think what?" he asked, his face taking on lines of suspicion.

"It would be best if . . . if I didn't . . ." She composed herself mentally before finally blurting out, "I don't think we should see each other anymore, Jackson. I think it's the best thing for both of us. You should just forget about me and go on with your life." Brandeis bent her head in abject weariness.

Jackson was up and across the room in three strides. He came to stand behind her. He wrapped his arms around her and pulled her back to lean against him, wanting to enfold her so completely in his strength and freedom that somehow her pain could become his, his assurance hers.

"Brandeis . . ." he said, turning her gently to face him and kissing her hair.

She pulled away. "No, please listen to me. You're not being realistic about this. Do you really want a relationship with someone with all these problems?"

"Do you really think I'm that shallow, Bran? Everybody has problems," Jackson replied.

"You don't understand what happened to me!" Brandeis was suddenly angry. "You know why? *Because you're a man!* No one's ever held you down and forced you to have sex with him. You expect me to just wash it out and go on to the next one . . . You need a woman of substance. Oh, just forget it!" Brandeis tone became chilly as she stood and walked away.

"You're taking it all wrong," Jackson argued. "Do you think for a minute that I don't know what this has done to you? *My God,* rape is a devastating crime of violence, a terrible loss of will. I might be a man, but I've seen the victims of some of the clients I defend. *It makes me sick!* I do understand." He walked over to Brandeis and placed his arms tightly around her. Jackson slipped a finger beneath her chin and raised it so she looked him straight in the face. "You are every bit a woman of substance. A strong woman." He bent and placed a gentle kiss on her temple. "The kind of woman any man could love."

His lips touched hers. Brandeis tensed for an instance, almost enough to part his lips from hers, then slowly relaxed as his hand slid up her back and pressed her against him.

Brandeis pushed forcefully out of his arms. A flicker of apprehension coursed through her. "I'm sorry," she murmured, "I didn't mean to do that. I don't know what came over me."

He took her hand, squeezed it softly, and said, "You don't owe me an apology." He gave her a lighthearted wink. "You'll heal, Bran, and learn to trust again. I promise that you'll not be given more than you can bear." He suddenly appeared to be deep in thought, his eyes never leaving her face.

Brandeis was quiet for a moment. She wondered what he was thinking about.

Jackson thought she was not only beautiful, but also courageous; yet at the same time, she was so vulnerable. "Want to talk about it? I told you before, you can cry on my shoulder any time you want."

"No, not really. I just want to stop hurting, Jackson." Brandeis paused. "I didn't mean to tell you that." There was a pensive shimmer in the shadow of her eyes. She watched him warily as he sat on the sofa.

He tilted his head to study her. "Why not? Still shutting me out?"

Brandeis stood tight and tense in her own space. She was thankful that Jackson was now sitting down. Her breathing quickened at the thought of being in his embrace. She craved his touch, but cautioned herself. Jackson was a temptation she could not afford. "I just want to forget everything that's happened. I want to start new and get on with my life. I don't want to hurt anymore! Do you know what I mean?"

"I think I do. I could kill that bastard for what he's done to you!"

Brandeis looked at him to see if he was serious. He seemed to be.

Jackson stood and walked over to her. "Bran, there's something I've been wanting to tell you—"

"No, Jackson." Brandeis backed away from him. "No more serious talk, please. It's been a long day. I . . . I don't think I'm ready for what you might say." Brandeis sighed. She took his left hand in her right. "Well, I appreciate your coming here tonight. That's all I have to say, I guess." She squeezed his hand and leaned her head on his chest, listening with all her soul to the silence of the night.

"There is something going on between us, Brandeis," Jackson said. "I can't get my mind off you. I think about you all the time. You can admit it now, or you can wait. Just remember, it won't just go away. I love you, Brandeis, don't you know that?"

After one agonizing perusal of Jackson's face, Brandeis turned away from him. How could she talk when her heart was so full? Finally, the words came. "You don't mean that. You can't know what you're saying."

He seemed to hold his breath for a moment, then an almost imperceptible sigh escaped from him, and he shrugged. "I see."

"What about Monique?" She could have bitten her tongue. She hadn't meant to blurt out such a question.

"What do you mean?"

"Never mind," she replied, hoping to evade the issue.

But Jackson wasn't about to be put off. "Tell me what you mean. Why would you insinuate something so outlandish?"

"Outlandish?" she said querulously. *How dare he insult my intelligence! Oh, he was nothing but a dog!* She looked him straight in the face and said, "The other night, I went to your condo to apologize, mind you. I saw you and Monique through the window. In your kitchen. I saw her standing there stark naked. I didn't mean to spy, it was purely unintentional."

A large smile crossed Jackson's face. So, that's why she hadn't taken any of his calls. "And naturally, you assumed that we were lovers."

She raised her chin somewhat defiantly. "Well, what was I supposed to think?"

"She's a hooker, Bran." Jackson shook his head in disbelief. "I believe I have more scruples than that. Besides, I thought you knew me better than that. As a matter of fact, if you hadn't run away so fast, you would have seen me toss her out. Half-dressed, I might add."

Brandeis was pleased, but she was also ashamed that she had misjudged him. She smile hesitantly. "I shouldn't have jumped to conclusions," she murmured. "I know better than anyone that things aren't always as they appear."

"We dated briefly, during my undergrad college days," Jackson explained. "Before she decided to become a prostitute. It's long over. Besides, my interest is in you. Even if you don't love me now, I'm going to keep hoping that you'll start to trust me. I think somehow, some way, you will. Do you feel the same way?"

Brandeis said nothing.

"I'm not leaving until I get an answer." Jackson felt they had reached the point where their relationship had to be resolved. Strolling back over to the sofa, he sat down, arms crossed over his chest.

"All right," she said resignedly. "I'm not promising anything, Jackson, but you're right. There is something between us. I've been thinking about you, too. But I want you to know I'm not sure. I don't want to hurt you, and I don't want to be hurt by you or by anybody. I really enjoy being with you." She smiled at him. "I just wanted you to know that."

The hope spread from Jackson's mouth to his eyes, and as he fixed them on her, she raised a warning finger. "Remember, I promised nothing," she said. "We're going to take it one day at a time."

He grinned. "That's okay. I'll make the promises. They'll be enough for the both of us. You know, we never did have that dinner party at my house. You think we can try for this Saturday?"

Brandeis smiled. "Sure, we can do it this weekend. Can I still invite Carol and James?"

Jackson nodded. "At least now I understand why you've been so reluctant to be alone with me. I'd started to take it personally."

"I'm sorry, Jackson. It's been very hard to relax . . ."

Jackson suddenly jumped up and was across the room in quick strides. He stood before her, his hands on her shoulders. "I think I finally understand fully. You've never forgiven yourself for trusting Martin. You're afraid to risk love again, aren't you?"

Brandeis didn't answer. Instead, she began to cry.

Jackson pulled her to his chest and rested his cheek on her head. "You can't give up on love, Bran," he whispered, as a deep desire for her coursed through him. It seemed as though he could literally feel his love growing stronger. It filled him to capacity.

"Problems don't just vanish overnight or even after a year, Jackson," Brandeis argued. "I don't know how long it'll take for me to put the rape behind me."

"Honey, you have to try to trust again, no matter how terrifying it seems. I'm not going anywhere. Take your time, I'll wait." Jackson enclosed her in his arms.

He kissed her lightly on each cheek, then her forehead, pausing to see if he would meet resistance. Finding none, his mouth sought hers, and initially, his kiss was tender. But as passion surfaced full force, his lips then seized hers demandingly.

Brandeis surrendered breathlessly to Jackson's fervent kiss and his warm, demanding mouth awoke alien, primitive yearnings within her. She reached up and took off his glasses. Moving a trembling hand to the nape of his neck, she pressed him closer as her lips savored his.

He felt her body tense when she felt his erection. Jackson reluctantly ended their kiss and slowly pulled away. "I meant what I said, sweetheart. I'll wait. Now, are we really on for Saturday?"

"We're on." She inclined her head. "You sure you want to put your cooking out there for scrutiny?"

"I think I can handle it. Hey! If you're not ashamed of your cooking . . ."

Brandeis' body shook with laughter. "You're terrible!"

"Actually, I'm a good catch! Just ask your mother."

"Arrogant, conceited—"

Jackson kissed her passionately. "I think I'd better leave now before I get into trouble. Sweet dreams." His eyes bored intensely into hers. Suddenly, he reached out and pulled her back into his arms. His mouth came down on hers quickly, kissing her again, giving her no chance to turn away.

Brandeis had to fight her overwhelming need to be close to him. She longed to fling herself into his arms and beg him not to leave. Instead, she conceded to her good sense and said softly, "Good night, Jackson."

He studied her lovingly for a moment more, then he was gone.

The moment the door closed behind him, Brandeis settled down on her sofa and snuggled up to a pillow as she went through the motions of watching TV. She thought back over the years and saw the many ways Jackson already had proven how much he cared. So long ago, and yet, he was still so patient and understanding. She couldn't concentrate on the TV because she was so happy! *What a wonderful man!* Amused by the notion, she smiled sleepily as she snuggled into her sofa and pillow.

What a woman! Jackson thought to himself as he drove the short distance home. *I love her and I'm going to marry her.* Brandeis had become his life, his heart, and his very reason for living. He would not lose her to the past. He refused to let that happen. "We're going to get past this, baby. I'm going to make you forget all that pain," he whispered to himself.

* * *

Mona noticed her daughter's radiant face one night during dinner. She knew that Jackson had to be the reason for her exuberance. They had stopped to have dinner at The Captain's Table after an exhausting day of shopping at the Glynn Place Mall. It was an annual ritual for them to do their Christmas shopping together and both looked forward to it.

Mona observed her daughter critically. "I'm so glad to see your appetite's coming back. Maybe you'll gain back some of the weight you've lost."

Brandeis pushed back a wayward strand of dark brown hair. "Ugh! I hope not! I like my weight just fine." She pushed her plate away as if to emphasize her point.

Mona chewed thoughtfully. "I think you're too skinny. I bet Jackson thinks the same thing."

She giggled. "You're wrong. He likes me just the way I am."

Mona grimaced. "What does he know anyway? Love is blind."

"Mom!"

"Besides, he could stand to add a few pounds himself."

"He does not! I like him just the way he is." Brandeis wrinkled her nose at her mother.

"I wonder if you'll ever outgrow that little habit."

" 'Fraid not, Mom." She laughed as her mother rolled her eyes.

"I love seeing you like this. So happy. I think this year is going to be a good one for you."

"I'm happy. Very happy, Mom." Yes, she was blissfully happy and she finally felt as if she were fully alive, and not just going through the motions.

They finished the rest of their meal quickly and prepared to leave. Brandeis drove the short distance to her mother's house. Together, they unloaded the trunk, laden with brightly wrapped Christmas presents.

"I hope Jackson will like the sweater I bought him for Christmas," Brandeis said.

"I'm sure he will. I'm sure he'll like anything that comes from you. So, what else did you buy him?"

Brandeis put her hands on her hips. "What makes you think that I've bought him more gifts?" She paused to let Mona pass, then followed her up the stairs.

"I know you, dear." Mona paused at the top of the stairs. "Well, are you going to tell me or do I have to wait until Christmas?"

"Okay. Okay. I bought him another briefcase. The one he uses has seen its last trial."

"And?" Mona persisted.

Brandeis laughed. "*And* I bought him another black tie. It's a Peter Max tie. It's not real conservative, but I like it and so does Jackson. He's looked at it several times. The last time we went to the mall he decided to buy it, but it was gone." She smiled at her mother. "You should have seen his face when the salesperson told him the last one had been sold." Brandeis giggled at the memory. "He looked so sad. I almost broke down and told him that I'd bought it, but I didn't. I wanted to surprise him."

"It looks like you and Jackson are getting closer and closer," Mona said, later, as she and Brandeis looked at the pictures of bridesmaid's dresses Carol had sent over. They were sitting on the floor in Mona's den. Both had changed into oversized sweatshirts and leggings. Pictures and fabric swatches were everywhere. In a corner near the fireplace stood a six-foot-tall Christmas tree, neatly wrapped gifts were stacked under it.

"Yes, we are. Mom, it feels so good to be able to go out and just have some fun, again." Joy bubbled in her laugh and shone in her eyes.

"I'm so happy for you. Jackson is a good man. He loves you, you know." Mona's smile broadened.

"Mom! How do you know that? Did he say something to you?" One thing for sure, Brandeis knew she was deeply in love with Jackson Gray.

"Hasn't he told you yet?" Mona asked.

"Well, he sort of mentioned it a while back, but I wasn't

ready to hear something so serious. I wasn't sure we were going to be able to get past what had happened to me. I was afraid I wouldn't be able to return his love. Besides, we've only been dating for five months.''

"Don't worry, dear. He loves you. It's written all over his face." Then, as if to change the subject, Mona pointed to another dress and said, "This dress is stunning. It'll look great on you."

"But will Barbara be able to wear a dress like this? I know Robyn and I will. Margaret, too." Brandeis pointed to a picture in front of her mother. "But Barbara. I don't know. Especially since she's had that boob job."

"Oh, that's right. For the life of me, I don't know why she wanted them so big."

Brandeis shrugged. "I don't know, either."

Mona handed a picture to Brandeis. "Well, this one is better suited for her. It's not as pretty as the other one but it'll do." Mona ran her slender fingers through her hair, as she asked, "What time are Carol and her mother coming by? I need the measurements of the other bridesmaids."

Brandeis looked at her watch. "In about an hour. They're having dinner with James and his family."

"Oh, that's right. Mamie has a bee in her bonnet about not being invited. Lord knows she fussed all this morning over her still being a part of James' family, too."

"But she's his uncle's ex-wife! Mr. Willie is James' dad's brother. Mamie was only related by marriage."

"I know, but she was still highly offended. Especially since Willie is taking that twenty-five-year-old woman he's been dating. That reminds me, Mamie said she saw you and Jackson at Freemans Jeweler's, in the mall. She said the two of you were picking out engagement rings. She also said to make sure you invited her to your wedding."

Brandeis laughed so hard, tears started to fall. "She's such a busy body. Yes, we were in Freemans. Jackson needed a new watch and he wanted my input. We looked at rings, necklaces, watches, everything. Jackson and I are *not* engaged, Mom."

Mona looked a little disappointed.

Brandeis laughed.

"Well, a mother can hope, can't she?"

Brandeis laughed harder and dodged the square flanged pillow her mother threw at her. Suddenly serious, she said, "I really wished I could have saved myself for my husband. My virginity was the most precious gift I could've given him. Now, I have nothing! Helen says I shouldn't feel this way. She says that when I weigh all else I have to offer, Jackson couldn't ask for a better wife."

Mona reached over and placed her hand on her daughter's. "She's right, dear. You have yourself, your love, and your friendship. The situation you're in was not of your doing. Jackson understands this, and he's not judging you. Don't do this to yourself. The hymen may not be in place to act as a physical barrier, but my darling, you're still a virgin, for goodness sake." Noting the confused look on her daughter's face, she continued, "You've never been made love to, not the way a man does, when he loves and cherishes you. When you make love for the first time with someone you love, you'll know the difference."

"Mom, I'm in love with Jackson and it's such a powerful feeling," Brandeis admitted. "I think about him every waking moment. Sometimes it's scary and I start to panic, but when we're not together, I miss him terribly."

Mona nodded her understanding. "Why don't you tell him?"

"No! I can't do that." Brandeis looked at her mother as if Mona were insane for suggesting such a thing.

"Why not?" Mona pressed.

"Because after that one time, he hasn't said anything of that nature to me. I don't want to make a fool of myself. I can't expose myself like that to him."

Mona just nodded. "I see. But have you considered that he may feel the very same way you do?"

She shook her head. "No. He always seems so calm and controlled."

"I don't know why you two are so afraid to share your feelings with each other," Mona grumbled. "Seems to me you're taking the longest route to the shortest distance."

"What do you mean by that?"

"It simply means that I'll be sewing for another wedding real soon."

"Mom! Let's not get ahead of ourselves. Jackson and I are getting closer and closer but we're not *that* close, yet."

Mona wagged her finger at her daughter. "Mark my words, young lady. I'll be helping you plan your wedding within the next six months."

Brandeis wrinkled her nose at her mother. "I'm not going to hold my breath." She dodged a second pillow Mona sent flying her way.

"Smarty!"

"Merry Christmas, sweetheart."

Brandeis blushed as Jackson planted a kiss on her full lips. "Merry Christmas, Jackson. Mrs. Davis. It's so good to see you." She wrapped her arms tightly around Jackson's mother, a tall woman both proud and feminine, graceful and stately.

"It's been a while, hasn't it? You look lovely, Bran."

"Oh, for goodness sake, Bran. Let Raine and Jerry come in out of the cold," Mona called from the dining room. Untying her apron, she strolled into the living room, arms open.

While the two women hugged each other, Jackson pulled Brandeis into his arms and planted a quick kiss on her lips.

"Hello, beautiful."

"Hello, yourself." Brandeis reluctantly pulled away from him. "Mr. Davis, please have a seat. We didn't mean to ignore you."

Jerry Davis, a pudgy man with a permanent smile plastered on his face, chuckled heartily. "Oh, don't you worry none 'bout me. I'm glad to see you kids so happy."

Jackson put his arm around her once more. "We are very happy."

Brandeis could only nod.

Mona waited until everyone was seated and comfortable, then she and Brandeis served eggnog. Brandeis took her seat next to Jackson on the sofa. Once more, she felt his arm wrap around her, cushioning her like a cocoon.

Raine Davis produced a brightly colored, gift-wrapped package from a large shopping bag and handed it to Mona. Jackson also presented Brandeis with a huge gift box. She plopped down on the floor, grinning as she ripped through the wrapping.

Raine chuckled and nudged Mona. "I see Bran still gets excited opening presents."

Mona nodded.

Brandeis was a little surprised to find another wrapped gift inside of the box. Glancing up at Jackson, she smirked and said, "Ha-ha! You think you're so smart, don't you?"

Jackson laughed.

Inside that box, she found yet another gift wrapped box. Everyone laughed at her puzzled expression. Opening the box, Brandeis was not surprised to find another box.

"I can't believe you did this to me, Jackson."

"I know how much you like opening presents. I thought you would get a kick out of this."

"Oh, I'm going to get a *kick* out of this, believe me!" There was no way he could mistake her meaning.

Her expression turned to delight upon opening yet another box, this one was small. Grinning, she opened it and peeked inside. Her eyes widened. "I don't believe it!" She opened the tiny box and pulled out a stunning two-carat tennis bracelet. "Oh my God! This is beautiful. Jackson, this is . . . this is so beautiful! Thank you."

"*Thank you!* Honey, you'd better get up and give that man a big hug and kiss. I taught you better than that. As

a matter of fact, I'm going to give him a big hug and kiss."
Mona jumped up and planted a big kiss on Jackson's cheek.

Brandeis sat in his lap and kissed him softly on the lips.
Whispering, she said, "I'll give you a better kiss when we're
alone."

"I'm glad you like it. Thank you for my gifts. I love all
of them. I especially needed the briefcase."

"Do you really like the sweater? When I saw it in the
store, I thought it had your name written all over it."

"I love the sweater, the tie, and the briefcase, sweetheart.
I love everything." Holding up the tie, he added, "I see
you had a surprise up your sleeve, too. You knew how badly
I wanted this tie."

She giggled. "I almost broke down and told you in the
store that day. You looked so sad. Thank you so much
for the bracelet, Jackson, but you didn't have to get me
something so expensive."

He placed a finger to her lips. "I wanted to buy this for
you." A devastating grin showed his perfect white teeth.

Neither one of them noticed when Mona, Raine, and
her husband left the room.

Brandeis heart fluttered from his nearness. She loved
him desperately, wanted him to hold and kiss her.

Jackson could stand no more. An animal-like sound
erupted from his throat as his hand slid down her back.
She went limp the moment his mouth captured hers.
Demanding, hot and ravenous, his tongue met hers boldly.
She kissed him back with a hunger that matched his own.

Chapter 11

The months flew by and winter turned into spring. Jackson spread the beach towel on the ground in precisely the spot Brandeis directed. Taking a seat beside her, he watched as she unloaded the picnic basket—fried chicken, potato salad, biscuits, fruit, lemonade, plates, eating utensils, and glasses.

"This is a feast." Jackson sighed, admiring her handiwork.

"I hope you enjoy it. Now settle down and let's get started. We have to get back to Brunswick in time to get dressed for the concert."

"We've got plenty of time, sweetheart. I suggested this picnic because I know how much you like it here on Jekyll. I thought it would be the perfect ending to our vacation. As for me, I needed this week off and away from the office."

"I needed this time off, myself. I made the mistake of telling Carrie that I wasn't going out of town, though. She called me practically every day this week."

"You shouldn't have answered the phone. I screened all my calls. My secretary only called twice."

Brandeis smiled. "That's because Fran is reliable and

doesn't mind working. To Carrie, working is just a way to pass the time. She wants to do as little as possible."

She handed Jackson a glass of lemonade. Without a word he touched his glass to hers, his eyes twinkling with silent promises. She felt her heart flutter as she sipped the cool tangy drink and recklessly allowed herself to consider what lay ahead for her. For them.

Jackson plunged in, heaping their plates with a little of everything.

"Jackson."

"Yes . . ." The words left him as he turned around to hand her a plate. She'd tossed her hair back from her face and was watching him through those wide amber eyes. Her lips parted as though she was about to speak, but she didn't say anything. He didn't either. He wanted to kiss her.

Brandeis couldn't remember what she was about to say. The look in his eyes sent a feverish heat through her. She wanted him to kiss her. She wanted to feel his arms around her.

Her stomach was too much aflutter to allow her to do more than nibble at her meal. Finally, Jackson took the glass from her hand, set it beside her nearly untouched plate, and pulled her to her feet.

"Come on. Let's take a walk by the ocean."

Brandeis started to protest, but her hand felt too good encased in his. She didn't dare glance at him. Their closeness was like a drug, lulling her to euphoria. Her heart skipped to her throat.

Jackson gently drew her to a halt. She chanced a look and discovered his eyes searching her face. Her lips parted involuntarily. She knew he intended to kiss her.

He embraced her as though they had been separated for a lifetime. When he closed his lips over hers, she seemed to melt into him, opening her lips, clasping his head, pulling his face nearer, nearer. All fear vanished. This is where she belonged. She pressed herself closer, feeling complete, feeling safe. Here in his arms she was whole again. Tears of pleasure slowly found their way to her eyes.

Cupping her chin, he searched her upturned face. "Bran, how do you feel about me?"

Brandeis covered her face with her hands and Jackson wondered if he had misinterpreted her tears. Was she crying because she couldn't return his love? He stood there in suspense, daring only to keep his arms around her as he waited for her to speak.

"Jackson," she said, her voice and mouth tremulous, "I've thought about everything I've ever wanted in a mate. The love, the friendship and fun. When I saw you again, I knew it was you. I knew that somehow, I had to open the door to let you into my heart. Only you. It was never anyone but you. I knew then how much I loved you and have for so very long. I will love you forever." She closed her eyes and put her lips up to his. She lifted her hand and placed it on his cheek.

"I never knew a man could be like you, "she whispered. "I never thought I could feel so close to another person. I love you so much."

Jackson let out a long, audible breath. "I love you, too, baby. You don't know how long I've wanted to say those words to you. I've worked so hard, hoping to convince you that I'm the man for you. To prove that I would be a good husband. You do know that I want to be your husband, don't you?"

"You w-want to m-marry me? But, but . . ." She gazed into his eyes.

Jackson pushed stray tendrils of hair away from her cheek. "No buts. I thought you'd have figured it out by now. I told you I wasn't going to give up on you. I know we belong together. Marriage is the next logical step." His lips brushed against hers as he spoke.

His kiss was slow and thoughtful. Their tongues met, danced, delved. Passion reeled and pounded through her veins, throbbed at her throat, pulsated in the lower, intimate regions of her body.

Her emotions whirled and skidded. Her voice was barely above a whisper. "I love you, Jackson."

As his hands moved gently down the length of her back, the degree to which she responded stunned her while shattering the hard shell she had built so carefully.

She pushed gently away from Jackson. "I'm sorry, I just can't . . ."

Jackson could have kicked himself. He was pushing her too fast. "It's okay, sweetheart. I wasn't thinking . . . I should've known better."

She quickly waved aside his hesitation. "No. No, I'm not going to look back. I'll get through this because I want to be your wife."

"Does this mean we're engaged?" Jackson asked. His voice was full of hope.

"It most certainly does not! I want an old-fashioned romantic proposal."

Bending down, one knee embedded in the sand, Jackson held out his hand. Brandeis placed her hand in his.

He held her hands against his chest, and took a deep breath.

"Darling, I love you with all the depth my soul offers. I will love you forever. I'll seek always for your good and want nothing more than to love you better and better. Will you do me the honor of marrying me?"

Tears spilled down her cheeks but Brandeis didn't care. She was giddy with happiness. A smile curved softly at the corners of her mouth. "Hmmm, I'll have to give it some thought."

Jackson grunted in pain. "Can you think quick? There's a shell cutting into my knee."

Brandeis giggled at the grimace on Jackson's face. Bending to plant a kiss on his forehead, she whispered, "Yes, I'll marry you."

Jackson was not through surprising her yet. Taking her hand, he pulled a small box out of his pants' pocket. Opening it, he took out an emerald cut diamond engagement ring and placed it on Brandeis' finger.

"When . . . when did you get this?" It was the same ring

she'd admired a couple of months ago when they'd picked out a watch for him.

"I went back to Freemans the day after I bought my watch. I thought it might come in handy one day." He laughed. "I wanted to give it to you at Christmas, but I didn't think you were ready."

"It's beautiful, Jackson." Brandeis put her arms around him and hugged him tightly. "I thank God for you."

She thought back to the conversation she and her mother had had just before Christmas. Mona had predicted they'd be planning a wedding within the next six months.

"You and my mother have been conspiring against me, haven't you?"

Jackson frowned. "No, why do you say that?"

"She predicted our getting engaged right about now."

"Did she really?" He grinned. "Mothers have a way of noticing when young men follow around after their daughters, wearing their hearts on their sleeves. You had me walking around looking like a love sick puppy, so I guess it really wasn't hard to figure out. Everybody knows how crazy I am about you."

"Is that so?" She was grinning, too.

"Well, everybody but you."

"Jackson, I knew you cared. I just didn't want to make assumptions," she confessed.

"You don't know how many times I wanted to tell you. I just wasn't sure you were ready to hear it."

She was a vision of sweet innocence that fired an instant desire in him. His dark eyes surveyed her hungrily. It took all his willpower to control the burning desire consuming him, but he knew he had to force himself to do so. He didn't want to scare her.

"Shall we head back to make sure the ants haven't carried off our food?"

Grinning, Brandeis glanced up at him. "Yes. Suddenly, I find myself starving." She wasn't sure if it was for food or for his love.

* * *

Monique awoke early and began the routine that characterized all her days. She did a brief, hard, aerobic workout, pushing herself until she had maintained her heart rate at more than twice the normal for fifteen minutes. She carefully exercised her neck, back, arms, and fingers, and did over a hundred sit-ups without effort.

In her line of work, a woman with a toned body and large, firm breasts could make a lot of money. To Monique, money was everything. Not being a fan of school, she'd dropped out in her tenth year. She didn't stop studying though. Monique had determined to educate herself as thoroughly as any college graduate. For years, she would go to the campus bookstore at Brunswick College and buy books on various subjects. That's where she'd met Jackson. He was taking a summer class for extra credits while on break from Howard University. She had been seventeen at the time. He had offered to help her with her independent studies and tried to encourage her to go back to school. She'd never gone back though. Monique didn't want to go back.

Monique knew she wanted to make a lot of money without doing a lot of hard work and without benefit of a college education. Becoming a call girl seemed the only solution. She simply decided to start a business. A call-girl business.

Her exercises finished, Monique moved to the bathroom and turned on the shower. She stood under the coursing cold water for a long time, feeling her senses awaken for the new day. When she emerged, she put on her short terry-cloth robe, wrapped her wet hair in a towel, and went down the hall to her kitchen.

Monique fixed herself a glass of fruit juice and a bowl of cereal with skim milk. She left her breakfast on the counter to go in search of her newspaper. Her paper carrier always left it hanging on her front door, in a clear plastic bag. After retrieving it, she returned to the kitchen.

Settling down at the breakfast counter, she drank her juice as she perused the newspaper. Suddenly, she gulped. In the society section was a smiling photograph of Brandeis Taylor. She and Jackson were engaged! Her eyes blazed with fury as she reread the announcement.

Monique threw the paper to the floor. She seemed held in a spell, frozen with some dark emotion. Conflicting emotions crossed her face.

"This should be *my* wedding," she spat.

Bitterness ate at Monique's insides. Her stomach felt as if it held smoldering, glowing coals. No amount of water or juice soothed the burning that seemed to reach clear to the marrow of her bones.

Crossing over to her balcony, shoulders rigid, she wrapped her arms around her waist and stared sightlessly through the sliding glass door. Her liquid brown gaze was turned inward to the truth that had forged her past and fashioned her future.

Having sex with a variety of men had never bothered her. It was simply a means to an end. She wanted to live a certain way and prostitution provided her with the means to do so. Monique never pretended otherwise.

"Whore." She spat the word out, the feel of the word in the empty room, hollow. As hollow, she thought, as her life. She knew what she was and she wasn't ashamed of it. It was a road she had chosen to travel. The only man who ever made her consider giving up the life was Jackson Gray. It was his face she saw each time she was with a john. He was the only man who made her feel like a woman, and not just a paid receptacle for a stranger's lust. Illusion had no appeal for her, particularly since she knew it could cause disappointment. While most whores combined their cynicism about society with a credulity about pimps, Monique depended on no one but herself. Thus she could evaluate people with pitiless dispassion.

She knew a lot of so-called ladies married for money and security. Love had nothing to do with it. They were no better than her, Monique thought. She didn't want their money, expensive clothes, big houses . . . She had money and could have all those things, easily. She could get them for herself. The only thing missing in her life was love. From the first moment she'd seen him, her heart had belonged to Jackson.

A brittle laugh escaped her when she considered just how dull and luckless her existence was. Monique shut her eyes briefly.

"I wonder if Jackson and Brandeis have the kind of love that lasts forever," she mused aloud. "I'll find out, some day." Right now, she would bide her time. Monique had to think about what she was going to do. Monique had to come up with a plan.

Brandeis was stunning in the romantic ivory satin wedding gown designed by her mother. The gown featured an off-the-shoulder, short-sleeved bodice sprinkled with pearl and crystal beading over intricate hand embroidery. The Basque bodice flowed into a glorious full skirt, trimmed with matching beading and embroidery.

Brandeis stood still as Mona pinned the crystal and pearl encrusted hair accessory carefully on her daughter's head of spiral-like curls. Brandeis had opted against having a veil.

Carol handed Brandeis a pearl necklace to wear. "These will go perfect with your gown."

She was astonished. "Carol! You bought these to wear with your gown."

"I know but I want you to wear them with yours, first. Think of it as your something borrowed. Mrs. Taylor, you really outdid yourself with this gown. Bran looks like the perfect June bride. I can't believe you two planned this wedding in just under three months. I can't wait to see what you create for me."

"You're going to be a beautiful bride, Carol," Brandeis said, hugging her dear friend. "Thank you so much."

Carol looked splendid in a sleek, floor-length, mauve-colored crepe dress. The halter styled neckline crisscrossed in back and was accented by two rhinestone buttons. The other five bridesmaids, who consisted of friends from college wore identical dresses. Each gown was one shade darker than the next, the darkest gown burgundy.

Mona's stylish ivory crepe ensemble featured a sleeveless sheath with elaborate pearl and rhinestone embroidery along a square neckline. Her coordinating jacket was adorned with matching embroidery and dazzling center link buttons.

Jackson's mother, Raine, decided on a mauve crepe dress that featured a V-back enhanced by pearl and rhinestone buttons and a satin bow at the waist. She hugged Brandeis and welcomed her to the family before leaving to check on Jackson.

Finally, Mona shooed everyone out so that she and Brandeis could have a few moments alone, before the ceremony. Tears in her eyes, she took both of her daughter's hands into her own. "My darling Brandeis," she said. "I'm so happy for you. I've waited so long for this day. I wish you much love and happiness. I'm so proud of you and it's been a joy for me to be your mother. Now, I hand you over to your husband. I pray that he will find the same joy I do in having you in my life. Remember that."

"Oh, Mom. You're going to make me cry. I love you, too." Brandeis picked up a tissue and gently dabbed her eyes. She handed another tissue to her mother. "You're going to ruin your makeup if you don't quit."

A soft knock at the door interrupted them. Mona's brother, Kane, peeked in. "They're ready."

Brandeis took a deep breath, exhaled and said, "It's time." She smiled at her mother. "This is some way to spend a Saturday evening, huh?"

"Sure beats watching old reruns on television," Mona agreed, passing manicured fingers over her french roll. Standing tall and elegant, she blew a kiss to her daughter and whispered, "I'll see you after the wedding."

Kane looked from his sister to his niece. "Well, Bran. I've come clear from California to give you away. Let's get with it!"

Brandeis laughed at her uncle's gruff remark. His bark was far worse than his bite. She touched her forehead slightly in a mock salute to the retired Marine. "Yes, sir, Uncle Kane. Let's go."

Together they made their way out into the narrow hallway leading into the main entrance of the church.

As the two double doors of the church opened, Brandeis was stunned by the sight of the sanctuary lit by the flickering light of tapers in white iron candelabra, festooned with pink and white roses and feathery green cypress boughs.

Kane Abbott held out his arm to escort his favorite niece down the aisle. He felt honored she'd chosen him out of four uncles to give her away. She had always been like a daughter to him. Kane blinked hard to keep the tears from falling down his weathered face.

As Brandeis walked toward the altar on her uncle's arm, Jackson thought her the most beautiful woman in the world. She looked radiant.

Jackson's best man and college buddy, Billy, leaned over to whisper in his ear. "Man, oh man! She's a beauty, Jax. You're one lucky man!"

"I know," he whispered back.

Brandeis watched Jackson as she approached him. He was so handsome in his black tux that her breath caught in her throat. Tonight, there were no shadows across her heart. As she thought of her father, a lone tear rolled down her cheek. He should have been here to walk her down the aisle. It was then she spotted Helen Thayer standing next to Dr. Myers. Brandeis smiled at them both. She quickly pushed all sad thoughts down deep. Today, she would begin a new life with a new name. She would not dwell on the past.

She moved slowly down the aisle toward the tall, lithe figure who totally held her attention as if they were they only two people in the church. She reveled in his open admiration of her.

Jackson stepped down to meet Brandeis as she and Kane neared the altar. When she kissed her uncle on the cheek and turned toward Jackson, Jackson couldn't see anything but Brandeis. He reached out and caught her hand in his, and for a moment, they simply looked into one another's eyes. Together, they stood before the minister.

The silence grew deeper as everyone took their seats. The minister cleared his throat.

Jackson kept his eyes on Brandeis' face. As the minister read the vows, Jackson saw her beautiful amber eyes flood with tears, and he wanted to hold her. He barely heard the minister as he spoke. He was mesmerized by Brandeis. When it came time for Jackson to recite his vows, Billy had to gently nudge him.

After the vows and the prayer, Brandeis waited for precisely the right moment. Softly at first, and then with growing power, she begin to sing, alone and unaccompanied by the pianist.

Jackson, surprised at first, gazed at Brandeis through loving eyes. He'd had no idea she was going to sing to him. He was enraptured by the way she lit up from the inside when she sang, radiating love and joy. Her singing transfigured her from a beautiful woman into something almost ethereal. A goddess. As she sang, her heart spoke to his, telling him of the love they shared for always and forever. An endless love.

Mr. and Mrs. Jackson Gray welcomed their guests at the reception, held on St. Simons Island. The banquet room was decorated in splashes of pink, mauve, burgundy, ivory, and gold.

Standing in the receiving line, Jackson leaned over and whispered to his bride, "You look beautiful, Mrs. Gray."

"Why thank you, Mr. Gray. You look quite handsome yourself."

"I'll tell you a secret," Jackson said softly. "I only dress this way for weddings. How about you?"

"I totally agree, sir." She placed her hand behind his neck and urged his lips to hers.

They soon sat down to a dinner of fresh garden salad, chicken breasts sautéed with a crab cream sauce and topped with Georgia white shrimp, mixed vegetables, and rice pilaf.

Standing with his champagne glass extended, Jackson said, "I propose a toast to my bride. May she find true happiness with me as I have found with her. May she also realize what a good catch I am."

Brandeis clinked her glass against her husband's. "As he has realized about me," she added.

Their guests laughed and clapped. Out of the corner of her eye, Brandeis saw her mother dash a gloved hand across her face in an attempt to stop the flow of tears. Brandeis blew her mother a kiss. When they were seated once again, Carol and Billy gave their toasts.

After dinner, Carol announced it was time for the couple's first dance as man and wife.

"Jackson, when are you going to tell me where we're going?" Brandeis asked as he twirled her around the dance floor. They were soon joined by other couples.

"I've told you that we're going somewhere tropical. Tomorrow, when we're at the airport, I'll tell you more." Jackson cocked his head to the side. "Don't you like surprises?" He had a boyish grin on his face.

"Sometimes. But I only like good ones."

"This *is* a good surprise. Now, are you ready for the honeymoon of your life?"

"Yes." Soon they would leave the reception and head to Jackson's condo where they would spend their wedding night. *Their wedding night!* Brandeis' stomach tensed and she felt disturbing quakes in her serenity. She took a deep breath and tried to relax.

Chapter 12

Brandeis huddled in front of the mirror on her dressing table. The small lamp on her vanity burned brightly in the dimly lighted room, elaborately decorated in shades of seafoam green and dusty pink. As a gift to them, Mona had redecorated the entire condo for Brandeis and Jackson, incorporating their favorite colors throughout the house.

With nervous hands, Brandeis dropped her brush among her perfumes and creams and cosmetics. She took the hairpins from her hair and threaded it with her fingers. Her hair was like silk against her skin. She massaged her temples, easing the tension that had begun to form there.

The reception had lasted until shortly after midnight. They had been at Jackson's condo for half an hour. Upon arriving there, Brandeis headed immediately upstairs to the master bedroom. Her belongings had been moved there less than a week ago, when she'd moved out of her apartment. Brandeis had stayed with her Mom until her wedding.

She paused in removing the rest of the pins from her hair and raised her eyes. Jackson was reflected in her mirror. His image seemed soft to her, wavering and blurred around the edges.

Her fingers returned to the pins in her hair. When they fumbled, failing to pluck out the last few, she swore softly.

"Let me, sweetness," he said. Jackson came up behind her and touched her shoulders. He unclasped the pearl necklace and laid it on the vanity. His fingers returned to touch the curve of her throat.

Brandeis took in his bare chest, the rippling muscles and the way his silk boxers enveloped his body. Heat flowed through her body as she drank him with her eyes. Her gaze wandered to his hands on her bare skin. His fingers were long, the nails trim. Next to them, the line of her collarbone was delicate. Even the lightest pressure from him was like a brand on her flesh. Eyes closed, she leaned back, resting her head against his hard, flat belly. His fingertips grazed her throat, sending a shiver through her.

Soon, she felt his hands in her hair. The pins were removed easily and her hair fell about her shoulders. His fingers combed through the curly mass.

"Better?" He asked quietly.

"Mmmm."

Jackson knew how to interpret that. He continued to thread his fingers through her hair. "If I keep this up, you're going to have a sore head in the morning."

Desire for her coursed through his body. And seeing her in that ivory gown of silk charmeuse with a bodice of lace, left nothing to his imagination. He kept telling himself to go slow, but hell! He was only human and his wife was so damned sexy.

As if she could read his thoughts, Brandeis opened her eyes, sat up and picked up her hair brush. She ran it through her mane in vigorous strokes.

Watching her reaction—half anticipation, half dread—Jackson's own heart was gripped in a vise. A tense silence enveloped the room. It loomed between them like a heavy mist.

He kissed the top of her head and whispered, "I'll sleep

in the guest room tonight." He said the words tentatively as if testing the idea.

Brandeis' knuckles whitened as she clenched the brush more tightly. She stared at him out of wide amber eyes. She swallowed with difficulty and found her voice. "W-why?"

"I think it would be better."

Awkwardly, she cleared her throat. "Better? Jackson, I—"

"It's okay, sweetheart. I'm willing to wait until you're ready to make love to me."

"Jackson . . ." How could she explain her guilt over not being a virgin? Her feelings of shame and degradation?

"Honey, I love you and I'm trying to be considerate. I'll see you in the morning." Jackson kissed her again, this time on the mouth. He hesitated, measuring her for a moment. For a brief moment, he thought he tasted the salt of her tears. Forcing that notion out of his head, he walked to the door and was gone.

Tears spilled down her cheek as she whispered, "But I don't want you to be considerate."

Husband and wife spent their first night sleeping apart.

Jackson slipped into the bed with Brandeis. He planted kisses all over her face as he whispered, "Wake up, sleepyhead."

She stretched sexily and smiling, sat up in bed. She was surprised and somewhat disappointed to find him fully dressed.

"Good morning, Jackson."

"I love you, sweetheart." He drew her into his arms. "I missed you so much last night. You don't know how much I wanted to rush in here and make love to you. I won't rush y—"

Brandeis held a finger to his lips. "Would you please be quiet and let me talk. I love you, too, and I appreciate your being patient with me. I admit I'm a little apprehensive about making love, but it's not in the way you think. I . . . I'm afraid I won't please you. I want you to make love to me. I need you to make love to me."

Jackson was quiet for a moment. "Baby, I'm so sorry about last night. I thought . . ."

"I know what you thought. And you were dead wrong." She laced her arms about his neck, kissing one corner of his mouth.

He fervently returned her kiss full on the lips, and drew her so close that their bodies seemed inseparable. "Are you sure, honey?"

"Make love to me, Jackson." Her arms roamed boldly over his wide shoulders, across his chest, and then up and down his back. She felt the clean, earthy aroma of him suffuse her as she tasted him again and again with her lips. She yielded to the searing need which had been building for months.

Then, he began to undress her. He removed her gown quickly, anxious to see her naked beauty. Jackson's eyes raked over her loveliness. "Bran, honey, you're so beautiful. You're absolutely perfect."

"Do you mean it, Jackson?" Suddenly, she felt more like a woman than ever before.

"Yes. I mean it." He stood and stripped off his clothes hastily, his passion raging.

Brandeis was impressed by his masculine physique. She exulted at the male strength, the cleanliness and beauty of him. In her opinion, he, too, was perfect.

Undressed, Jackson stretched out beside her and took her in his arms. As his mouth crushed against hers, she freed her mind of worry, and lost herself in the throes of ecstasy. She felt transported, as if on a soft and wispy cloud.

His tongue caressed her sensitive nipples as their hands traveled hotly over each other, every caress, every touch, adding more fuel to their burning desire. As Jackson roused her passion, his own grew stronger. His hand seared a path down her abdomen and onto her thigh. His touch was light and painfully teasing. He paused to kiss her, whispering his love for each part of her body. His expert touch sent her to even higher levels of ecstasy.

Brandeis reached out to explore that male part of him as he whispered words of encouragement.

Jackson continued his kisses and caresses until her inexperienced body was ready to receive him. His body moved to partially cover hers.

She gasped as bare chest met bare chest. Skin to skin, they were as one. It amazed her to find such closeness comforting. Their bodies moved softly against one another, and their caresses were a perfect music of familiarity and strangeness, for they knew each other well, and not at all.

Then, bracing himself above her on fully extended arms, Jackson gazed down into her lovely face, "I love you, honey. I wouldn't hurt you for the world. If you want me to stop, just say so and I will."

"I know, Jackson," she whispered. "I'm not afraid." She caressed his face. Brandeis didn't see Martin's face when she looked upon her husband and she felt no hesitation at satisfying the yearnings mounting inside her.

He delved deeply into her moist depths. He stayed still inside her for several moments, waiting for her body to recover from the shock of his invasion, then began a slow, rhythmic motion that rocked her against the mattress. She gripped him with soft hands beneath his waist, helping him to come deeper into her. Brandeis moaned as he began to move inside her and the power of his strokes bespoke his joy at being her husband. Soon, she felt a sweet ache building between her thighs.

Instinctively, her body understood his rhythm and her thrusting hips met his in perfect timing. Their bodies were in exquisite harmony with one another. Passion streamed through her like a river, sweeping her into a whirlpool of indescribable splendor.

Abandoning themselves to their passion, wondrous sensations coursed through the lovers as, together, they sought and achieved a mindless rapture.

Tears ran down Brandeis' flushed cheeks as her body tumbled over cresting waves of ecstasy. Brandeis was finding herself as a woman, clean and feminine and desirable. Jackson kissed the tears away before he, too, was consumed by pleasures that defied description.

Jackson moved over, and stretching out beside her, he urged her into his arms. She placed her head on his shoulder and snuggled intimately.

Brandeis shivered in his arms for a long moment as her body pulsated with the aftermath of love. She'd never in her life imagined that anything could be so overpowering and so wonderful at the same time. Perhaps her mother was right, it was because Jackson was her husband now. There had been no guilt, no shame in their lovemaking, just pleasure. Her energy spent, she lapsed into sweet dreams that took up where reality left off. She was blissfully happy.

A tender smile crossed Jackson's lips as he peered at his wife, sleeping soundly in his arms. He marveled at the feelings of possessiveness that overcame him when he stared at Brandeis.

"I'll never let anyone hurt you again, sweetheart. I promise."

"It's so beautiful! Martinique is so lovely. Look at all the flowers." As they drove from the airport, Brandeis admired the tropical island.

Hibiscus, bamboo, and wild orchids decked the woodlands while a variety of flowering trees rimmed the hills. On the way to the hotel, Brandeis saw plantation fields with crops of bananas, pineapples, sugarcane, and coffee.

"The Carib Indians called the island Madininia, *'the island of flowers'*" Jackson explained. "In a couple of days, I'll take you to the Caribbean Arts Center, on the seafront."

"That'll be great. Where do most people do their shopping? I want to take home some souvenirs for Carol and Mom."

"The main shopping district is in Fort-de-France, along rues Antoine Siger, Victor Hugo, and Schoelcher."

"How many times have you been here?" Brandeis asked. "You seem to know the island very well."

"Twice. Remember, my father grew up here. The last time I came here was about five years ago. I decided back then, when and if I ever married, I'd bring my bride here for our honeymoon. We're going to spend a week in Martinique then fly to Grenada, the island of spice."

Jackson pulled up in front of the hotel. A bellman quickly approached to assist them.

Brandeis threw her arms around her husband, holding him tightly. "This is so perfect, Jackson. You're a wonderful man. A very special man. One I love with all my heart." She kissed him passionately. She could see the desire in his eyes. "I think maybe we should hurry and check in. I'm in need of a nap. How about you?"

Jackson responded huskily, "I'm in need of you. We'll nap eventually."

They settled into their room and Brandeis admired the view of the ocean from the balcony of their suite. "I love the ocean," she said.

Jackson put his arms around her from behind, his chin resting on her head. "Yes, I know. I love it, too. That was one of the reasons I returned to Brunswick. I missed St. Simons Island and Jekyll."

He could feel her body starting to tremble. "Are you cold?"

"No, but I think we should go inside." She turned around in his arms. Wrapping her arms around his neck, she stood on her toes to offer him her mouth.

"You know, I think you're right. We should go inside. As a matter of fact, I think we should go straight to bed." He stretched and feigned a yawn. "I'm getting sleepy, how about you?"

She feigned a yawn also, covering her mouth with her hand. "Yes, I'm feeling pretty tired myself. I'll race you to the bed." She was off and running in a flash.

Jackson wasn't far behind.

They made love for the rest of the evening, only stopping to order room service.

The next day, Jackson took Brandeis to the Court of Justice building where she photographed the statue of Victor Schoelcher, the man responsible for freeing the slaves in the French West Indies in eighteen forty-eight.

Brandeis took pictures of churches, buildings, shops, children, and of the beaches. By the end of the day, Brandeis had photographs of such places as Cathedrale Saint-Louis with its Poyzantine decor and stained-glass windows and the Musée Departemental de la Martinique.

They had dinner at La Grand Voile. Seated in an open, second-story balcony overlooking Fort-de-France, Brandeis smiled at her husband over candlelight.

"This place is paradise! I love it here."

"So do I," Jackson said. "I'm glad you love it as much as I do."

"The only problem is that my French is terrible." She laughed.

Jackson placed long, slender fingers over hers and whispered, "I think the way you speak French is sensual. It really turns me on."

"Jackson!" She glanced around to see if anyone could hear their conversation. She saw the lusty gleam in his eye and blushed. The heat of desire spread through her body like a fire out of control.

He knew what she was thinking about and he smiled. She was still so innocent. Jackson wondered if she realized just how desirable she was to him.

They ate quickly and returned to their suite. As soon as they closed the door, their hands worked furiously to be rid of the layers of clothes separating them. Jackson picked Brandeis up and carried her over to the king-size bed. Brandeis pulled him down on top of her. He eased himself inside.

Moaning, she urged him to take her with even more force, and he rammed himself harder and deeper in answer to her plea. She rose to meet his movements with thrusts as hard and forceful as his own.

"Oh, Jackson, Jackson," she moaned. Her body was no longer her own. All control was lost. It was intolerably beautiful, and so sensual, so slow, that she gave him her shudders, her spasms of ecstasy, a dozen times before she felt the great swell of his need upraise her, thrusting her higher and higher, until strange cries she had never heard before sounded in her throat, and delights unimagined sang through the heart of her. With a final thrust, all energy drained from his body.

At daybreak, they dressed and took a stroll on the beach, walking toward the first glow of orange peeking above the horizon. The waves broke gently, thirty yards out, and rolled quietly onto the shore. Brandeis ran boldly into the sea, then retreated furiously when the next wave of white foam approached. Jackson sat on the sand, grinning as he watched his wife dart in and out of the ocean. It made him feel good to see her so happy.

A couple of days later, they traveled from Fort-de-France to the southern half of the island, where they stopped at Trois-Ilets, the birthplace of Empress Josephine.

The rest of their week in Martinique was spent taking long walks on the beach, shopping and dining on island specialties such as *columbo,* an Indian dish of currylike seeds cooked with beef, chicken, or pork and eaten with rice; *boudin,* a spicy blood sausage; and *callaloo,* a soup made from greens and West Indian herbs.

In Grenada, they shopped at Tikel, where Brandeis bought her mother and Carol spice baskets, a hand-woven pannier of palmleaf filled with cinnamon, nutmeg, ginger, vanilla, cloves, and other native spices. They ventured down Cross Street and viewed the art works of Canute Caliste and Elinus Cato.

"Grenada has some of the most spectacular waterfalls I've ever seen," Brandeis said as she held her camera to her face.

Brandeis lowered her camera and smiled at her husband.

Jackson put his arm around her waist. "I love seeing you this happy. I hope I can keep you smiling and delighted for the rest of our lives."

"Just love me, Jackson," Brandeis said. "I just need you to love me."

They ventured back to the Twelve Degrees North, an elegant eight-unit resort. Staying there afforded them the use of the resort's own private beach as well as maids to cook all meals and do the laundry.

Brandeis eyed her husband as they sat in La Belle Creole, a restaurant at the Blue Horizon Cottage Hotel. He looked so handsome in a crisp linen shirt and khaki pants. It was their last night in Grenada and dining out seemed the perfect end to their honeymoon. One of the maids at Twelve Degrees North had recommended the restaurant. They dined on lobster à la Creole.

"Jackson, this has been the best honeymoon any bride could want. I never dreamed I'd have this much fun. Swimming, shopping, long walks on the beach. All the things I like to do best. Thank you so much for bringing me here."

Jackson's smile reached all the way to his eyes. "I'm glad you enjoyed it. I wanted to make this a honeymoon you'll never forget."

After one unforgettable month of marriage, Brandeis never thought she could be so happy. She glanced at their wedding photo on her desk and smiled. Then, she spied the stack of cases on her desk. Sighing, she decided it was time to stop daydreaming and get back to work. Facing her monitor, she keyed in her password, then proceeded to type.

Brandeis picked up her ringing phone without taking an eye off her computer screen. "Brandeis Gray speaking."

The voice she heard made her breath come short.

"Well, well, well. I see congratulations are in order." His voice heavy with sarcasm.

She sat up straight as shock flew through her. But that

shock yielded quickly to fury. It was impossible. Martin would never call her after all this time. But he had.

"M-Martin!"

"Yeah, it's me baby. How have you been?"

Her face was marked with loathing. "You've got some nerve! Why are you calling me?" Could fate and chance be so capricious as to taunt her this way? How could his voice have sprung from that banished time to summon her once again to a suffering that two years of living had all but buried?

"You've been on my mind. For a while, actually. I've missed you," Martin said.

"We really don't have anything to talk about—"

"Yes, we do." Martin cut her off. "I'm still crazy about you. I know I left in a hurry, but I couldn't take FLETC anymore. They were giving me so much crap. It had nothing to do with you."

Brandeis recognized a breezy, somewhat sheepish tone in his voice. "Is that a fact?" she replied coolly.

"Why did you have to go and get married, baby? I told you I was gonna marry you. I just had to get away for a while. You know, to go clear my mind."

"Martin, I've had enough of this conversation. You may have forgotten that you raped me the night before you skipped town, but I haven't. You rotten bastard! Do not—"

"What the hell you talkin' about, woman?" There was an edge to his voice.

Brandeis' tone hardened. "You heard me. You raped me!"

"Look! You're not the only girl to give up her virginity before her wedding night," Martin argued. "You're just mad because I up and left town the day after we made love. I know how it looked but I really cared 'bout you. I told you I'd marry you one day, but not at that time. I wanted to get to know you better."

Brandeis was livid. "I didn't give up my virginity! *You took it!*" Anger filled her to the core. "How dare you tell me that you wanted to wait to get to know me better. You should have gotten to know me better before you raped me!" Brandeis heard the horrible bitterness in her voice.

"What!" Martin yelled. "You know what . . . you're crazy. I can't believe you're acting this way. Women have sex all the time and they don't go crying rape. I bet half the women in your church aren't virgins . . ."

"I don't care what you say, Martin. I didn't want to have sex with you that night. I tried to tell you over and over, but you wouldn't listen to me. It was *rape!*"

"I didn't rape you and you better not be telling lies like that to no one," Martin warned. "Do you hear me, girl? You wanted me as much as I wanted you. You just worried 'bout what them ol' church biddies think. Don't worry 'bout them. God cares 'bout what's in your heart. Having sex before marriage don't make you a bad person. I bet your husband didn't care whether or not you was a virgin."

Brandeis slammed the phone down. The nerve of that son of a—

Carrie knocked on her door. "Brandeis, Mr. Matthews wants you to come to his office. He called when you were on the phone." She watched Brandeis intently.

"Is there something else, Carrie?"

"Um, no." Her eyes never left Brandeis' face.

Why is she still standing there, staring at me. It's as if she knows something. But what? "If that's all, I need to go to Mr. Matthews' office."

Carrie turned and left without another word. Brandeis didn't miss the smile on her face as she left. *What was Carrie up to?* No need to linger on it. She had another problem. A bigger problem. Martin!

Chapter 13

Martin swigged his gin. He couldn't get Brandeis out of his mind. She was a lying bitch! Going around telling people that he'd raped her. He never had to rape anyone before. If anything, they begged him to love them. Brandeis wanted him, too. He could tell from the looks she'd give him. It's all that going to church all the time mentality. Those church women had her thinking it was a sin to have premarital sex, but it hadn't stopped a few of them from coming on to him. Even the preacher's daughter had flirted with him.

"I've got to set her straight. I can't have her going around spreading those sort of rumors around," he said to the empty room. He tilted the bottle to his mouth once more. He was still hot for the woman. *I bet she still wants me, too. I'll pay her a visit one of these days, just for old time sakes.*

Martin staggered to his bedroom and took off his clothes. Looking down at his nude body, he smiled. He thought his features were so perfect, so symmetrical, that any more delicacy would have made him too beautiful for a man.

Admiring himself in the mirror, he bragged, "No I don't have to rape anybody." Placing his hand on that male part of him, he murmured, "Woman beg for this all the time. I have to fight them off. No woman has ever said no to me and really meant it. About anything. Not even my dearly departed mama. She would've given me the world if she could have." Martin knew it was his mother's way of trying to make up for the love he'd never received from his father.

He closed his eyes and tried to forget the man that had done nothing but cause him pain. As a child, Martin was very sickly, whereas his brother was healthy as a horse. While Matt participated in sports, Martin sat on the sidelines. His father always considered Martin a weakling. Even said he was too pretty to be a real man. A nothing! Rage flowed through Martin's body like blood coursing through his veins. He hated his namesake. Hated him with a passion.

Staggering over to the bed, he lay down. Again he thought how handsome he was. From the time he was a young boy, women were attracted to him. He was given everything he ever wanted. At the age of thirteen, one of his mother's friends introduced him to sex. All women wanted him. Even Brandeis. She still wanted him. He would make her admit that she still loved him. This time, he would make her beg.

Jackson walked into his living room and placed his brief-case on one of the wing chairs. Loosening his tie, he ventured into the kitchen. Brandeis was sitting at the counter, staring into space.

"Bran?"

She was so caught up in her thoughts of whether or not to tell Jackson about Martin's phone call, she hadn't heard her husband come in. "Huh? Oh, hi, honey. I didn't know you were home."

"I can tell. What's got you so preoccupied?"

"N-nothing." Brandeis decided not to tell him about the phone call. Martin was a part of her past and she didn't want to relive the pain. She wanted to forget it ever had happened herself. She walked over to assist him in taking off his jacket. "How was your day? I know you were in court today . . . with Marc. How did it go?"

Jackson took a deep breath. "Marc Wiley was found not guilty of rape charges." He held up his hand to halt Brandeis' comment. "Before you get upset, Peggy admitted under oath that she'd lied. She said she threatened Marc with the bogus rape charges in order to break up Marc's marriage. She was furious when he broke off the affair, instead."

"Oh." Her voice rose in surprise. She pulled away and walked over to the window.

Jackson walked up behind her and put his hands on her shoulders. "Are you okay, honey? I know you really wanted to believe he was guilty . . ."

"I'm fine, Jackson. I guess I jumped to conclusions where Marc was concerned. I'm glad he's not going to be punished for a crime he didn't commit . . ." Her voice broke. "I'm so ashamed. I all but had him convicted."

Jackson held her in his arms. "Considering what you've gone through, it's understandable."

Her conversation with Martin drifted back to mind. She pushed it to the recesses of her mind. *I'm not going to think about this right now.* "I made beef Stroganoff for dinner. I hope you're hungry."

"I'm hungry, but it isn't for food."

He reached up and tugged at the black and white barrette that held her hair back. Curls came tumbling down around her shoulders. He leaned into her, his mouth covering hers in a long, searching kiss, his tongue exploring the sweetness of her mouth before darting around hers.

His fingers stroked her soft breasts, drawing a moan from deep in her throat.

Brandeis shuddered as delicious waves washed over her. "Then it is my duty to see to it that you're deprived of nothing, my hungry husband." She pulled away and led him to the den. Brandeis slowly and methodically undressed him, her lips nibbling down the long column of his throat and across his broad shoulders. Ever so gently, she ran her fingers through the crisp curls on his chest, then licked the hard male nipple, smiling in satisfaction at his groan of pleasure. Brandeis continued her tender assault, nipping across his taut abdomen, the muscles jumping reflexively at the feel of her soft teasing lips. She stopped and played havoc with his senses as she did a sensual striptease. Each time he reached for her, she backed away.

When she was completely nude, she resumed her trail of fiery kisses over his lower abdomen, deliberately brushing his groin. Jackson groaned. She nibbled at his thighs, her tongue flicking, feeling the powerful muscles tense. Then she sat back on her heels, her hand wrapping around him, sensually stroking his immense, throbbing hardness that stood so proudly before her.

Jackson's blood was surging through his veins like liquid fire, his senses reeling, his body trembling with delicious agony. His hands tangled in her hair as he jerked her head upward. "I can't wait any longer. I want you now!"

His mouth took possession of hers and Brandeis responded mindlessly to his deep, passionate kiss. Together they fell to the floor. Brandeis felt the hot, moist tip of him against her womanhood. She feverishly arched to meet him, welcoming him with a glad cry, sheathing him as he drove deeply inside her, her muscles rippling about and caressing each inch of his length.

Their union was a fierce coming together. Brandeis met each powerful, searing stroke with one of her own. Their bodies rocked, their mutual passion blazing as they grew frenzied in their urgency. They climaxed in a hot, tumultuous eruption that sent brilliant fireworks flashing through their brains.

They lay, shuddering from their soul-shattering experience, their breathing ragged, hearts racing, too exhausted even to move. Finally, Jackson kissed her temple, relieved her of his weight.

Brandeis smiled seductively up at him, a warm gleam in her eyes. "Satisfied, my darling husband?"

"My hunger for you will never be satisfied. However, my need for nourishment has not been fulfilled," Jackson said.

Brandeis picked up his shirt and threw it at him. "You're so romantic!"

Jackson chuckled as he headed to the downstairs bathroom. "Join me in the shower. I'll show you how romantic I can be."

After dinner, Jackson helped wash and put away the dishes. When the last plate was placed in the cabinet, he picked Brandeis up and carried her upstairs to their bedroom. "Now for dessert . . ."

Two weeks later, Marlena brought in a letter for Brandeis. It was marked personal with no return address. The address on the envelope was typed. She opened it. She could not believe it. Martin had the unmitigated gall to send her a love letter. As if nothing out of the ordinary had taken place. As if he hadn't raped her!

She read the letter twice before folding it neatly and putting it in the pocket of her pink blazer. Brandeis intended to destroy the letter once she left her office. He had the nerve to complain about her hanging up on him Shuddering, she recalled Martin's pledge of love. Once again, he explained his reasons for leaving Brunswick so quickly, citing his dismissal from the U.S. Marshals and FLETC as the reason for disappearing. The way Brandeis figured it, Martin had been afraid she'd press charges so he'd left town. Now, Martin had the nerve to apologize for leaving her so abruptly. Brandeis almost laughed. Did he think she was an idiot?

She wondered if he really thought he could win her back, despite the fact that she was married now. He had no idea how much she hated him. How could he actually believe he could win her affections? *But how did he find out about my marriage in the first place?* Brandeis wondered.

She perused the envelope the letter had come in, but there was no way of knowing where it had come *from*. The postmark was illegible. It was obvious Martin still feared she'd press charges against him. Brandeis had prayed Martin had forever disappeared from their lives. She didn't want to alarm her mother or Jackson.

Why did you have to come back to haunt me? You got what you wanted, now please leave me alone, Brandeis cried silently. She decided she would stop by and see Helen Thayer today. Maybe she could give her some advice.

Since her marriage, Brandeis hadn't felt a need to resume her weekly counseling sessions, but now, it warranted a second thought.

Jackson arrived home the same time as his wife. He waited as Brandeis retrieved her briefcase and locked her car.

He put his arm around her and kissed her. "Hi, sweetheart."

"Hi. I didn't expect you home so early," Brandeis said. "After work, I stopped over at Mom's house. If I'd known you were coming home, I would've had dinner ready for you."

"I thought I'd come home and cook dinner for *you* tonight," Jackson said. "I know how tired you've been. You have been working some long hours. I thought I'd surprise you tonight. By the way, I love you, dearly."

Brandeis looked up at her husband. "I love you, too. You are so good to me."

"I won't ever let anyone hurt you again," Jackson promised.

Brandeis was quiet for a moment. She thought about the letter from Martin and the phone call. She wanted to tell Jackson about them both, but then, she hadn't heard any more from Martin in the last week. She decided to say nothing for now.

After dinner, they settled down in their bedroom to watch television. Brandeis tried to concentrate on the movie, but her mind kept drifting back to Martin. She refused to give him the power to control her life once again, but still, he invaded her mind.

Jackson noticed the grimace on his wife's face. "What's wrong, honey? You look a little upset."

"N-nothing's wrong. I was just t-thinking about something. There's nothing wrong." Brandeis smiled. She felt trapped and vulnerable, but wasn't willing to confide in Jackson yet. She feared the questioning would continue.

Doubt flickered in Jackson's eyes, but he said nothing more.

A few minutes into the movie of the week, Brandeis fell asleep. Jackson picked up the remote control and turned down the volume on the TV. Jackson watched her sleep, searching her face in silence. *What is she hiding from me?* he wondered.

Getting out of bed, he walked softly toward their walk-in closet and grabbed his robe. He put it on and headed downstairs.

The soft navy and burgundy padding of the sofa cushioned him as he situated himself comfortably. Flames crackled in the fireplace. A number of law books were stacked haphazardly on one corner of the coffee table and the rest of the surface was covered by magazines and journals. Questions sliced through him like a freshly sharpened blade. Jackson thought he'd finally earned Brandeis' trust. Apparently, he was wrong. She was hiding something from him, but what? Leaning forward, he rested his elbows on his knees. Why wouldn't she confide in him?

When he felt he could no longer hold his eyes open, he put out the fire and returned to their bedroom. Brandeis hadn't stirred from her slumber. Jackson went to the closet and pulled out a hanger. A pink blazer belonging to Brandeis fell to the floor. As he bent to pick it up, he caught sight of a folded piece of paper falling to the floor. He was about to return it to her pocket when a feeling of dread swept through him like a tornado. Looking at the piece of paper, Jackson debated with himself whether or not to read it. Curiosity won over and he quickly scanned the letter. It was clearly a declaration of love from Martin, and it was dated almost two and a half weeks ago.

Jackson felt as if he'd been kicked in the gut. *What in hell is going on?* Martin stated that he knew about her marriage. He expected Brandeis to walk out on her marriage. He apologized for leaving her the way he did. Especially after they'd made love. *Made love!* Had Brandeis really been raped? Or, was she simply trying to strike back at Martin somehow, as the letter suggested? Jackson wished he knew. Deep down, he didn't think Brandeis would lie about something as serious as rape. But when scorned, there were women who stopped at nothing to get revenge. Peggy Roberts was such a woman. But would Brandeis go that far? One never really knew.

He heard her whimper and quickly returned the letter to her pocket. Back in bed, Jackson lay awake for a long time, wondering why she'd never mentioned receiving the letter or the phone call. He hated himself for doubting her, but the facts simply didn't add up.

From what Martin stated in his letter, Brandeis was angry because of the way he'd ended their relationship. He accused her of trying to get even with him. Something like betrayal gripped Jackson's insides, chilling his blood and filling him with a rage rooted in his soul. He thought again of Marc Wiley's case. Only Peggy admitted she'd lied. *Would* Brandeis lie about something like rape? Jackson shook his head. She was not that kind of person. But why would she keep all of this a secret from him? What was she trying to hide? He wanted some answers.

The next morning, Jackson was sitting quietly at the dining room table, his tired eyes scanning the pages of the *Brunswick News,* when Brandeis came downstairs. Settling back for a moment, he removed his glasses. Jackson rubbed his eyes and sighed.

Brandeis seemed surprised to see him as she entered the kitchen. She sensed his disquiet, her questioning gaze following his movements. He slowly put the newspaper down and proceeded to clean the lens of his glasses, his eyes never leaving her face.

"Jackson? Is something wrong?" A sense of dread suddenly covered her like a cloak.

He hesitated, measuring her for a moment. "I need to know something and I want the truth." Before she realized what was happening, Jackson was up and looming over her. "What is going on between you and Martin?"

Brandeis was perplexed. "I-I d-don't know what—"

"Don't lie to me, Bran!"

She shrank back from him. "D-don't . . ." She put her hands up as if to ward off a blow.

Jackson saw the fear in her eyes. "I'm not going to hit you." He backed away from her. "I didn't mean to scare you. I just want the truth."

Taking a deep breath, she tried to relax. "Please Jackson, tell me what you're talking about." *You know what he's talking about,* her heart whispered back.

In response, Jackson held up the letter.

A deadly silence saturated the room.

Brandeis swayed. She held onto the chair with all her might. Summoning all her strength, she pulled it out and sat down. She sucked in a shallow breath and lowered her head, trying her best not to cry. Her hands, hidden from sight, twisted nervously in her lap.

"I know what you must think, Jackson," Brandeis said. "Please listen to me. It's not like that. Not the way that you're thinking."

"Then why didn't you tell me about it?" Jackson's expression was a mask of stone.

"I didn't want to bring Martin into our marriage. He's been in *my* life for the past two years. Two horrible years.

I didn't want him in my life with you,'' Brandeis said, an almost imperceptible note of pleading in her voice.

Jackson squinted critically. "Then why in hell would you keep a letter from him? A love letter, of all things. And why would you hide it from me?''

Brandeis kept her features deceptively composed. "I was going to throw it away.''

Jackson spat a string of curses and turned away in frustration. He turned and stared at her from across the room, and damned himself for putting that wounded expression in her eyes.

Brandeis stood and walked up to him. Her hand moved to rub his smooth cheek. "Why don't you trust me, Jackson?''

Jackson removed her hand and walked away. "I want to, but when I find out my wife is keeping love letters from her rapist—''

"Please don't use that tone with me. I've done nothing wrong,'' she snapped.

"You actually believe that? That you've done nothing wrong! How in hell can you say that?'' Fury spread through his body like a fire. "You call keeping this letter from your husband nothing!''

Jackson's fiery, angry look was unfamiliar to her. Brandeis tried to keep her body from trembling. "Jackson, that's not what I meant. I'm tired and I don't want to fight anymore.'' Feeling suddenly weary and light-headed, she grabbed the back of a chair as her head began to swim and her stomach churned. "Can we talk about this later. I really don't feel well.'' Brandeis sank down slowly into the chair.

Jackson could tell that something was wrong. Brandeis looked as if she were trying to keep from passing out. "What's wrong?'' he asked.

"I don't know. I just don't want to argue with you anymore.'' She pushed her hair back. "I feel sick . . .'' Brandeis pleaded for help with her eyes, unable to say more as wave after wave of nausea washed over her.

As soon as he helped her up, she rushed to the bathroom. Jackson winced at the sounds of her vomiting. "Do you want help?" he called. Her moan could have meant anything; he took it as a refusal.

"Are you all right?" he called again. His anger had disappeared in the wake of his concern.

There was no moan this time. There was no response of any kind. Jackson was standing outside of the door when he heard Brandeis' running water, then the sounds of her brushing her teeth. She was fine, then.

Jackson walked into the bedroom and sat on the bed. Resting his elbows on his knees, he supported his head in his hands.

"Do you feel better?" he asked when she came out of the bathroom. His voice was quiet, yet held an undertone of coldness.

As casually as she could, Brandeis answered, "Yes. I think I've been pushing myself too hard lately. I hope my ulcer isn't acting up again."

"Why don't you stay home today and get some rest," Jackson suggested.

"I think I'm going to do just that," Brandeis replied in a low voice, taut with anger. "Tonight we can pick up where we left off."

"As a matter of fact, after my meeting this morning, my calendar is clear. I'll come home early. We can talk then."

"That's fine."

"Get plenty of rest this morning." Jackson picked up his briefcase and headed toward the door.

"Jackson, I love you. I just wish you would trust me!"

He whirled to stare at her, quick anger rising in his eyes. "Why don't you trust *me?*"

Denial flew from her. "I d-do."

Jackson stormed from their bedroom, leaving Brandeis to stare after him and weep.

"I'm sorry," she whispered. "I love you, Jackson, and I'm so sorry."

* * *

Brandeis glanced up from the book she'd been reading when Jackson strolled casually into the room. She took a steady breath. "I-I didn't know you were home. I didn't hear you come in."

Jackson started to undo his tie. "How are you feeling? Do you need another prescription of Tagamet?"

Brandeis took another deep breath to bolster her resolve. "I'm feeling better. I thought I'd wait a few more days before calling Dr. Myers. Maybe it's not my ulcer."

Jackson seemed to study her thoughtfully for a moment, then asked, "What else could it be?"

"It may just be the stress . . . of everything."

"What? The stress of hiding things from me?"

"Jackson! I've apologized already!"

"I know. And you expect me to just forget about it. Just like that, because you apologized!"

"No, Jackson. I don't expect you to just forget about it. I'm simply asking you to understand why I did what I did."

Jackson sat on the bed beside her. "Do you still believe you've done absolutely nothing wrong? Do you really believe that I shouldn't be angry right now?"

"Yes," she said quietly. "Don't you understand? I didn't want Martin to have any control over our marriage—"

He interrupted her. "Honey, you're giving him power over us by hiding things from me. Right now, we're fighting! If you'd come to me in the first place, this would not be happening."

"I don't agree, Jackson. You don't trust me. That's what this is really about."

He stood. "This is ridiculous! You . . ." He threw up his hands in resignation. "You know what? Never mind! It's pointless!"

Brandeis crawled out of bed slowly. She moved to stand behind Jackson. "Honey . . ."

He whirled around. "Look, it's obvious we're not going

to agree on this. I'm through with it." Jackson started to undress. "I'm going to take a shower."

She tried to smile seductively. "Want some company?"

"No, I think I'd rather be alone."

"That's a first!" Brandeis turned away before he could see how much his remark wounded her. Picking her book off the bed, she headed out of the room. "I'll leave you to your shower." She left, slamming the door behind her.

Chapter 14

On her way to the office the next day, Brandeis tried to reassure herself that she'd done the right thing by not telling Jackson about the call and the letter. Last night, Jackson had decided to sleep in the guest room. Although it hurt her deeply, she assured herself that maybe it was for the best. She would give him time and let him cool off first. Then, she planned to sit him down and explain why she didn't want Martin to have a place in their marriage. It was something she was still trying to come to terms with herself.

Brandeis walked into her office and put down her brief-case. She prayed Martin would have the good sense to stay out of her life. Brandeis didn't want to relive the pain. She sat at her desk and prepared to start her work.

Suddenly, her stomach turned. The smell of coffee was making Brandeis nauseous. For a brief moment, she wondered if her ulcer was acting up again. All that worrying over Martin in the last few weeks. She refused to make herself sick, like before. She stood up, intending to close the door to her office in an effort to shut out the coffee aroma. A feverish wave of nausea swept over her. She closed her eyes and leaned against the side of her desk to keep from falling.

Just as she was feeling her way back to her chair, Carrie came in. "Brandeis, are you okay?" she cried, rushing over to assist Brandeis.

"Yes, I'm fine. I just got a little dizzy, that's all. Thanks for your help."

Carrie watched her closely. "Sure. Anytime. How long have you been feeling like this?"

"For the last two weeks. I have an ulcer. I get nauseous, have dizzy spells, and sometimes pain in my stomach."

Carrie was thoughtful for a minute. "Have you had any pain lately? Are you sure it can't be something else?"

"No, I don't think so. Why?"

"Oh, no reason. I've heard there's a virus going around, so you should probably go see your doctor. You know, just to be sure it's your ulcer. I'll leave you alone for now. You don't have any appointments until noon. Why don't you go to see your doctor this morning?"

"Thanks, I'll consider it." When Carrie left, another wave of nausea hit Brandeis and she laid her head on the desk. After it passed, she reached for the phone.

Jackson took off his glasses and cleaned the lenses with a handkerchief from his breast pocket. Brandeis knew by now the action was more indicative of the fact that he was thinking than of his glasses being smudged.

"Hi, Jackson," she said brightly.

He glanced up toward the door of his office. His eyes narrowed and his back became ramrod straight. "Come on in, Brandeis. You can close the door behind you."

Brandeis walked over and sat on her husband's lap. "How's your day going?" There was defiance in her tone as well as subtle challenge. She knew he was still angry with her.

Jackson gave a fatalistic shrug of his shoulders. "It's

improving. I can see you're feeling much better. Did Dr. Myers say whether or not it was your ulcer again?"

Brandeis could not keep the grin off her face. "It's not my ulcer. I haven't had my cycle since we got married. I've missed three months." She laughed at Jackson's skeptical gaze. "You're as bad as me! I guess we both missed the obvious. I'm going to have a baby."

Jackson looked as if he couldn't believe his ears. "You're p-pregnant?"

"Yes."

"Oh, man! You mean, I'm going to have a baby?"

"No. *You're* going to be a father. *I'm* going to have the baby. Are you clear on this?" She laughed at the wondrous expression on Jackson's face. "It's okay." Forcing herself to be strong, she took a deep breath and leaned into him, kissing him fully on the mouth. "I love you anyway."

He was suddenly very serious. "I really want this baby."

"I see," she said in a tight whisper. Didn't he care about her? Didn't he want to know if she was happy sad or scared about the pregnancy? Oh, God, why couldn't he love her enough to trust her? She struggled to keep her tears at bay.

Brandeis let none of her anguish show on her face as she hugged the knowledge of a child to her heart. She refused to let Jackson's anger destroy her happiness.

Oblivious to her feelings, Jackson grinned. "I'm going to be a father. Imagine that!"

"I'll make something special for dinner tonight, to celebrate."

"No. I'm going to take you to dinner tonight," Jackson said. "To celebrate our good fortune."

Brandeis was hopeful. "Can we invite Mom and Carol?"

"Sure. Don't forget about James. Is there somewhere special you'd like to go? Or should I just pick a place?"

"I'll let you decide. Just surprise us. I've got to head back to the office, so I'll see you when you get home." She kissed him gently on his cheek. "I love you. Please forgive me, Jackson. I really believed I was doing the right thing by not telling you—''

Jackson kissed her lightly on the lips. "I don't want to talk about this now."

Brandeis stood up then. "But we have to talk about this. I don't want this dark cloud hanging over our marriage."

Sudden anger flashed in his eyes. "Look. I don't want to talk about Martin. You've just told me I'm going to be a father. Don't spoil this day for me."

Brandeis could tell he was trying to control himself. Gone was his good humor, and in its place was anger. Jackson leaned back and closed his eyes, indicating that their conversation was over.

"Can we get past this, Jackson?"

"Sure. Let's just forget about it."

"Can you honestly do that?"

"Ummmm," he grunted with no more than a brief glance at her. "I said, it's forgotten."

Clearly, it wasn't. Jackson was brooding over what had happened, trying to figure out if she was telling the truth.

Brandeis waited for him to say something more, then finally, started to prod. "It isn't forgotten."

"For the last time, forget it!" he snapped. "Why do you want to dwell on it?"

She rolled her eyes. "Because I'm not crazy. It isn't forgotten."

Jackson shook his head and closed his eyes.

Brandeis wished she hadn't pushed the subject. She hated seeing him so sullen.

"I love you, Jackson."

His eyes remained closed and he said nothing.

Clayton walked in just as Brandeis was leaving. He spoke briefly with her and stepped aside to let her exit. "Your wife is such a sweet lady," Clayton said when he was alone with Jackson. "You two make a nice couple. I can tell she makes you happy."

"Clay, she's pregnant. We're going to have a baby."

"Congratulations! That's wonderful news. My wife and

I will be praying for you both to be blessed with a healthy baby."

"Thanks, Clay." Jackson smiled. "I really appreciate that."

Jackson knew that the issue of Martin was far from resolved, but he vowed he would not upset Brandeis throughout her pregnancy. Nothing would harm their unborn child.

That evening, as she readied for dinner, Brandeis examined her marriage. She knew that every passing day they ignored their problem would only serve to broaden the gap between them. She didn't want to exist in a world where Jackson wore two faces. At night, he would be cold and indifferent, but in the daytime, around family and friends, he would be gentle and loving. She couldn't bear to see his torment, knowing she was the cause of it.

Just then, Jackson walked into the bedroom. He nodded at her but said nothing.

"Can we please talk, Jackson?" she asked, sitting on the bed and looking up at him with a soft amber gaze.

His smile was sensual. "I can think of something else I would rather do before we meet everyone for dinner."

Brandeis did not trust his seemingly light mood. "I'm serious, Jackson."

"So am I." He crossed the room and knelt down in front of her and pressed her hands in his. "I know I haven't been easy to live with."

"I just want everything to be all right with us. The way it used to be."

"I would like that, too. Bran, I didn't start this—"

"How many times do you want me to say I'm sorry?" She struggled to keep her temper under control.

"I know you said you were sorry, but do you really think I can just forget that my wife hid a love letter from her rapist?"

He saw the flash of pain in her eyes and quickly added, "Look, it's just not that easy, Bran."

"You're never going to forgive me, are you?"

Seconds ticked away as they stared at each other.

Finally, he shrugged his shoulders and walked away, as if he had been only half-listening to her.

Brandeis could feel her heart drumming and wished he would just hold her.

He loosened his tie and sat down at the desk. "As far as I'm concerned, this subject is closed for now. I would appreciate it if you would not mention it again."

Fighting tears, Brandeis moved toward the huge walk-in closet. "I'll go get dressed for dinner, then."

Jackson moved across the room and pulled her into his arms. At first she was cold and unyielding, but when his lips brushed against her mouth, Brandeis melted against him. Where Jackson was concerned, *she* had no control over her emotions.

When he laid her back on the bed, her eyes were laced with desire. As his hands moved across her breasts, she pulled him down to her.

Their problems were forgotten as their passions ignited and they slipped into a world where only desire existed.

"Jackson, I want to go to the bathroom! I feel as if I'm about to explode. I'm only five and a half months, but I feel as if I'm ready to burst. I can't imagine having a sonogram at seven or eight months. They tell you to drink three tall glasses of water three hours before the sonogram, then they have you come to the hospital and wait *another* half hour before someone will even see you."

"I'm sorry, baby. I can imagine how uncomfortable you are."

"It's hell!" Brandeis shifted, fighting the urge to yell, "just forget it" and take off running to the nearest bathroom.

"We shouldn't have to wait much longer, sweetheart,"

Jackson whispered. He reached over to pull her close to him.

"I wouldn't squeeze too tightly if I were you," she said irritably. "I'm liable to embarrass all of us."

Jackson stared at her, then burst out laughing.

A young woman who appeared to be in her late twenties called for Mrs. Gray. Brandeis stood and walked briskly behind the woman down a long narrow hallway. The woman introduced herself as June and led Brandeis to a dressing room where she handed her a blue hospital gown.

"As soon as you're dressed, come to room B."

A few minutes later, Brandeis was positioned on a table, listening as June explained the procedure.

June worked silently and quickly. Then, she excused herself and left the room. Within minutes she was back, with Jackson in tow. "So, are you ready to see your baby?" she asked as she perched on her stool.

"Yes, we are." Brandeis held her breath as the lab tech turned the monitor toward her and Jackson. Although she felt like her insides were about to burst, she couldn't wait to see her baby on the screen.

"I'm going to give you some ultrasound photos to keep."

"Thank you, June." Brandeis marveled at the tiny fingers that suddenly balled into a fist. Then, he opened his little legs.

Jackson laughed and said, "It's a boy. I can tell it's a boy. I have a son!" He kissed Brandeis and said ever so softly, "We have a son, honey."

Brandeis could not stop the tears from flowing. "Yes, we have a son."

"Here are your pictures. Your doctor will get the results in a couple of days and give you a call. You can relieve yourself and get dressed. Congratulations!"

"Thank you," they said in unison.

Brandeis quickly dressed and they left the hospital. Jackson was quiet during the ride home. Brandeis' attempts at making conversation went unanswered.

When they got home, Brandeis stood before their bedroom window, thinking of the past months. For the most part, Jackson had avoided her. At home, he had been almost overly polite and very distant. When confronted, he blamed it on a heavy case load. She stared out at the tiny rose garden she and Jackson planted shortly after they became engaged. Tension mounted inside her as she turned around, her eyes locking with Jackson's.

He stared at her. Her face was lovely, framed by her hair spilling about her shoulders. Jackson came to stand beside her. His shoulder brushed against her and she moved away.

"What's wrong. Why do you look so sad?"

"How can you even ask me that?" she said. "You know damn well what's wrong."

She could feel the heat from his body, and as always, his nearness disturbed her peace of mind. Looking up at him, she allowed her anger to sparkle in the depths of her eyes.

He gripped her by the shoulders. "I don't want you upset. It's not good for the baby."

Brandeis shook her head slowly. "It's upsetting me *not* to talk about our marriage. We are having a problem, Jackson. We've had this problem for months now. You're still upset with me about Martin's letter and phone call. We need to resolve this issue. You don't trust me and we need to talk about it." She shrugged his hands away. "If you don't want to talk about saving our marriage, then please stay the hell away from me. I can't take this tension between us anymore!"

Jackson reached out, took her arm, and pulled her against him. "I am trying to be considerate. I don't want to make you unhappy."

"But you *are* making me unhappy, Jackson. I can't stand it."

He placed his hands on either side of her face and looked deeply into her eyes. "I'm sorry, Bran. Do you realize how I felt seeing that letter?"

Her eyes were clear and sparkling with honesty. "I know that it must have hurt you, but that was not my intention.

I know *my* heart feels as if it's been torn out. I can only imagine yours must feel the same way."

He surprised her when he pulled her into his arms and held her tightly against his body.

She shut her eyes, swallowing the moan that began in the region of her heart. It would be so easy to give him what he wanted, to lie next to him and pretend everything was good between them. She couldn't. Somehow, once and for all, she had to make him understand.

"Nothing has changed, Jackson," she whispered, tears gathering in her eyes. "I can't go on giving you my body and receiving only snatches of momentary pleasure. Don't ask me to do that. It hurts too much, loving you and . . . wanting more, wishing that you . . ."

Her misery was complete, draining her of the last of her strength. "If you have any feelings for me, please leave me alone." Brandeis gave herself up to her tears, not caring if he watched or not. As exposed as she felt, his angry stares didn't matter. Nothing mattered. Her pride and her dignity were in shreds.

His arms tightened and he caressed the top of her head with his jaw. "Don't cry, I can't bear to see you so upset. I shouldn't have put you through this. I'm sorry, baby. So sorry."

"I'm sorry, Jackson," Brandeis murmured. "I handled everything wrong. I should have come to you in the beginning. I realize that now."

"I want no more secrets between us. Is that understood?"

She smiled through her tears. "No more secrets. I promise."

Chapter 15

"You're just starting to gain weight, Brandeis. All we have to do is make your dress just a little fuller here. See, you can't really tell." Mona adjusted the waist of Brandeis' dress.

Brandeis assessed herself in the full-length mirror. "You're right. Actually, I think it looks better this way. What do you think, Carol?"

"I like it this way, too. No one at DKD's party will be able to tell you're pregnant."

"That's great. I didn't want to have to go out and buy another dress. Did Mom tell you that she found a picture of a wedding dress that would be perfect for you?"

Carol shook her head. "I can't wait for this wedding to happen. I'm so excited!"

"We can tell," Brandeis said.

"Have I been talking nonstop about it?" Carol looked embarrassed.

Brandeis and Mona exchanged looks. "Yes," they replied in unison.

Mona rushed to reassure her. "But that's all right, dear. Every bride should be excited."

Brandeis nodded in agreement. "I was sooo excited when Jackson and I got married. I'm sure I got on your nerves."

Carol laughed. "Actually, you seemed pretty calm to me."

"I wasn't though. I was so nervous. I talked Mom's ear off about dresses and favors . . . and Jackson. So, talk about the wedding if you want to. It's a special time in your life."

"Good! Cause all I can *think* about is my wedding."

Mona told Carol about the wedding gown while Brandeis walked over to the sofa and sat down.

Carol glanced over at her friend. "What's the matter, Bran?"

"Nothing. I was just thinking about my own wedding again. Mom did such a wonderful job. It was beautiful, romantic, all the things I want yours to be."

"Your wedding *was* lovely. It was so emotional. Especially with your uncle crying as he walked you down the aisle. I was fine until I saw him."

"Kane has always been a romantic," Mona said above the low hum of the sewing machine. "I declare, I was doing okay until Brandeis started singing to Jackson. When I saw the tears in his eyes, I couldn't stop mine from falling."

Carol nodded as she took a seat next to Brandeis. "I'm so glad you're happy, Bran. It was a long time coming. Just think, in less than six months, we're both going to be old married ladies. Can you imagine that?"

Brandeis shook her head, "Oh, no! Speak for yourself!" She tried to sound cheerful, but deep inside she longed for the closeness she and Jackson once shared. They were close, but the oneness they shared during the beginning of their marriage was gone.

The last time she'd felt their special bond was when she and Jackson viewed their son on the monitor during her ultrasound. By the time they'd arrived home, the feeling seemed to have evaporated into thin air. At the time, she'd wondered whether she had imagined it.

"Are you and James planning to start a family right away?" Mona asked.

"Yes. We want two children and we want them to be close in age."

"Jackson and I have talked about having another one when this baby is about two. We're hoping the next one will be a gir—" She stopped. She hadn't meant to let them know the sex of the baby. Well, maybe they missed her slip.

"You're having a boy!" Mona jumped up and pulled Brandeis up from the sofa. She jumped up and down in a very unladylike fashion, out of character for the usually demure Mona.

Babies make people do some of the silliest things, Brandeis thought to herself. "Yes, I'm having a boy. Jackson and I agreed to keep it a secret from the two of you, but leave it to me to divulge a secret. Jackson's gonna kill me!"

"We'll act surprised," Carol offered.

Brandeis laughed. "It's okay. We just wanted to hold out and keep you two in suspense until the last moment. We know how much you both wanted us to have a boy."

"Now, Bran. We would have loved a little girl just as much as we love little Gary."

"Little Gary! His name is going to be Brandon," Mona argued.

"See. This is why we weren't going to tell you. I know this may sound kind of old-fashioned, but *Jackson and I* have decided on a name. Our son will be named Brian Jerome Gray."

"Ugh!" said Carol.

"That's so *common!*" Mona sniffed.

"I never realized you were such a snob, Mom. Besides I think it sounds better than Gary Gray or Brandon Gray. Well," she amended, "Brandon Gray doesn't sound bad, but Jackson prefers Brian."

"What makes him think he has any say so in this?" Mona wanted to know. "He's just your husband. I'm your mother, Carol is your best friend."

"Mom!" Brandeis' mouth dropped open. "I don't believe you!"

"She makes a good argument. I wouldn't put my best lawyer up against her." Jackson strolled into the room, only stopping to plant a kiss on his mother-in-law's forehead before heading to his wife.

"How are you doing?"

His tone was somewhat formal and it grated on her nerves. She struggled to keep the sadness out of her voice. "I'm fine, Jackson. How long have you been standing there?"

He settled down beside her. "Long enough to know that you told them, we're having a boy. I knew you wouldn't be able to keep it from them."

"It kind of slipped out. Are you mad?"

"No. I kind of told my mother, too." He had the good sense to look sheepish.

They all laughed.

That night while Jackson was working, Brandeis grew bored and a bit restless. Catching sight of the new rolls of wallpaper border she'd purchased earlier in the week, Brandeis decided now was as good a time as any to start decorating her son's nursery.

After a quick search, she found just the right chair and went to work trying to position the border on the wall.

"What the hell are you doing, Brandeis? Get off that damn chair!" Jackson growled. He gave her a condescending glance and reached to help her down.

"Have you no thought for this baby?" he demanded in an irritated voice. Jackson scooped her up in his arms and carried her to their bedroom.

"I'm sorry! You don't have to treat me like a child." She said raising her chin.

"Then stop acting like one!" He sat her gently down on the bed. Then Jackson lay down beside her.

Tears sprang to her eyes. "I was only trying to hang the border, Jackson."

"Please let me do that. I don't want anything to happen to our child."

"That's all you care about, don't you? Your precious baby."

He surprised her with a smile that touched the corner of his lips and danced in his eyes. "I'm not going to fight with you, Bran. I was told by the doctor not to upset you, so I'll leave you alone."

When he reached out his hand to touch her face, she flinched away.

"I'm tired, Jackson, and I'm a little short-tempered." Brandeis squeezed her eyes tightly together. She heard him stand up.

"I can tell. Get some rest."

She lay still long after she heard the door close and the sound of Jackson's footsteps fade down the hallway. Tears ran down her face as she resisted the urge to run after him.

Brandeis waited for what seemed like hours, but in reality was only a few moments. Jackson returned and prepared for bed. She watched him in silence.

After settling in bed, he took her in his arms. This time she was too tired to resist.

"Bran, do you still want to go to law school?"

Brandeis was quiet, so quiet, Jackson wasn't sure she'd heard him. "Bran?"

"Yes. It's been my dream for so long. Jackson, I want to be a lawyer. I want us to open our own law office, be partners. Gray and Gray Law Offices, what do you think?"

"I think that's a wonderful name."

"But, Jackson. I'm going to have a baby. I have to be home with him, for the first year. There's no law school in Brunswick. I don't really want to go away to school and I don't want to be away from you and Brian. As it is, we can't seem to get past . . ."

"Don't worry, baby. We'll get through this and you're going to go to law school. I'll make sure of that. Right now, you're going to get some much needed rest."

* * *

As Brandeis handed her credit card to the sales clerk to pay for her purchases, Mona browsed around the store one final time.

"They really have a nice selection of career-oriented maternity clothes. You made some great selections. I really liked that black dress on you."

"It's my favorite, too," Brandeis said. "I was beginning to wonder if I'd ever need maternity clothes. Then, I wake up one morning and I'm nothing but belly."

"But you look beautiful, dear." Mona reached for the shopping bags. "I'll carry these."

"Mom, thanks, but I can carry my own bags."

"Bran, I'm not going to take the chance of you going into labor while we're in Savannah. Jackson would have such a fit."

Brandeis laughed and reluctantly handed over both shopping bags. "What are you going to do if I decide to buy more?"

"I'll just have to pull my brand new car up to the door."

"Do you really like the car, Mom?" The gleaming black Lincoln Town Car with leather seats and an assortment of accessories was an early Christmas gift from Brandeis and Jackson.

"Oh, honey. I love that car! I hope you and Jackson know how much I appreciate it. I just wish you'd let me take over the payments."

"Mom, Jackson paid for the car. There are no payments."

"Oh," Mona said.

"You deserve it. You've been such a good mother and a friend," Brandeis said. "I wanted to do something for you. I've been saving for the last four years to get you a new car. Jackson put up the rest of the money with what I'd already saved. We love you, Mom. I hope I can be half the mother that you are to me."

"You're going to be a good mother," Mona said warmly. "I just know it."

"I had a great teacher. Just think, Mom, your first grandchild."

"I know. I'm still trying to decide what I want to be called. I think I want to be called Grandmother. Definitely not Grandma."

"I like Grandma myself."

"Don't you dare teach my grandbaby to call me Grandma," Mona warned, pointing her finger in jest.

Mona drove along River Street. They admired the nineteenth-century restored buildings that now housed specialty shops, restaurants, and popular nightspots. She pointed out that they used to be warehouses and cotton broker offices.

"Nineteenth-century Savannah grew and flourished with cotton. Cotton proved to be Savannah's salvation before and after the civil war. My great-grandmother was once a slave on one of the plantations here in the city," Mona went on. "She ran away during the Civil War and headed north. After the war ended, she returned to her beloved Savannah. As a child, I used to love sitting on my grandmother's lap, listening to her tell our history. It filled me with such a strong sense of pride in my family."

They pulled into the parking lot of the River House, located on the historic waterfront. Mona and Brandeis ate there every time they came to Savannah, both favoring the nautical atmosphere of the restaurant.

Minutes after entering the restaurant, they were shown to their table. Neither one saw the lone man with green eyes sitting in the far corner and staring at them.

Martin couldn't believe his eyes. Brandeis was pregnant! He mentally calculated back to her wedding date. That was less than seven months ago. Should she be that far along? He didn't think so, but he guessed it was possible. *Looks to me like she didn't wait 'til her wedding night with him,* he thought jealously.

He wondered if she was still believed he'd raped her.

He had to find out. Martin didn't want her going around telling lies like that. It could ruin him. Signaling a nearby waitress, he ordered another beer and settled into his seat to wait until the right moment to approach Brandeis and her mother.

An hour later, Brandeis and Mona got up to leave, Martin got ready to follow. A few minutes later, he caught them off guard at their car.

"Hello Brandeis, Mrs. Taylor."

"What do you want?" Mona said angrily.

Martin ignored Mona's question. Looking directly at Brandeis, he said, "I need to talk to you, Brandeis . . . *alone."*

"I'm not leaving her alone with you!" Mona yelled.

"Please, Brandeis," Martin implored. "I don't think you want to have this conversation in front of your mother."

"Martin, I told you on the phone," Brandeis said coldly, ignoring her mother's gasp of surprise, "we have nothing to talk about. And furthermore, do not write me anymore letters. *Now, leave me alone!"*

"I think we need to talk," Martin went on, as if Brandeis had not spoken. "About our future."

"Our what?" Brandeis shuddered. "You are really sick."

Martin reached out to touch Brandeis' arm, but Mona stood in his way.

"Obviously, my daughter doesn't want to talk to you. If you don't leave, I'm going to call the police."

Martin turned to face Mona. "Mrs. Taylor, I'm not doing anything to your daughter. All I want is to have a conversation with her." Turning to Brandeis again, he asked, "What have you been telling your mother about me?"

"I told her the truth!" Brandeis cried. "That you raped me!"

"You're a lying bitch!" Martin shouted.

Before Brandeis realized what was happening, Mona slapped Martin across the face. *"Don't* you call my daughter a bitch ever again! Do you hear me, you . . . you *lunatic!"*

Martin rubbed his reddening cheek. "Don't *you* ever put your hands in my face again!" he threatened.

Mona stood as close to him as she possibly could, her hands balled into fists. "You don't scare me, you beast! You listen to me and hear me well." Pointing a finger in his face, she said slowly, "If you ever come near me or my daughter again, you'll rue the very day you were born! Bran, give me your cell phone. I'm going to call the police."

Martin glared at them both before turning and stalking off.

Mona unlocked the doors of the car. Quickly, they got in and drove off, watching to see if they were being followed. When they felt sure they weren't in any danger, their tension slowly eased.

"I can't believe you did that, Mom. You slapped him." Brandeis shook her head.

"Nobody talks that way about my daughter. The nerve of him. That, that *rapist!"*

Brandeis laughed in spite of herself. "Way to go, Mom! And thank you for trying to protect me. I really appreciate it."

"What's this about a phone call and a letter?" Mona asked.

Brandeis sighed. "Right after Jackson and I got married, Martin called the office one day. I told him then not to bother me again. I didn't hear from him again until he sent me a letter at the office. He keeps insisting that he loves me and that we belong together."

"Does Jackson know?"

Brandeis sighed again. "Oh, Mom, I didn't tell him but he found out anyway. He was so angry. I've tried to make him understand that I didn't tell him because I didn't want to upset him—or you, for that matter. I just wanted to keep the past in the past."

"I understand that," Mona said, "but I really don't think you should keep something like what happened today from Jackson. I don't trust Martin."

"Mom, he only confronted us because we ran into him," Brandeis argued. "He never called me after that one time, and he never wrote to me again, either. I didn't want Jackson to think about . . ."

"Bran, honey, do you think Jackson's going to think badly about you?"

"Jackson has had four rape cases," Brandeis said slowly. "Only one man was convicted of rape. In two of the cases, the women lied. In the other case, the woman never showed up in court. She just suddenly left town."

"But what does this have to do with *you?*" Mona pressed.

"Jackson may think that maybe *I* lied about being raped," Brandeis said. "I know you don't think so, but look at it, Mom. I was dating Martin. I invited him over to my apartment and we were kissing. After I was raped, I never pressed charges. I didn't even tell anyone until a couple of weeks had passed. By then, Martin had left town. The whole situation could be construed as my being bitter over being dumped."

"I don't beli—"

"Mom, don't you get it?" Brandeis cried. "In one of Jackson's cases the woman lied for exactly that same reason. Why *wouldn't* he doubt me?"

Mona knew her daughter well enough to know there wasn't anything she could say to make her believe otherwise. Only time would give her more faith in Jackson. She silently prayed Brandeis' reluctance to confide in her husband wouldn't cost them their marriage.

Carrie propped her left foot on the sofa as she polished her toenails peach. The doorbell sounded as she prepared to polish the nails on her right foot.

Damn! Who can this be? she wondered. She wasn't expecting anyone. Quickly tying the sash of her silk, turquoise robe around her waist, Carrie walked over to the door and peeked out. A wide grin spread over her face. "Martin! I can't believe it!" Throwing open the door and forgetting her wet toenails, she jumped into his arms, hugging him tightly.

"Well, hello there, baby! I guess you're glad to see me." He planted a kiss on her full lips as he gently sat her down. He surveyed the neat and pretty apartment. Nodding his approval, he sat down next to Carrie and placed a foot on her coffee table.

"I guess I should've called you first, but I just hopped in my car and drove straight here. I've been thinkin' a lot 'bout you and me. About our future. In fact, I decided to move back to Brunswick." He absently rubbed his chin. "Yeah, I kinda like this little ol' town."

Carrie could not believe her good fortune. Martin was moving back to Brunswick. He was moving back just to be with her! She had lusted after him from the first time she glimpsed him with Brandeis. Now, Brandeis was safely married and very pregnant. She didn't have to worry about her going after him. Carrie had him all to herself.

Striking her most seductive pose, she purred, "I'm so glad you're back. But what about your job? Are you going to try to commute back and forth? I told you that I'd move to Savannah. There's nothing *in* this town. Savannah has more opportunities for us."

Martin decided not to tell Carrie that Brunswick had one very important thing Savannah didn't. Brandeis. "I didn't want to take you away from a good job," he said instead. "My job is crappy. I'll try to get on at the pulp mill."

"My dad and my brother both work there," Carrie said excitedly. "They can probably put in a good word for you. I'll give them a call tomorrow."

Martin wrapped his arms around Carrie and pulled her close to him. "I knew I could count on you." He gave her a passionate kiss that left her breathless. "I need another favor from you," he said.

"What is it, honey?"

"I need somewhere to stay. Can I stay here?" Martin smiled that irresistible smile. "With you?"

Carrie was giddy. "You can stay with me as long as you like."

"One thing though," Martin went on. "You can't tell anyone. Especially Brandeis."

"Why? She can't stop you from moving back to Brunswick."

"Because I told you Brandeis was probably gonna try and say I raped her after I dumped her for you. After I saw you that first time, Carrie, I couldn't get you out of my mind. When I broke up with her, she said she would cause trouble for me. She said she'd have me arrested for rape."

"Don't worry," Carrie promised. "I won't tell a soul. I just want to throttle that uppity bitch for what she's trying to do to you. Maybe now that she's married, she'll forget about trying to hurt you."

Pulling Carrie closer to him, Martin flashed her a sexy smile that made her heart turn somersaults.

"Yeah, maybe. Right now, girl, I don't wanna do no more talkin'. I want some of you."

"Say no more, darling." Carrie pulled away and led him into her bedroom.

They fell together on the bed, naked and hungry for each other. Martin grinned as he forced Carrie on her knees and he entered her from behind. As he heard her passion-filled moan, he thought about how easy it had been to win Carrie over. She was so man-hungry, she'd fall for anything. His excitement built and he admitted that Carrie was one great lay.

"What did you ever see in her?" Carrie asked afterwards, as she and Martin lay in bed. "Brandeis has always thought she was too good to be around me. That Miss Goody Two-Shoes. I can't imagine her having sex at all."

"It's all a front," Martin said. "She likes sex all the time. We stayed *in* bed more than out. I just didn't make enough money for her."

"It shouldn't matter to you," Carrie said vehemently.

"You tell me she's telling people you raped her. I can't believe she's saying that!"

"I'll take care of the lying bitch!" Martin grabbed the bottle of gin he'd placed on the bedside table and shoved it to his mouth.

"Honey, I'll never do something like that to you," Carrie promised. "I was so happy when you stopped seeing Brandeis. I always thought you were too good for her."

Martin grinned. "Shut up and kiss me."

"How was your day in Savannah?" Jackson walked in the apartment and planted a kiss on his wife's forehead. "Did you have a good time with Mom?"

"I-it was fine, honey. I spent lots of money." Brandeis made a conscious effort not to stutter. She didn't want to tell him about her confrontation with Martin. No need to cause any more problems in their marriage. She knew Jackson had not forgiven her for not telling him about the phone call and the letter from Martin.

"So, I guess that means I have to work harder," Jackson said.

"I'm only teasing, honey. I only spent what was necessary."

"Is that supposed to make me feel any better?"

"Well, yes. No. I don't have any idea. Do you want to see what I bought? Then you can decide for yourself."

"That's fair," Jackson said.

Brandeis modeled her purchases in front of him. Saving the best for last, she finally modeled a black gown with spaghetti straps that criss-crossed in the back, and a lace bodice with a full sweeping skirt. She turned slowly. Her hair, gleaming and straight, fell to one side.

"Well, what do you think?"

Jackson pulled her into his arms. "I think you look stunning. I love this gown."

"I was hoping you would say that. When I saw it, I just

had to have it. The good thing is I can still wear it after I have the baby."

"Good," Jackson murmured as his lips met hers, devouring her with hungry kisses.

They undressed each other with feverish haste, alternately moaning with delight and giggling like children as they tried to undo stubborn buttons and hooks. They reveled in rediscovering each other's bodies, consumed by the need to touch, taste, and enjoy.

Jackson guided her upstairs where they headed straight to their bed. He lay back on the bed with Brandeis astride him, glorying in her abandon. She rocked her hips against him, running her palms over his shoulders and down his arms. He gripped her swollen breasts, fondling them until she felt her nipples go rigid and her face glow.

Together, they rode the waves of passion. For the longest time they gazed into each other's eyes. It was Brandeis who finally broke the silence.

"I love you with all my heart, Jackson. I want you to remember that."

"I love you, too, baby," he whispered. "I'm glad we have no more secrets between us."

Brandeis remained silent.

Chapter 16

The next morning, Carrie was on the phone, whispering, when Brandeis walked in. When she saw Brandeis, she quickly hung up. In recent weeks, Brandeis had noticed her acting strangely and receiving suspicious phone calls. This morning, she'd received a dozen red roses. When Brandeis asked who they were from, Carrie just smiled and walked away. Brandeis surmised she was probably having an affair with a married man.

"Hello, Brandeis. How are you feeling?" Carrie asked, appearing in the doorway of Brandeis' office several hours later.

"I'm feeling just fine, Carrie. Why do you ask?" Carrie reminded her of a grape. She wore a purple dress with a huge green collar, purple hose and purple shoes.

"You're looking remarkably well for being pregnant. I just wondered if you feel as good as you look."

"Thanks, I think."

"Brandeis?"

"Yes," Brandeis answered, unsure of what to expect next.

"Can I ask you a personal question?"

She carefully observed Carrie's face before answering. "You can ask anything you like. I must warn you, I may not give you an answer."

"I was wondering how long you and Jackson dated before he asked you to marry him?"

"Why?"

Suddenly, Carrie became animated. "Well, I'm dating someone and he's been talking about marriage. We haven't been together very long, though."

"Do you love him?" Brandeis asked.

"Oh, yes. I love him to pieces."

Carrie's smile lit up her whole face. Brandeis could tell Carrie was very much in love, but something bothered her. It was then Brandeis noticed the bruise on Carrie's neck. Clearly, she'd tried to hide it under makeup. "Well, that's all that matters. Right?"

"Brandeis, how did you know that Jackson was right for you?" Carrie went on. "Is it because you loved him with all your heart? Was that enough?"

"No, I think marriage is about more than love," Brandeis said, noticing another bruise on Carrie's arm. "I think you really have to take your time and get to know a person."

Carrie shifted uncomfortably under Brandeis' now serious gaze.

What's going on with Carrie? she wondered silently. "Was there something else you wanted to know?"

"No. Not really." Carrie bit her lip and then said, "Brandeis, pregnancy really does agree with you."

"Thanks, Carrie. And I hope things work out for you." Before Carrie turned away, Brandeis glimpsed just a hint of sadness passing over her features.

Carrie smiled. "It will. He tells me all the time that he loves me and I'm good for him. Imagine that. Me, being good for somebody."

There it was again. The barest hint of sadness. Brandeis thought it best not to respond.

Brandeis' groans grew, and one look told Jackson that after an agonizing prolonged active phase, she was at last in transition. She did not know how much time passed. Each pain that ripped through her body seemed more intense than the last. The doctor signaled the nurse to prop Brandeis up so gravity would help move the baby down and out.

"I can't do it, Jackson. I can't do it!" Brandeis gave way to the natural feelings accompanying the hard labor of transition, the most difficult part in all the birth process. She was irritable, panting and shaking wildly.

Jackson murmured comforting words and caressed his wife's forehead and cheeks. "Yes, you can, honey. You're doing fine, the baby's fine. Soon we'll see him. We're going to be able to hold our son. I can't wait, can you?"

"I hate this pain!" Brandeis glared at Jackson. "You should be the one having this baby!"

"Keep it up, Brandeis," the doctor encouraged from her post. "This is the worst it's going to get. You're going to begin pushing very soon. Before you know it, the newest member of the Gray family will be in your arms."

Brandeis shrieked, then looked at the doctor with frightened eyes. "Yes, yes," she mumbled straining and twisting. Jackson soothed her until she stilled.

"I'm-I'm sorry. I didn't mean what I said. I'm glad you're here, Jackson. I love you." Brandeis' words dissolved into a sharp cry.

"You're doing great, Brandeis," the doctor called out. "Keep it up!"

"No more!" Brandeis cried. "No more—"

"Your baby is coming! Now, bear down! With all your concentration, bear down!"

Brandeis bore down so hard her whole body trembled from the effort. She thought she would pass out from the pain. She groaned as Jackson looked at Dr. Myers worriedly.

"One, two, keep bearing down, Brandeis! That's it!" Soon the doctor had the tiny baby in her hands.

"You did it, Bran! You did it!" Jackson was overjoyed and relieved. He'd hated seeing his wife in such pain.

The nurse cleared out the baby's mouth and nose, and the child's wail soon filled the air. She wiped the baby and quickly evaluated him before transferring him to a clean blanket and then to his mother.

"My baby! My baby!" An exhausted Brandeis held out her arms for the crying infant. After a good first nursing, she held her son to her cheek.

"He's beautiful," Jackson said quietly. He sat on the bed near Brandeis. His hands shook and eyes dimmed at the sight of maternal bonding before him.

"He looks exactly like you, love. He's the spitting image of you," Jackson exclaimed with intense pleasure. "Thank you for such a handsome son."

"Thank you for saying that, Jackson." Brandeis was tired but she didn't want to sleep. She wanted to enjoy this time with her family. She raised her hand and placed it on her husband's cheek. "You really are a wonderful man. I'm so blessed to have you in my life. To have you as my husband."

Jackson kissed her tenderly on the lips. "I'm the blessed one here. A beautiful and loving wife who has just made me a father. I love you with all my heart."

Brandeis held her tiny son close to her heart and murmured soft words of love. "Hi, precious. We've been waiting so long to meet you. I'm so glad you're here, Brian Jerome Gray . . ."

Jackson kissed his wife and sleeping son. "Your wonderful husband has to go call your mother and Carol. I'll put Brian back in the bassinet. You get some rest."

"No, I want him to be here, right next to me."

"That's fine. After I make the calls, I've got to run an errand. I'll be back within the hour."

When Brandeis woke up, it was already dark. Jackson was sitting in a chair next to the bed, dozing. She marveled at how handsome he looked. She heard the faintest whimper. Turning her head in the direction of the sound, she saw her tiny son. He was so beautiful. She saw the blanket move and knew he was coming out of his slumber. Brandeis gingerly eased her feet out of bed. Just as she was about to try to stand, Jackson was by her side.

"Honey, you've just had a baby!" he whispered. "You've got to be careful. Do you have to go to the bathroom?"

"No, I was going to get my baby," she said softly. "I thought he was waking up. The nurses must have taken him from me when I fell asleep."

Jackson assisted her to the bassinet. He lifted Brian and gave him to Brandeis.

"Where's Mom?" Brandeis asked, cuddling her new born son. "I thought she would've been here by now."

Jackson nodded. "She is. She and Carol went to get something to eat. They should be back soon."

Jackson leaned down to kiss his wife. "I've been wanting to do that all day."

"Me, too. Jackson, I don't think I could've made it without your being there."

"We're a family, baby. You and I and Brian are a family."

"A real family," Brandeis repeated.

Jackson looked deep into her eyes. "Honey, we've always been a real family. Our son is just proof of the bond between us."

Carol stood still as Mona fussed with the train of her gown. Brandeis provided the finishing touches to Carol's hair. She applied a light mist of hair spray and then surveyed her handiwork. Next, she pulled ribbons here and there as she secured the pearl-encrusted headpiece on the top of Carol's head. Finally, Brandeis straightened out the long attached veil. "You look so beautiful, Carol," she said.

"T-thank y-you."

Brandeis was about to put away the curling irons and sprays but stopped to look closely at her friend. She hadn't realized just how quiet Carol had suddenly become. She was even trembling now. "Carol. What's wrong?"

Carol's eyes were clouded with tears. "N-nothing's wrong." She sniffed. "I've waited so long for this day. Now that it's here, I'm scared to death!"

Mona placed a loving arm around Carol. "Are you having second thoughts, dear?"

Carol shook her head emphatically. "Oh, no! It's nothing like that! I love James and I want to marry him. It's hard to explain. It just all seems too good to be true."

"I think I understand," Mona said, stroking Carol's back. "Your life seems so perfect now and you're happy. But you wonder if it's going to last, all of this happiness."

"Yes, that's exactly what I'm feeling," Carol admitted.

"Carol, I'm going to tell you the very same thing I told Bran. No one knows what the future holds, but whatever happens, always remember this. People make mistakes. All the time. It is up to you to find the strength to accept all that you cannot change, then, go on. Just do the very best that you can. That's all anyone can expect. You and James love each other dearly. I believe that no matter what happens, you two will have a good marriage."

"Mom's right, Carol," Brandeis said. "Marriage is scary yet it's wonderful. Look at everything I went through with Martin's harassing me. I made some big mistakes, but Jackson has been very patient with me. My biggest mistake was not being able to trust myself or Jackson with my feelings. It was so difficult. Especially my wedding night."

Carol and Mona glanced at each other.

Mona placed a nervous hand to her chest. "Your wedding night?" she said. "What happened? We just assumed everything went okay."

"Well, it started off okay, but . . . I kind of tensed up. Before we even got in bed. Anyway, Jackson decided to sleep in the guest room."

"What!" Mona and Carol cried in unison.

"Oh, I didn't want him to, but I didn't stop him," Brandeis said. "I was a little bit angry at first, but when I thought about it, I realized Jackson was only trying to put me at ease. He knew what I'd gone through and he wanted me to feel comfortable with him. He loved me enough to wait until I was ready to make love. It reaffirmed to me that marriage is about giving and taking. He had given me so much, and was patiently waiting for me to return that love."

"But you got pregnant so quickly. We . . . we assumed that . . ." Mona blushed and could not continue. She smoothed nervous fingers down her peach chiffon dress.

"He came to wake me the next morning," Brandeis said with a smile. "I made it known to him that I was ready to be a wife to him, in every way."

Carol clapped her hands. "You go girl!"

"Your wedding day is a day of new beginnings," Mona pointed out.

"And hidden blessings," Brandeis added. "Carol, you're going to be a good wife and mother." Brandeis hugged her friend. "Now, no more tears. While you touch up your makeup, I'll go check on your parents."

Twenty minutes later, everyone was lined up for the wedding processional. Before Brandeis headed up the aisle, she turned to Carol, with her thumb up, and whispered, "You go girl!"

Brandeis opened the trunk of her car and was in the process of putting her groceries inside when Martin walked up beside her.

"Hi, honey."

"What in hell are you doing here? Get away from me!" Brandeis cried. She searched the lot frantically, hoping to find someone to help her if needed.

Martin held up both his hands. "I'm not trying to cause you problems. I just wanted to tell you how good you're lookin'. I saw you last Saturday when you were leaving the church, after your friend Carol's wedding. You just had that baby in March and I can see you already lost all that weight.''

Brandeis shook her head. She could not believe his gall. "You just don't catch on, do you? I don't want to talk to you. We have nothing to discuss.''

"Yes, we do. I love you, Brandeis. I think about you all the time. You can leave that fancy lawyer and marry me. I'll be good to you. We're good together, don't you remember?''

Brandeis laughed harshly."I really think you're psychotic.''

"What's so damned funny? Here I'm declaring my love for you—''

"Martin. Listen to me,'' Brandeis said angrily. "I am very happy with Jackson. Why can't you leave me alone? I could have pressed charges a long time ago, but I didn't. If you persist in harassing me, I'm going get a restraining order.''

Martin grabbed her arms and jerked her to him. "I've had enough of the games. I want you and I know you want me, too.'' As if to prove his point, Martin covered her mouth with his.

The feel of his tongue made her nauseous. Brandeis felt nothing but revulsion for him. She pulled away and slapped him as hard as she could. "Don't you *ever* do that again, you bastard! If you ever come within twenty feet of me, I'll see that you are placed in the jail!''

Martin gingerly rubbed his stinging cheek. "You better be glad I'm not kicking your ass. If you—''

"Go to hell, rapist!'' Brandeis wrenched open her car door and jumped in, leaving Martin standing alone, hissing furiously.

Monique was out of fruit. She grabbed her purse and car keys and ran out of her apartment. She headed to Wynn Dixie since it was the closest store to her apartment. Passing a silver Mercedes, she thought of Jackson. That witch Brandeis, had made him a father. It didn't matter. She was going to find a way to get even with them. Their happiness would not last. She would see to that. Jackson Gray was hers!

As soon as Monique turned into the parking lot, she spied Brandeis, talking to a gorgeous man. He looked familiar, but she couldn't place him. Monique parked her car and decided to watch them for a while. From the expression on Brandeis' face, this could prove to be very interesting. She settled back in her car and observed the couple.

Monique could barely believe her eyes when she saw them kissing. She watched as Brandeis slapped him hard. *Wow, that must've hurt like hell,* she thought.

As soon as Brandeis sped off, Monique quickly pulled into the parking space next to Martin's car. She got out smiling. "Hello." Monique pointed in the direction Brandeis has just taken. "Wasn't that Brandeis Gray I just saw you kissing?"

Martin looked at the curvaceous woman from head to toe. He licked his lips and smiled. "Who wants to know?"

She returned his lustful gaze. "My name's Monique. Monique Allen. What's yours?"

"I'm Martin St. Charles. I'm a close friend of Brandeis'."

"Obviously. That's too bad." She turned to walk toward the supermarket.

He grabbed her arm and pulled her toward him. "Why do you say that?"

The force of his response caught Monique off guard. "Because you're wasting yourself on a married woman. You're much too good-looking for that."

"She's gonna leave him," Martin said defensively. "He doesn't do for her what I do."

"Really? I find that very hard to believe."

Martin's face contorted in anger. "What? You think I can't fu—"

Monique held up her freshly manicured fingers. "No,

no, that's not what I mean at all. Hey, calm down. I'm on your side.''

"What?"

"I'm into Jackson Gray. I didn't realize Brandeis was unhappy with him.''

"Well, I suggest you start swinging your hips in Mr. Gray's direction," Martin said. "He's gonna be a free man soon." Free or dead, it didn't matter to Martin. He intended to have Brandeis.

"Thanks for the advice," Monique replied. "Nice talking to you, Martin. Gotta run.''

Monique drove clear across town, straight to the offices of Davis, Kinard & Donaldson. Jackson was with a client when she arrived, so she waited.

Forty-five minutes later, he came out of his office with a young woman she didn't recognize. He spotted Monique and nodded hello. When his client left the office, he said, "Hello, Monique. What brings you here? Are you in need of an attorney?''

"I came to see you, Jackson. Can we please speak privately, in your office? Please?''

"Follow me," Jackson said blandly. "I have another client coming in around four o'clock. That gives you approximately thirty minutes.''

"I won't need that long!" Monique said, as Jackson closed the door of his office behind them. "I'm sorry about coming to your office this way, but there's something I think you need to know. I don't want to see you get hurt.''

Jackson pushed his glasses back on his face. He was clearly angry. "What the hell are you talking about, Monique?''

"I just left the supermarket and I saw your wife with a light-skinned man. They were kissing.''

Jackson waved his hand as if dismissing her. "Monique, I don't have time for this. My wife has friends. Don't jump to conclusions. It was—''

"I talked to the man," Monique said. "His name is Martin and he said that they we—"

"What did you say?"

"What? That I tal—"

"What was his name?" Jackson repeated.

"Martin. Wha—"

"You said you saw them kissing," Jackson asked, his hands flat on his desk. "Brandeis was kissing him back. Not fighting him?"

Monique sensed his discomfort and seemed pleased by it. She almost grinned.

"Are you sure about this?" Jackson pressed. "She seemed to welcome his kisses? Tell me!"

Monique was reluctant to admit she'd seen the entire exchange. It was obvious Brandeis had been repulsed by Martin's kiss. She'd seen Brandeis slap him, too. "Actually," Monique said, "she looked like she was enjoying it."

Jackson felt as if he'd been stabbed in the heart. There was no question Monique was enjoying the pain she was causing him. He could see it written all over her face.

Monique glanced over at the beautifully wrapped gift on his couch. "It's your first wedding anniversary, isn't it?"

"Yes, how did you know?" he said quietly.

"The gift for one thing, but I'll never forget your wedding day in a million years."

"Why is that?" he asked drily.

"Because it was a big slap to my pride. You married on my birthday!"

"I see."

"Martin told me that Brandeis planned to leave you. That she's going to leave you for him. He said she told him that you did nothing for her."

Jackson could not contain his fury any longer. "I believe you've said enough, Monique. I would appreciate it if you took your leave now."

Monique stood and practically skipped out the door

of Jackson's office. Under her breath she sang, "Happy Birthday to me. Happy Birthday to me . . ."

Jackson left shortly after she did. He sped out of the parking lot, but not before throwing his wife's anniversary gift in the dumpster.

Chapter 17

Martin slammed the door to Carrie's apartment. "Damn that bitch!"

"What's wrong with you?" Carrie was frightened. When she'd first met Martin, she was charmed by him. Lately, he was drinking more and more and getting meaner and meaner. Had he really raped Brandeis? She wondered. *No. Martin wouldn't do something like that. He can have his pick of any woman, she thought. And he chose me. He left Brandeis for me!*

"That bitch won't give me the time of day!" Martin mumbled. "She don't get it though. I always take what's mine. She's mine and always will be. I was her first. She is *mine!*"

Carrie shuddered. "What did you say? Are you talking about Brandeis? Have you lost your damn mind?"

"Shut up, wench!"

"Wench!" Carrie jumped at him. "I bet you did rape her. Brandeis wouldn't want a drunk like you."

Martin's hand reached out and grabbed her by the throat. "Now you talking crazy, girl! I don't need to hear this kind of talk. I don't need you. I got plenty women wanting to get next to me all the time. Hell, even you was begging for it. Here you were making passes at me while I was dating Brandeis. You're her secretary and all. You were eager to spread your legs for me. I could tell." He laughed cruelly. "I didn't even have to ask for it."

Filled with humiliation and fearing she would die, Carrie struggled to get away from Martin. Finally, he let her go. Sagging to the floor and gasping for air, she put her hands to her face and sobbed. He was crazy! She had to get him out of her apartment!

Martin saw the fear in Carrie's eyes. He could tell he was about to lose his meal ticket. Thinking quickly, he sank down beside, her, gently wiping the tears away from her face. "I'm sorry, baby. I'm really sorry. I never shoulda said those things. I only said them to hurt you. You hurt me by saying I raped that bitch. I left her to be with you. I care about you. I always have." He put his arms around her and held her close.

The Martin she knew and loved was back. Carrie released a sigh of relief. Deep in her heart she wondered which of the two sides she'd seen was the real Martin. She felt his gentle kisses along her face and neck. She could hardly concentrate.

After vigorous lovemaking, Carrie was still unsure of the sleeping man beside her. Easing out of bed, she tiptoed into her bathroom and examined her bruises. Makeup wouldn't be enough this time. She would have to wear high-necked blouses to hide these. Tears slid down her cheeks.

She feared Martin. Had he been using her to keep tabs on Brandeis? Carrie's jealousy of Brandeis was so intense, she'd been so eager to help Martin in any way she could. He was so obsessed with her. Suddenly, an idea popped in her head. Opening her medicine cabinet, she emptied her birth control pills into the toilet. If Martin got her pregnant, he would have to stay with her. He didn't seem to be the type who would walk away from his child. But then, Carrie only knew what he allowed her to know. He was very secretive when it came to his family. As far as Carrie knew, he had no living relatives. Marc Wiley once told her that Martin had had a brother who had died a long time ago. Marc had also told her that both his parents were dead.

"W-where are you, baby?" Martin called from the bedroom. "I need some good loving."

Carrie brushed aside her mounting fears. "I'm in the bathroom. I'll be out in a minute."

Brandeis placed the phone on the cradle. She was getting worried. Jackson should have been home hours ago. It wasn't like him to stay out without calling. She had phoned his office and was informed that he'd left hours ago. What was going on? Oh, Lord, what if he'd been in a car accident! Brandeis was about to call the police when she heard his key in the lock.

Jackson walked in. He glared at his wife, then without as much as a hello, he headed up the stairs.

Shock coursed through her veins. Jackson looked so angry. Brandeis followed him up the stairs.

"Jackson, honey, what's wrong?"

"I don't want to talk to you right now," he snapped.

Tears started to form in her eyes. Her voice quivering, she asked, "A-are you mad at me? P-please, what have I done?"

"Leave me alone, Bran." Jackson slammed the bedroom door in her face.

Summoning all her strength, Brandeis opened the door and walked in. She eased down on the bed and sat with her hands clasped in front of her, her head held high. "Jackson, don't treat me this way. I deserve better than this—"

His eyes met hers coldly. "And what in hell do I deserve? To find out my wife is getting phone calls, letters, and kisses from a man she claimed raped her!" Jackson pulled her to her feet. "Do I deserve that? Do you remember the promises you made to me? Do I deserve to be lied to like this?"

Brandeis turned away from him, her back stiff and straight. When she felt she had everything under control and wouldn't cry, she faced him and said, "No, Jackson, you don't deserve to be told lies. But please give me a chance to explain. I-it wasn't l-like t-that. Please l-listen to m-me."

Jackson held his hands outward. "I gave you all I had to give, Bran. I loved you with my heart and soul. Why?"

He saw her lips moving, but he wasn't listening to her. He couldn't hear her above the breaking of his heart.

"J-Jackson, please. I wasn't kissing him. He k-kissed me. I slapped him and threatened to call the police. I was going to tell you about it as soon as you came home tonight."

"Just like you were going to tell me about the letter and the phone calls? Damn, Brandeis! You lied to me. You had no intention of honoring your promise. Well, you wanted to explain. What do you have to say for yourself?"

Brandeis said nothing. She couldn't.

"Someone saw you today at the supermarket," Jackson went on. "They said it looked like you were enjoying your kiss. They said Martin told them you were leaving me. That you wanted him. That I did nothing for you."

"You can't possibly believe that!" Brandeis cried. "Jackson, you've known me all of my life. Do you think I would be kissing my rapist! Whoever told you that is a *liar. Martin* is a liar!"

"Is he? Look, Bran, I know you cared a great deal about him," Jackson went on. "I realize you may have been angry about his leaving the way he did. If you want him, just say so. I'll step aside."

"Jackson, the man raped me!"

"Did he, Bran?" Jackson sneered. "I wonder." He reached for her and pulled her to him. His hand moved down to her waist. Untying the sash of her dress, he pushed the material aside, baring her bra.

"Let me go," she cried. "I don't want you to touch me."

"Don't you?" Jackson bent his head and his lips lightly touched hers. He felt her body go tense when his hand cupped her breast. When it slid down her stomach, he heard her intake of breath. Looking into her eyes, he saw the battle taking place there. She wanted to tell him to leave her alone, but her body reacted strongly to his caresses. "I think you want very much for me to touch you, Bran."

She gazed into dark eyes that were burning with a slow passion. "No Jackson . . . no," she whispered, knowing she could not resist him. "Please, don't do this . . ."

His mouth moved across her face. He breathed in her ear, "Was that the way you said no to Martin?"

"You bastard!" Quivering with fury and pain, Brandeis did not stop to think. She brought up her hand in a swift motion that caught Jackson by surprise, striking him across one cheek and sending his glasses flying clear across the room.

He immediately caught her hand before she could repeat the act, and his voice was a low, savage growl. "That's the second pair of glasses you've broken. *Make that your last!"* He turned his back to her.

Hurt and feeling defeated, she could only stare at him through tears. She watched as he changed into a pair of black jeans and a T-shirt. He grabbed his car keys.

She stood facing him, trying to block his exit. Brandeis was crying so hard she could hardly speak. "D-don't l-leave, Jackson. We need to talk."

"I can't talk to you right now. Hell, I can't even bear to look at you."

Brandeis flinched, but her chin tilted proudly. "So, you've condemned me already."

"No, you've condemned yourself, Brandeis."

"Are you coming back?" She asked, praying her voice wouldn't tremble.

"Why?" he asked nastily.

Brandeis stood, tears glimmering on the tips of her lashes as she struggled for something to say that wouldn't come out sounding pitiful and foolish. The hurt and humiliation was crushing. "I have no defense. Neither do I have control over what people say or do, Jackson," Brandeis said. "I can only repeat my innocence. It's up to you whether or not you believe me. But you won't even listen to me."

He headed for the door and was gone.

"Oh, Lord! What have I done?" Brandeis whispered to the empty room. Hot tears scalded her eyes as she scrubbed the back of her hand across her moist cheek. She collapsed on the bed as deep sobs racked her body.

Jackson stood in the hallway, knowing he had deeply hurt Brandeis. He had read the torment in her eyes and he could hear her heartrending sobs. Why had he said those things to her when all he wanted to do was take her in his arms and tell her that he loved her? If she was telling the truth, he was a fool to have allowed Monique to provoke him into a jealous rage. He had not been able to stand the thought of another man's hands on Brandeis. He wanted to find Martin and tear him from limb to limb.

Brandeis was still awake when he came home a few hours later. He eased into the darkened bedroom and stealthily made his way to the bathroom.

"You don't have to tiptoe on my account."

"You're awake," he said quietly and turned on the light.

She sat up in bed. "How could I sleep with something like this between us?"

He met her gaze, but there was no tenderness in his look. "I'm tired, Bran." He paused, let his head drop and continued, "We'll talk in the morning. I'm going to sleep . . . in the guest room."

"Jackson, no! I love you and I need you. Dear Lord, I don't want our marriage to be like this . . . all this anger and hurt. I just want you to love me."

He seemed unmoved by her appeal, his eyes cold. She watched as he turned out the light and the room fell into darkness. "Good night, Bran. We'll talk in the morning."

"Jackson . . ." Brandeis' chin quivered. Never had Jackson been so heartless.

"What?"

"Happy first anniversary."

Jackson stalked out, slamming the door behind him.

A half hour later, Brandeis summoned her courage and headed to the guest room. She had to talk to Jackson. Her marriage depended on it. She grabbed the gift she'd bought him and took it with her.

"Jackson," she whispered. She knelt down next to his bed, placing a feathery touch on his bare shoulder. His muscles were so tense. "Jackson, are you awake?"

After finding himself unable to sleep, Jackson had been staring at the ceiling. Now, he turned his head to face her. "What is it you need, Brandeis?"

"I don't need anything. I can't take the fighting and the mistrust. I—"

"Go to bed, Brandeis." In the bright moonlight he could see the flimsy nightie she wore, meant to destroy a man's resistance. Not one of her charms was hidden from his eyes.

"I told you to go to bed," he repeated more forcefully when Brandeis made no move to leave.

"I want to be with you," she murmured, and reached out to stroke his smooth cheek. Brandeis handed him the brightly wrapped box. "Here is your anniversary present."

Jackson threw the gift on the floor and grabbed her wrist. "I want you to stay away from me. I don't want to be around you right now."

Brandeis paled, but pride would not allow Jackson to see how much he'd wounded her. "My thoughts exactly!"

Brandeis walked with careful steps to the door. She felt Jackson's eyes on her and hoped her composure would not crack. Brandeis couldn't bear the thought of Jackson's seeing her weep like a lost child, even though she felt like one.

"Brandeis," Jackson said when she'd opened the door to leave. She paused without turning around to look at him.

"Yes?"

"You can return the gift. I have no use for it."

Brandeis stiffened and closed the door behind her. Her humiliation and pain threatened to choke her. She went into her bathroom and ripped off the beautiful lingerie with careless hands. She flung it to the floor. She'd bought it especially for their anniversary. Now, she hated it.

"I canceled all of my appointments this morning," Jackson said at breakfast the next morning. "You wanted to talk. So talk!"

"Jackson, I'm so sorry," Brandeis began. "I was going to tell you about the kiss, honestly. I've never lied to you. How can you take someone else's word over mine?"

"What about the letter and the phone call?"

"I wasn't going to tell you about them but not for the reason you thi—"

He cut off her explanation. "Is that the only time you've seen him?"

"No," Brandeis admitted.

"What?"

"Mom and I saw him in Savannah, when we were shopping for maternity clothes. He came up to us in a parking lot." Brandeis hastily added.

"What? Why am I just hearing about this?" Jackson cried.

"I didn't want to upset you. I just wanted to forget about everything," Brandeis said.

"You accused the man of raping you!"

"I know what I said! You don't believe me, do you? You think I was only trying to cover my tracks about not being a virgin. Right? Mom was in Savannah with me. If I were having an affair, do you think I'd take my mother with me?"

"You two are awfully close," Jackson said.

"You bastard!"

"This is getting nowhere." Jackson strode toward the door, then stopped and turned back to her. "For the record, I *don't* think you've been honest with me about Martin. I believe you were angry after sleeping with him and being dumped by him. Maybe you thought you'd find yourself with an unwanted pregnancy. I don't know. Right now, all I can think about is divorcing you and taking my child.''

Brandeis watched the door close. Jackson didn't believe her. *He wants a divorce! He wants to divorce me!* Hurt welled up in her heart and spread like a fever through her body. Jackson's words struck her more brutally than his hand would have done.

She made her way up the stairs to her bedroom. Pulling out a suitcase, she began to pack. She placed a hand over her mouth to drown out the crying.

The raw pain had eased sightly and was duller now, more easily dealt with. At first, nothing had helped. Then, Brandeis had begun taking her life one day at a time, making it through the day and then congratulating herself for it, spending as much time with Brian as possible. She also started seeing Helen Thayer again.

She hadn't seen Jackson in two weeks. However, a few days earlier, he had called to let her know he was going to Atlanta for a conference. He had called daily to check on Brian, though he never had more than small talk for Brandeis.

"Mom, he's crawling!" Brandeis clapped her hands as Brian, wobbly at first, then gaining confidence, made his way to her. *I wish your father could see what a big boy you've become,* she thought.

"He's getting so big. Come to Grandmother, sweetie." Mona sat down on the floor beside her daughter, motioning for Brian to come to her. He looked her way, then toward his mother. He grinned a toothless grin and sat up.

"He's very diplomatic." Brandeis smiled at her son.

The doorbell rang and Mona jumped up. "I'll go answer the door."

Brandeis continued to play with her son while downstairs, Mona opened the door to a tired Jackson.

"Hello, Jackson."

"Hello, Mom." He managed a small smile. "How have you been?"

"I'm fine but I've missed you." She took his hand into hers.

"I've missed you, too."

"Brandeis and the baby are upstairs. Why don't you go on up to see them?"

"She may not want to see me."

"She loves you, Jackson."

"I love her, too."

"Then go on up. Visit with your wife and son. Let me know if you want me to come get Brian."

Jackson kissed Mona on the cheek and hugged her tight. "Thanks, Mom."

Mona patted him on the back and sent him upstairs.

He found Brandeis sitting on the floor with her knees bent. She was watching Brian play with a soft toy.

"Mom, who—"

"It's me."

Brandeis cast a hesitant glance at Jackson.

"What is it?" she asked in a suffocated tone, and he moved jerkily. His gaze was hot, and he swallowed twice as he tore his eyes from her face.

Jackson wondered why he had ever allowed doubts to come between them. "I'd just forgotten how incredibly lovely you are," he said in a tight voice.

"Oh." A shiver ran down her spine and she hugged her knees lightly to her breasts.

The movement brought Jackson's attention to her denim shorts, her thighs smooth and firm, tapering to the most luscious calves.

"Brian's crawling some."

"Really?"

"Yes, but he's still not very sure of himself yet." Brandeis couldn't look at Jackson. If she did, she would throw herself at him, begging him to love her.

Jackson was having trouble not throwing himself at Brandeis. He'd always been able to maintain control, until her. How could he have ever doubted her? How could he ever make things right?

She lifted her heavy lashes to gaze up at him. She saw the bleak expression in his eyes. Caught by the naked pain, Brandeis grew still.

"Jackson?"

He sat down beside her. "God, don't look at me like that." He groaned and buried his face in the curve of her shoulder. Tangling his fingers in her hair, he grounded his mouth over her lips until she couldn't draw in a breath.

She pulled away gently.

Brian crawled over to Jackson's hard, lean thighs. Brandeis watched as her husband propped the drooling baby against him.

"Didn't want to feel left out, slugger?"

Brandeis couldn't help but laugh. "You're not going to look very intimidating sitting in a courtroom with baby drool all over your Armani suit."

An unwilling smile tugged at Jackson's mouth. He sat Brian on the rug beside him, grinning when the baby let out a howl of protest.

"I want you to know that you and Brian didn't have to leave," Jackson said. "It's as much your home as mine. If you want me to leave, I will." *I wish I could ask you to come back, but I don't know how,* Jackson cried silently.

Brandeis struggled to hide the pain she was feeling. She had hoped . . .

"I-I guess I'd better leave," Jackson said. "I just got back in town and haven't been to the office yet. I'm sure there's a pile of work on my desk. I wanted to see how you and Brian were doing. Do you need anything? Money?"

Yes! Damn you! I need you. I want my husband back! she pleaded. Brandeis shook her head.

Jackson kissed her cheek and got up to leave. He looked back at her. She had turned to Brian as if he were not there. *She doesn't want me back,* Jackson thought.

Brandeis couldn't look up for fear of Jackson's seeing her tears of anguish. She didn't want to give him the thrill of knowing how much rejection had hurt. *Mom was right. You trust, you love, then you hurt . . .*

When Jackson was gone, Mona walked into the room and sat next to her daughter. "I hope—"

"He doesn't want me back," Brandeis said. She felt as if she'd been kicked in the stomach. "Mom, he doesn't want me back." Tears rolled down her cheeks.

"Sweetie, Jackson is angry and hurting right now," Mona said. "Give him some time to sort things out. He loves you. I don't believe he's going to just give up on your marriage."

"He's already had two months!" Brandeis cried. "Before I left him, he said he wanted to divorce me and take Brian."

"He was trying to hurt you back, for what he thinks you've done. Bran, don't give up on your marriage," Mona urged. "Don't let this misunderstanding tear you two apart."

"It's not me, Mom."

"I know, sweetie. But I also know this man loves you."

"He used to . . ."

"I'll watch the baby tonight," Mona offered. "Why don't you go home and cook a nice dinner for you and your husband. Fix yourself up real pretty. Sit down and talk to Jackson. Make things right between the two of you."

"Do you think it'll work?"

"Of course I think it'll work! I suggested it."

"Thanks, Mom," Brandeis said, her eyes bright with hope.

"Now, go freshen up. I'm taking the three of us to lunch."

Jackson rushed out of the shower and quickly dressed. He had a plane to catch in less than four hours. He estimated it would take him about an hour and a half to get to Jacksonville, Florida. From the airport there, he would fly to Washington, D.C. He tried to call Brandeis, but no one answered at her mother's. Jackson made a mental note to buy Mona an answering machine.

He looked around once more, to determine whether or not he was forgetting anything, then headed downstairs. Jackson wished Brandeis was going with him.

Three hours and forty minutes later, Jackson peeked over his newspaper when he heard a familiar, sugary voice. Monique.

"Well, talk about a small world. Hi, sugar."

Jackson smiled, but without warmth. "Hello, Monique. What are you doing here?"

"You mean on this plane, sugar?"

"Yes."

"I'm not following you, if that's what you think. I have family in D.C. I'm spending the weekend here. What about you? Needed to get away, huh?"

"I have a business meeting in D.C."

"Oh. Mind if I sit next to you?" She looked around. "I think I'm the last passenger and that seat's empty."

"Suit' yourself. I must warn you though, I'm not good company right now."

"Why don't you let me be the judge of that?" Monique grinned and settled in beside him.

Jackson turned to her, his look pleading. "Monique, I need to know something. Did you lie to me about what you saw in the parking lot that day? I know you wanted to renew our relat—"

"No," Monique said firmly. "I saw your wife kissing a man named Martin. We spoke briefly and he said he and your wife were lovers. I told you all of this already. Look, Jackson. You're a handsome man. You don't have to put up with a cheating wife."

"I would prefer that you didn't refer to my wife in those terms," Jackson said coldly.

"A spade is a spade." Monique placed a soft hand on

his. "I know it hurts, Jackson. And I'm sorry. I just felt you needed to know."

As soon as the plane took off, Jackson closed his eyes and pretended to sleep for the duration of the flight. He didn't want to give Monique the satisfaction of seeing him in pain.

Just before they landed, Monique nudged him and whispered, "Jackson, I'm staying at the Hyatt Regency. If you're staying near me, we can share a cab."

"I'm staying at the Hyatt, too" Jackson mumbled. "That's fine."

She put her arm around his. "Don't shut me out, Jackson. I know you need somebody . . . to talk to," she added quickly. "I hope we're still friends."

"Monique . . ."

Anger flashed in her eyes. "Jackson, get a grip! I'm not pushing for anything. You've made yourself perfectly clear. You're in love with your wife. Even though she doesn't deserve it!"

Chapter 18

Brandeis glanced out of the window. It was getting dark and still no sign of Jackson. Perhaps she should have called him at the office. It was after five now and no one would answer, except for the answering service they subscribed to. She placed a hand to her upswept spiral curls. Mona had insisted on Brandeis getting her hair and nails done. Her mother had paid for everything, including the dress she was wearing. Brandeis put a manicured hand to her stomach as it rumbled.

Glancing over at the table set for dinner, she tapped her three-inch heels against the polished hardwood floor. Outside, the shadows lengthened. Brandeis was trying to keep from bursting into tears. She fought against feeling a sense of abandonment and desolation.

Brandeis looked at her watch. It was after eight. Jackson should have been home by now. Did he know she was here? He couldn't have. Her mother promised not to tell. She sank down on the plush and comfortable sofa, brushing away tears. Was her marriage truly over? Brandeis didn't think she could survive her heartbreak.

Closing her eyes to ease the tension, she fell asleep on the sofa.

She was awakened by the ringing telephone. It stopped before she could get to it. She knew the answering machine would pick it up, so she went back to sleep.

The next morning, she awakened with the sun shining brightly through the windows. The empty plates on the table greeted her. Brandeis called her mother.

"Morning, Mom. How's the baby?"

"He's still sleeping. He's such a good baby."

"Did Jackson call last night?"

"Yes. I told him to call you at home. He had to leave right away for D.C. He said he tried to call before he left, but we weren't home."

"I remember the phone ringing, but I was so tired, I just let the machine pick it up. I'll check to see if there's a message. Thanks, Mom. I'll be home as soon as I shower and change."

Brandeis checked the machine. She listened to the first two messages and finally, the one from Jackson. He explained his quick business trip and left the hotel number and his room number. Sadly, she noted he didn't say he loved her.

Monique decided she was going to seduce Jackson. He was a very passionate man, and she was sure she could arouse him. Dressed in a clinging knit dress, Monique admired herself in one of the hallway mirrors. She stopped at Jackson's room and knocked. She smiled when he opened the door.

"Hi, sugar. How'd your meeting go?"

Jackson forced his eyes away from her large breasts. He instantly regretted his decision to let her come by his room. "It went fine. How was your day? I'm a bit surprised to hear from you. I thought you'd be spending time with your family."

"I spent the whole day with them. That was enough. They're a bunch of church folks."

"There's nothing wrong with that," Jackson replied.

"No. But they don't do nothing. Just talk about the Bible. I know a lot about a lot of things, but when it comes to the Bible, I know nothing about none of it."

Jackson laughed. "You're something else."

"And you know it!" Monique crossed her legs, causing her dress to rise even higher. "Do you have any ice, Jackson? I'm dying for a glass of water." She leaned forward, giving Jackson a close-up view of her breasts. "I brought my own bottled water, but it's hot."

Jackson leaped up quickly. "I'll go and get some."

She almost laughed. "Thanks, sugar."

Jackson was gone all of two minutes when the phone rang. Grinning, Monique reached over and drawled sleepily into the receiver.

"Hullo."

She smiled when she heard a gasp of shock on the other end.

"Who is this, please?"

"This is Monique. Is this room service? We ordered our food twenty minutes ago—"

"Hell no! This is not room service! Monique, where is my husband? I want to speak to him now!"

"Brandeis, Jackson is in the shower. He told me about your cheating on him with Martin. He's hurt and very angry. If he wants to talk to you, he'll call you back. Otherwise, we don't want to be disturbed."

The phone line went dead.

Monique was just hanging up when Jackson walked back in the room. He froze. "Did you answer my phone?"

"Why, no," she lied. "I was checking to see if I had any messages."

Relief washed over his face. Brandeis would never believe that this was just a coincidence. Right now, his marriage was on shaky ground. Something like this could destroy it.

"Monique, I don't think this is such a good idea," Jackson said. "I think you should leave now. As a matter of fact, I'm going to change hotels. Enjoy the rest of your weekend."

Bitterness marred her beautiful features. "You must really love her," she said bitterly.

"I do."

Monique felt no pangs of remorse for what she'd done to hurt Jackson's marriage. "Jackson. She doesn't deserve you." His pain was written all over his face. Monique walked over to him and pulled his head down to hers. She pressed her lips to his but there was no response. Undaunted, she slowly pulled away. "I'll see you around, sugar."

Monique left and walked back to her room. She went to the window and opened it slightly, taking in a deep breath. Then, she covered her mouth with her hand, trying to stifle her sobs. When she had regained her composure, she continued to stare out at the darkening sky.

She bit her lips and tasted her own blood. Finally, she shook her head and went to her bed. Jackson would come crawling back to her. Brandeis would never forgive him for going away for the weekend with a known whore.

Jackson left the airport and drove straight to Mona's house. Brandeis' car was not there. He wondered if she was with Martin?

"Hello, Mom," he said when Mona opened the door to him.

"Hello, Jackson." Mona ushered him inside.

"I wanted to see Bran. I think it's time we had a serious talk . . . about our marriage."

"I think that's a splendid idea," Mona said.

"Mom, I love Bran," Jackson said. "I've been open and honest with her. It hurts that Bran felt she couldn't be truthful with me."

"What do you think she lied about?" Mona asked.

"I'm not sure . . . About the rape, I guess. I mean, why would she protect a man who raped her?"

"Did you ever think that maybe she was trying to protect you or herself?" Mona said.

"Protect me? From what? And why would she protect herself this way?"

"Jackson," Mona explained, "women in my family have always placed a lot of value on virginity. I raised my daughter that way. Brandeis was one of the few women in today's society who chose to wait for that magical wedding night. When that dream was ripped apart by Martin, she felt betrayed, used, cheap, and dirty. She no longer trusted her own judgment when it came to men. Not to mention the men themselves." Mona placed Jackson's hand into her own.

"You came back into her life and helped her to live again. You treated her like a queen. Bran was afraid of losing your love and respect. *She was raped, Jackson.* She didn't lie about it. Bran wanted to keep Martin buried because she feared you would think she lied. Like some of the woman who accused your clients of rape."

Jackson was quiet and thoughtful for a moment. "I acted like an ass, didn't I?"

"I wouldn't say that. I—"

They heard the front door open.

"What are you doing here?" Brandeis asked. Her eyes were filled with fury. "You've got a lot of nerve—"

"What is wrong with you? I came by to see if we could go somewhere and talk," Jackson said.

"We have nothing to talk about! I want you to leave. By the way, you can also have your divorce, but you're not getting my son."

"I realize I've been unfair to you, but—" Jackson began.

"I don't care anymore. By the way, did you enjoy your little trip?" Brandeis said sarcastically.

"What are you talking about? I called our house when Mom said you were over there. I left a message—"

"I know you weren't alone. Don't try to make a fool out

of me, Jackson!" Brandeis cried. "You were with Monique in Washington, D.C."

"We were on the same plane, Bran," Jackson said. "She was spending the weekend with her family in D.C."

"I'd say that was some coincidence."

"Bran, listen to me . . ."

"Like you listened to me?"

"Honey, I'm sorry. I should've listened to you, but when Monique said—"

"Monique . . . ? Wait a minute! It was Monique, wasn't it? *She* told you that I was kissing Martin. I remember seeing a little red mustang when I looked in my mirror as I was driving off. She parked right next to his car. You believed a whore over your wife! Then the two of you end up on the same plane, going to D.C. the exact same weekend, and when I call, she answers the phone in your room! How in the hell did she get in your room?"

"Maybe you called her room by accident," Jackson said, helplessly. "I moved to another hotel on Saturday evening."

"Jackson, I *called* Saturday evening. Monique said you were in the shower! What was she doing in your room? For that matter, why would you even consort with a whore?"

Jackson felt as if he'd been punched. "She just came by for a visit. Look, Brandeis, even though she is a prostitute, I tried to be her friend. Is there something wrong with being nice to people even if we don't approve of their choices?"

Brandeis was shocked speechless. "Even if the person is trying to ruin your marriage? Oh, Jackson, there is nothing else to say except that I want a divorce! I don't want to be married to you! You have the nerve to judge me, but you don't want me to be judgmental when it comes to Monique. You are seriously tripping!" Brandeis shouted.

"You don't want to try to work this out," Jackson said, putting his hand to his head. "It's all a big misunderstanding. Nothing happened between us!"

"Answer one question for me, Jackson. If I hadn't found out about Monique, would you have told me?"

"No. Probably not. I understa—"

Brandeis didn't want to hear anymore. "Now, would you please leave?"

"Can I at least see my son?"

"Go ahead."

As soon as he turned the corner to go upstairs, Brandeis fell to the sofa in tears.

Mona sat next to her, gently rubbing her back. "Think long and hard before you decide you want a divorce, dear. Look again to see if your marriage is worth saving."

"Mom, I can't trust him and he doesn't trust me either," Brandeis whispered.

"Take a few days and think about things. Please," Mona said.

Upstairs, Jackson cradled his sleeping son and cried.

"Jackson why don't we go somewhere and have a drink?" Clay suggested to his supervisor and friend.

The two men were in Jackson's office, discussing an upcoming trial. Legal pads and pencils were scattered all over the table. Jackson had been going through a copy of *Shepard's United States Citations*.

"Sure, why not. It's not like I have a wife to go home to," Jackson said somewhat bitterly. He put the book aside. "I guess we've done as much as we can tonight. We'll finish this tomorrow morning." He stood up and put on his black pinstripe jacket as Clay gathered up his materials and placed them in his briefcase.

They drove separate cars to Applebees. It was not crowded and Jackson was grateful. He didn't feel like being around a lot of people.

Grabbing two seats at the bar, they both ordered beers. They were in the midst of discussing the upcoming trial when Jackson overheard his wife's name. He turned around and found a well-dressed, light-skinned man with green eyes, sitting next to a young girl at the bar.

"Yeah, that bitch going around telling people I raped her. Her ass couldn't wait to give it to me. If anything she raped me—"

A muscle flickered in Jackson's jaw but his face was a marble effigy of contempt. He locked eyes with Martin, his dark eyes blazing with his barely restrained anger. In a flash, Jackson was standing.

"What the hell do you *want?*" Martin said.

"I *want* you to stop spreading lies about my wife! I *want* you to stay away from my wife!"

Martin stood up. He swayed a little but quickly straightened up. "Well! If it isn't Jackson Gray, Esquire. Finally, we meet." He eyed Jackson up and down. His tone mocking, he added, "Tell your wife to stop telling lies on me. She started this! She's just mad cause I dumped her. I had her more than once. She couldn't wait to give it up and I—"

Before Martin could finish, Jackson's fist buried itself in his midsection. Blow after devastating blow jarred bone and flesh. Jackson leveled a blow that knocked the air out of Martin's lungs. Before he could turn his opponent into a human punching bag, Clay and several of the waiters grabbed him.

"Don't, Jackson. That son of a bitch isn't worth it." Clay pulled him away. "Come on, let's get out of here."

Martin struggled against a numbing pain. He wiped the trickle of blood from his lips. "I'll make that bitch pay for all the trouble she's caused me," he vowed spitefully. "Yeah, Jackson, I had your wife! I'll have her again. She wants me. She told me so that day she kissed me. Do ya hear me? She kissed me. She wanted it then! Bitch can't get enough of me!" His tone had changed to a harsh snarl. "You'll both be sorry!"

"You miserable son of a bitch!" Jackson turned around and growled. "I'm warning you. Stay the hell away from my wife!"

Clay pushed him toward the door. "Let's get out of here, Jackson. You know he's just trying to piss you off. Next, he'll probably try to sue you."

"Let the bastard try! I'm gonna break his fu—"

"Jackson! Brandeis wouldn't like this. Don't stoop to his level."

"You're right, Clay. You're absolutely right. But you know what, Clay? It felt damn good!" Jackson felt good, better than he'd felt in weeks. Tomorrow, he would visit Brandeis. It was time to bring his family home.

Martin slammed the door as he entered Carrie's apartment, his body still sore from the beating he'd received.

"Martin, honey, I'm so glad you're home. I've got something to tell you," Carrie called from the bedroom. She walked out wearing a black lace teddy. She took one look at him and exclaimed, "What the hell happened to you?"

He scowled at her through his good eye. "What the hell do ya think? I was in a fight."

Carrie poured him a drink from the bottle of gin he had bought two days ago. "With who?"

"Jackson Gray."

"What?"

"Look! I don't feel like talking about it. He just better be glad I didn't kill his punk ass!"

"Why don't you get undressed, Martin. I'll run a bath for you," Carrie said. "Soaking for a few minutes may help relieve some of the soreness."

Carrie wondered why Martin and Jackson had been fighting. *Was it over Brandeis?* she wondered. It had to be. They didn't know each other personally. She *knew* the ice princess had to try to find a way to ruin her happiness. But not this time. Carrie placed a protective hand over her stomach and smiled.

She heard Martin moving around and knew he had finished his bath. She hoped his disposition was better.

The bath had helped relieve some of the pain, but it

did nothing whatsoever to improve Martin's disposition. He lay on the bed, mumbling to himself. He called to Carrie to cook something for him and bring him another drink.

Carrie debated whether or not the time was right to give Martin her news. She'd almost abandoned the idea when he brought it up.

"You said you had somethin' to tell me. What's up?"

Carrie took a deep breath and said, "I'm going to have a baby."

"You're what? Naw! You didn't just say you were pregnant!" Instantly, Martin was on his feet and grabbed her by the shoulders. "How can you be pregnant? I thought you told me you were taking birth control."

"I was on the pill." She shrugged. "I guess it just happened. Maybe my pills weren't strong enough." Carrie was disappointed. She thought Martin would be happy about the baby. Especially after he'd obsessed so much about Brandeis and her child.

"I'll give you some money for an abortion. You'd better tell your doctor you need stronger pills or something."

"An a-abortion. W-why do you want me to have an abortion? You don't want this baby? You eat, sleep, and drink Brandeis' brat, but you want me to abort our baby!" Carrie cried.

"You don't get it, do you? She's mine, has always been mine. I was her first!"

Carrie cringed. *Oh, no. He must have raped Brandeis. It was all true. He wanted Brandeis, not me. He never wanted me and he doesn't want our baby.* "You bastard, you used me!"

"No, I didn't. I just took all you had to offer," Martin said nastily. "Look, I never did love you. The way I figure it, if you were so easy for me, you'd be easy for any man. I don't want no woman I can't trust."

Carrie slapped him with all her might. Never had she felt so humiliated. Everybody thought she was no better than a whore. Her long nails left a trail of blood across his face.

Martin shoved her against the wall. "I told you before, don't you ever hit me again, bitch!" He hit her hard with his clenched fist at the soft point where the curve of her breasts joined her collarbone. Her cry of pain echoed in the apartment. The force of the blow knocked her away from the wall.

Carrie came at him again. "I want you outta here! I'm glad Jackson beat the crap outta you. Get out of here, you low-life pig! Don't you ever come near me again!"

"You don't have to tell me twice. I hated being here, but it was an ends to a means," Martin said with a sneer. "I don't need your whoring ass anymore. I gots me a good woman. She just don't realize it yet. She didn't realize she wanted me as much as she did. I had to prove it to her."

"You raped her, you monster!" Carrie screamed.

Martin slapped her hard. "Don't you say that again, girl," he said harshly, his fingers buried in her hair. He released her and she staggered backward toward the sofa.

Martin was on her before she could find her feet. His second blow was a brisk slap to her ear, his third, a hard punch in the center of her back.

"Rapist! She didn't want you and you couldn't handle that. You had to rape her—"

Martin slapped her again and again. Carrie fell to the floor, trying to protect her face. His foot connected with her stomach. Pain such as she'd never known engulfed her. "Oh, God, please save my b-baby," she moaned as darkness settled over her.

Chapter 19

Brandeis awoke with a start. Everything was cast in darkness, but she knew someone was in the bedroom with her. She did not have to be told that Jackson was nearby, because she could feel his disturbing presence in some inner part of her being.

She swallowed hard, fearing to face him. Slowly, her eyes became accustomed to the dark and she saw his outline where he was standing by the window.

"Jackson?"

"Yes, I'm here."

She wanted to run to him to feel his strength fill her whole being but she dared not. "But what are you doing here, Jackson? I guess Mom let you in."

She heard him move across the room until he was over her. "I suppose you could say I've come to right a wrong, sweetheart. I treated you unfairly. Last night, I took a long, hard look at myself, and I didn't like what I saw. I want no more lies between us."

"I haven't lied to you—"

"I wasn't talking about you, or me," Jackson said. "I was talking about others who have lied. I'm not willing to let their lies keep us apart anymore." Jackson sat gently on the bed next to her. He reached for her but she moved away.

"Jackson. I want . . . to talk. Nothing else."

"I just need to hold you." His voice was deep with emotion.

"I can't. Not yet."

"What happened to us?" Tears glistened in his eyes.

"I-I don't know. I can only speak for myself. I guess we never really trusted each other. I think I placed all the emphasis on being loved, rather than on loving . . . on taking, rather than on giving. I was so caught up in trying to keep Martin out of our lives, I never thought about how you would understand my actions. I can see why you thought I was hiding something."

"I love you, honey, and I do trust you," Jackson said. "I was so jealous and insecure. I didn't listen. I want you to come home. Our son needs both of us."

"He'll have both of us. No matter what happens."

"Do you still love me?" Jackson asked, reaching to take her hand in his long slender fingers.

"Yes, of course I still love you." Tears slid down Brandeis' face. To her amazement, tears were sliding down Jackson's face, too.

Jackson took his finger and traced the path of tears on her cheeks, then touched his own wet face, blending their tears together. Brandeis thought it was the most endearing moment of her marriage.

"Will you please come home, to me?" Jackson whispered. "To our life?"

He stroked her hand 'til she could think of nothing but the feel of his touch, the memory of what it felt like to have those knowing fingers caress the burning skin of her body.

"A lot has happened," she managed to respond, despite the ache of longing his touch was kindling in her veins.

"Bran, DKD has merged with a huge law firm in D.C.

They want me to head the Criminal Defense Department there. In D.C. I have to leave town in a couple of months."

"What?"

"I accepted because I'd hoped you would be coming with me. I thought you could attend law school somewhere in Washington."

"I d-don't know what to say. I didn't know you were planning to move away."

"Honey, I don't want to leave you behind," Jackson pleaded. "I love you, Bran. I want my family back."

"I have to think about this. About everything. We would have to resolve the problems in our marriage first."

Brandeis reached and turned the light on. She saw the bruise on Jackson's left cheek. "Oh my God, what happened to you? Were you in a fight?"

"Yes. I had a fight with Martin."

"Why? Did you confront him?" Brandeis asked nervously.

Jackson didn't answer. Instead he said, "Bran, I'm willing to listen. Please tell me about Martin."

"Martin called me at the office shortly after we got married. I told him not to call me anymore. I didn't hear from him anymore until I received the letter. When Mom and I went to Savannah to shop for maternity clothes, we saw him. Rather, he saw us and followed us to Mom's car. Mom actually slapped him for calling me a lying bitch."

"Your mother!"

"Yes," Brandeis smiled. "She tried to persuade me to tell you what was going on but I didn't want to relive the past. You and I were just getting back on track. I didn't want to ruin it. She gently touched his face. "In my own way, I was trying to protect you. I didn't want you fighting."

"Honey, I'm sorry about all the things I said," Jackson apologized. "I was so afraid of losing you. I needed to hurt you as much as I hurt. I remember well how you reacted when we started dating. I know you were raped, Brandeis, I never really doubted that. I'm so sorry."

"Jackson, so many times I questioned myself about what

happened that night with Martin," Brandeis admitted. "I wouldn't even admit to myself at first that it was rape. I didn't press charges because I was afraid of what people would say. I was afraid people would think I was lying. I know I should have and I think any woman who experiences date rape should press charges, no matter the outcome. It's something I know I'll always regret, not taking Martin to court."

"Can you ever forgive me?" Jackson said.

"Jackson, I forgive you. Will you tell me about Monique now?"

"Monique told me about seeing you and Martin in the parking lot. I guess Martin told her a bunch of lies. I don't know why she was really in D.C., but she came by my room on that Saturday. I was out in the hallway getting ice for a glass of water, not taking a shower. Honey, why would I have called you and left the phone number of my hotel if I was having an affair?"

Brandeis smiled ruefully. "I guess when you think about it, it all sounds really stupid. Can you ever forgive me?"

"Yes," Jackson said, "but I think we should do something right now."

"What?"

"We didn't get to celebrate our one year anniversary but it's not too late. We can start by saying our wedding vows to each other again."

"But . . . when?"

"What's wrong with right now? Right this minute."

Was there no end to the surprises he would spring on her tonight? Brandeis wondered.

"B-but what would we say? I mean, I can't remember the vows exactly," Brandeis said.

"Why don't we say what's in our hearts?" Jackson clutched her hand with both of his. "You go first."

Brandeis captured his eyes with hers. "I promise to be honest with you. To not keep secrets from you. To love you and to trust you."

"I promise to listen to you," he said. "To trust you and

to love you. I promise to remember what's important and to hold onto it always. May I hold you now?"

"You don't need to ask." Brandeis put her arms around him and kissed him. He pushed her gently back on the bed. He kissed her until she moaned and held him more tightly her arms curving around his broad shoulders. It was growing too difficult for Jackson to hold back his need, and when she whimpered softly, he twisted his lean body from the bed and stood beside it.

As he shrugged out of his shirt and unzipped his pants, Brandeis felt a surge of admiration and pride at his tall, muscular body, the long legs and lean hips. A wide expanse of brown skin with curling dark hair appeared as he pulled away his white shirt with an impatient jerk. He moved swiftly, with lithe, graceful motions.

"I never thought you would want me after I said all those cruel things to you," he admitted. A faint smile lit his face as he knelt on the bed beside her, his hands sliding up the hem of her gown. "I may not deserve your love, but I will accept it anyway."

She pressed her tear-wet cheek against his. "My dearest husband, you are the most deserving man I have ever known. I love and respect you with all my heart. Thank you for being my knight in shining armor."

He stared into her amber eyes, swimming with tears. "You have my word that I will be the man you can honor and love."

When he'd removed her gown, Brandeis arched her hips to meet him eagerly. There was no need for a lingering teasing of the senses; both of them were aching for sweet release. Winding her legs around him, Brandeis welcomed his body into hers with a throaty cry that made him lunge more fiercely into her velvety warmth. He drove into her with increasing tempo, a rising intensity that swept them both to a thundering climax.

Jackson's body sagged briefly against hers with the shivering aftermath, and he kissed her mouth in a tender brushing of his lips that made her smile.

Brandeis thought that she had never been so happy in her entire life. And when Jackson lifted his head from her lips and gazed down into her eyes with a hazy smile and whispered, "I love you," she knew it was for certain. "I'm glad mom went against my wishes and let you in."

"Jackson?"

"Yes."

"I want to go with you to Washington. Maybe it would be best if we leave here. As far as law school is concerned, I still want to go, but we really need to think things out."

"Honey?"

"We have Brian and we want other children. We've talked about wanting the children to be close in age. We can't do both. Not right now."

"Which is more important to you, Bran?"

"Can you wait until after law school to have another baby?" she asked.

"I don't have a problem with that."

"Are you sure?"

"Positive." Jackson smiled. "As long as that doesn't mean we're going to have to abstain from making love."

"But, honey. That's the only way we can be absolutely sure I won't get pregnant," Brandeis protested.

"We'll just have to take our chances." A faint smile tugged at the corners of Jackson's mouth. Gathering his wife closer, his hands stroked her full breasts. He lowered his head to brush his mouth over her aching nipples. "I love you, sweetheart . . ." he whispered.

Brandeis was concerned when she heard that Carrie was in the hospital. She remembered seeing bruises around Carrie's neck a few weeks ago. Carrie had been very secretive about the man she was seeing and Brandeis had respected her privacy. Although the two never cared much for each other, Brandeis had never wished any harm to come to her.

After work, Carrie was still very much on her mind.

Brandeis called her mother, then Jackson, and told them she planned to stop by the hospital to visit a coworker.

"Do you want me to pick Brian up at Mona's?" Jackson asked.

"If you don't mind. Oh, Mom has some leftovers from the Labor Day barbeque. I forgot to bring them home last night. Brian was . . ." Her thoughts drifted to Carrie. Who could have done such a thing to her? *Who were you dating, Carrie? Who on earth would do this to you?*

"Bran?"

"Oh, Jackson, I'm sorry. I was thinking about Carrie. I believe she's involved in an abusive relationship. I got a glimpse of some bruises on her neck a few weeks ago. And now, she's in the hospital. She's been beaten up."

"I hope she'll be okay," Jackson said, his concern evident. "Does anyone know who she's been seeing?"

"No. It's really very strange. She's been so secretive about him. Usually, she can't wait to brag about a new boyfriend."

"Maybe you should sit down and have a talk with her. Do you think she'll listen to you?" Jackson asked.

"I'm the last person she'll listen to," Brandeis admitted. "I hate to see her going through something like this."

"Try to get through to her, honey," Jackson urged. "That type of relationship is very unhealthy."

"I will," Brandeis promised. "I love you and I'll see you later."

"I love you, too."

"Who are the flowers from?" Carrie asked. She tried to sit up in bed, but the pain from her broken ribs stopped her.

"They're so lovely!" The nurse opened the card. "I think you should read this yourself." She handed the card to Carrie.

It's from Martin! He's asking me to marry him. A few days ago, it was all Carrie had dreamed of, but now, so much had been said and done. She still loved Martin with all of her being, but she knew he was crazy. *I'm not falling for your lies anymore,* she vowed.

Brandeis entered the hospital room and saw Carrie. The beautiful woman's face was battered. One eye was swollen and her lip had been split.

"Carrie?"

Carrie looked up and squinted through the eye that hadn't been bruised by Martin's blows. She already was so humiliated, and seeing Brandeis made her feel even worse. Was that concern she saw on Brandeis' face? No, it couldn't be. "What are you doing here, Brandeis?"

"I came by to visit with you. I hope you don't mind."

"Oh. No . . . I don't mind. Come on in and pull up a chair. I didn't mean to appear rude," Carrie said. "I'm just surprised you cared enough to come."

Brandeis sighed. "I *do* care about you, Carrie. You get on my nerves every now and then, but I don't want anything bad to happen to you. Especially something like this. How are you feeling?"

"I've been better. I guess you heard, huh?"

"Heard what?" Brandeis asked. "You know I don't listen to office gossip."

"No, I guess you're too good for that." A tear rolled down Carrie's cheek.

"Carrie, I didn't come to upset you. I came because I was concerned about you. I'm sorry." Brandeis turned to leave.

"Brandeis, wait! I'm sorry. I didn't mean what I said. It's just that . . . I've always been jealous of you." Carrie bowed her head, her bruised hands tightly clasped together.

"But why?" Brandeis pulled a chair next to Carrie's bed and sat down.

"You're pretty, you're educated, and just too good to be true. You always seemed to say and do the right things. It gets on my nerves, but deep inside, I wish I could be just like you. Good men always seem to flock to you,"

Carrie said. "All they want from me is sex. They want to sleep with me but not marry me."

Brandeis wasn't sure how to respond.

"I'm pregnant, Brandeis. I thought he would be happy about it, but he tried to hurt my baby." Carrie's voice broke. "I thought he loved me."

"I'm so sorry, Carrie," Brandeis said, touching Carrie's arm.

"He wants you, Brandeis. He's always wanted you and he still does."

"Who? Who are you talking about?"

"Martin. Martin St. Charles. I'm sure you remember him."

"Martin! You mean—"

"I started seeing Martin after you broke up with him," Carrie said. "He called me one day at the office and asked if we could meet for lunch. Martin said that you were upset about his dumping you. He said that he'd told you he wanted me and that you freaked out. That you threatened to accuse him of rape. He seemed so hurt, I believed him."

"Carrie, Martin did rape me," Brandeis said, looking intently at her colleague, "I wouldn't lie about something like that. You told him about my wedding to Jackson, didn't you? I always wondered how he knew about it."

"He always asks me about you. At first, I thought it was because he was afraid of your pressing charges against him. But he still wants you, Brandeis. That's why he dated me. He wanted to keep tabs on you. I was so stupid." Huge tears rolled down Carrie's bruised cheeks. "He's crazy, Brandeis. He acts like your baby is his. The other night, when Jackson beat him up, he said he was gonna make you both pay. He says you and the baby belong to him."

"What's he planning to do, Carrie? Has he said anything specific?" Brandeis was scared. She would call Jackson before she left the hospital.

"Just that he plans to have you and the baby back with him, where you both belong."

"Carrie, you need to stay away from him," Brandeis said.

"He almost killed you and your unborn baby. I hope you pressed charges against him?"

"Yes, I pressed charges," Carrie said, "I'm going to stay with my mother for a while. He's already called the hospital, but I left instructions that only my parents could be put through. My brother is here and he's keeping a watch for Martin."

"I'm glad to hear that," Brandeis said. "I have to go, but if you need to talk to someone, give me a call. Okay?"

"Thank you, Brandeis," Carrie whispered.

"Carrie, I'm so sorry about what happened."

"I'm sorry, too. I let things get completely out of hand. I hope you'll forgive me. I really believed he loved me and that he was telling me the truth."

"All is forgiven." Brandeis shook her head. "I know how sweet he can be at times. Please be careful. Not just for your sake, but your baby's, too."

"I'll kill the bastard if he comes near you again!"

"Jackson, please don't act this way. I'll stay as far away from Martin as possible. We have the restraining order. That should be enough."

"He may be stalking you, honey."

"I think he's just trying to aggravate me," Brandeis said. "It doesn't matter anymore because we're going to D.C. in a few weeks. He's Carrie's problem now. With Carrie pressing charges, maybe he'll do another disappearing act and leave town."

"Maybe you're right," Jackson said. "When the police went by Carrie's apartment, he was already gone. It looks like he's skipped town."

Brandeis put her arms around his neck and buried her face against his throat. "Jackson, I don't want to spend our evening talking about Martin."

Jackson held her snugly. "It's still hard for you, isn't it?"

"He's just a very painful memory. I tried to be so careful in my choices of men. I remembered what my mom went through with my father and I swore it would never happen to me. I was going to be so careful when it came to finding a mate."

"How can you remember what your mother endured? You were so young when your father died."

"I may have been young," Brandeis admitted, "but I remember as if it were yesterday the day we found out about the accident that killed him, his lover and . . . their child. The look on my mother's face . . . Jackson, it was heartbreaking."

"I'm so sorry."

She shrugged. "Mom says things like that happen. She says you trust, you love, you hurt, you cry, get angry. Then you learn from all of it, go forward and not look back."

"You're mother is a very special person," Jackson said, "I love her outlook on life."

"So do I," Brandeis said. "It's what's helped me through all my ups and downs. And now, I have you."

"Yes, you do." Jackson's mouth returned her kisses with a frantic urgency.

Chapter 20

Martin slammed the phone down. They wouldn't put any calls through to Carrie without screening them. With her brother guard-dogging her room, he couldn't get in to see her. She'd better keep her mouth shut. He'd thought about threatening her, but had since changed his mind. She would stay quiet as long as she felt he loved her. Martin knew what made her tick.

Earlier, he'd sent her flowers with a marriage proposal written on the card. He wondered if she'd gotten them. Although he had no intention of honoring that proposal, he wanted to pacify her until he could grab Brandeis and the baby and leave town.

Why hasn't she called by now? he wondered. He had hoped she'd lose her baby. He didn't want that child. Nevertheless, in his note he'd apologized and pleaded forgiveness. She was a sucker for stuff like that. She'd be thrilled by his proposal. Martin laughed. Woman were such fools over good looking men like him. Handsome looks, good hair, and a few sugary words could get you everywhere. Except where Brandeis was concerned. She was a challenge. He liked that in a woman.

Once he talked to Carrie, he'd have to get her to agree to drop the charges against him. He hated hiding out like this. "I gotta talk to her," he muttered. "Gotta find some way to convince her I'm serious." Clapping his hands together, he laughed. "I know just the thing." Grabbing his car keys, he headed out of the dingy hotel room.

The nurse brought a small package to Carrie. "This just came to you by messenger."

"What in the world—" Carrie opened the package to find a tiny gift box. In it, sat an exquisite solitaire diamond engagement ring. "Oh my!" *Is this really happening to me?* she thought. Her mind raced. *Could Martin really be in love with her? This diamond has to be at least three carats. You don't spend that kind of money on someone you don't love!*

Reaching for the phone, Carrie dialed the number of the hotel where he was staying. After a minute or two, she reached him. "Hello, Martin," she said nervously.

"Hello, baby. I called and tried to see you but no one would let me near you. I been going crazy thinking 'bout what I did to you and our baby. I'm so sorry." Martin sounded as if he were crying. "I was drinking a lot, but I quit. I promise, honey. I won't ever hurt you or the baby again, just give me one more chance."

"Do you really love me?" Carrie asked. She had to be cautious. "I need to know the truth, Martin."

"Yes. I love you more than life itself. I want you to be my wife. Screw Brandeis and her brat. We'll have a house *full* of kids."

"I love you, Martin," Carrie whispered. "I really do."

"I know that you do. I want you to be my wife. I want to see you, make sure you're okay. But I can't because of your family and the police. It's been hell for me."

"I'll take care of all that, Martin," Carrie promised. "I'm going home tomorrow. I'd planned to stay with my mother, but I'll go to my apartment. Tomorrow night, you can come over and we'll talk, okay?"

"Sure, baby," Martin said, "but I must admit I'm not so comfortable coming near you with a restraining order hanging over my head."

"I'm going to have all the charges dropped. But Martin, you need to understand one thing. I'm going to have my baby. I'm not getting an abortion and if you ever raise a hand to me again . . ." Carrie let the threat hang in the air.

"I want the baby. I want us." Martin's voice broke.

"Honey, are you okay?"

"I'm just so relieved. I couldn't live with the fact of killing my own child. I-I'm so s-sorry 'bout what happened."

"Oh, Martin. D-don't do this. We'll get through this," Carrie said. "You'll see."

"You wanted to see me, Brandeis? Why?" Carrie stood in the door to Brandeis' office. She had been out of the hospital for two weeks. Today was her first day back at work.

"Yes, would you please close the door." Brandeis smiled smoothly, betraying nothing of her annoyance. "I normally don't listen to office gossip, but I couldn't help overhearing that you're engaged to Martin. Have you forgotten what happened just last month, Carrie?"

"No, I haven't forgotten but people can change," Carrie said defensively. "As a matter of fact, I *am* engaged to him." She lifted her chin, meeting Brandeis' icy gaze straight on. "I'm going to have his baby. We're going to be married."

"You don't have to marry him just because he's the father of your child," Brandeis argued. "He almost *killed* you and your baby. Before that, he must have tried to choke you because you had bruises all over your neck. More than once. I saw them, Carrie."

"What? How did you see them? I didn't show them to anyone."

"I *saw* them. It was purely by accident. Carrie, you're in

an abusive relationship. Please get out while you still can. You don't need someone like Martin in your life. He's a very dangerous and volatile man."

"I can handle it," Carrie said. "Martin was drinking a lot then, but he's changed now."

Brandeis did not miss the way Carrie stirred uneasily in the chair.

"Carrie, he really did rape me."

Carrie's face paled with anger. "I don't want to hear that lie! Martin said you're only telling that lie because he told you that he wanted me. He left you for *me!*"

Shock rendered Brandeis speechless. Suddenly she laughed. "Carrie, you can believe whatever the hell you want. I'm just trying to give you some friendly advice."

Tears formed in Carrie's eyes. "Please, let me be happy, Brandeis. Martin loves me. You have Jackson. You two are leaving town anyway. What does it matter to you?"

"I really don't want to see you get hurt. Remember, you've got a child to think about." Brandeis voice softened. "You really love him, don't you?"

"Yes."

"In the hospital, you told me that Martin still wanted me. Do you remember saying that?"

"Yes. I-I know I said that, but I must have misunderstood what he was saying. He loves me. He loves *me* and he's truly sorry about what happened. I declare, Brandeis, do you think he would've bought me this?" Carrie held out her hand for Brandeis to see the gorgeous diamond.

Brandeis shook her head. "I guess you're correct. He must love you." Inside, she was still unconvinced.

"He says he's no longer interested in you," Carrie said, admiring her ring. "Hasn't been for a while. He says you've been harassing him."

Brandeis sighed. "I suppose it doesn't do any good to tell you Martin's lying to you. He's a good actor. Very convincing. I hope he's telling you the truth about his love for you."

Carrie nodded. "He is. No man spends this kind of money on a woman he doesn't love. I trust him, Brandeis."

"Well, I wish you luck. Congratulations on your engagement," Brandeis said.

"It'll work out, Brandeis," Carrie said, her eyes burning with determination. "He loves me and I love him. It's all gonna work out."

Carol gave Brandeis a tour of the house. "So, what do you think?"

"It's a beautiful house. I really love the kitchen."

"I do, too. We close in two weeks, on Halloween. Can you imagine? I'm so excited." Suddenly, Carol sobered. "I'm going to miss you so much, Bran," she said, quietly. "I wish you didn't have to leave."

"We're going to visit often, I promise. You know I'll miss my mom dearly. And I hope you and James will come visit us."

"We will. As a matter of fact, we're going to be in Landover, Maryland, in December, attending a tax seminar," Carol said.

"Great! Make sure you plan to stay for a few extra days. I want you to stay with us. I can't *wait* for you to see our house! It's a five-bedroom, two-story Colonial. Jackson found it the first time he was in D.C. It's in Arlington, Virginia."

"You mean, he bought this house during the time you two were separated?"

"Yes. He says he always knew in his heart we'd be together again."

Carol hugged her friend. "We all did."

Brandeis placed a hand on her stomach to quiet the low rumbling. "Well, I'm hungry. Let's go have lunch. Applebees okay?"

"That's fine."

"I'm really going to miss Brunswick," Brandeis said as she drove down Altama Avenue. She turned into the parking lot of Applebees. Just as she opened her door to get out, a red mustang pulled up beside her. Monique stepped out of her car and walked toward Brandeis.

"Brandeis, I want to talk to you," she said.

Carol stood next to Brandeis and tugged at her arm. "Why don't we just go inside. Don't listen to her. She's probably got more lies to tell . . ."

Brandeis was shocked at Monique's audacity. Striving for composure, she responded, "No, Carol. I want to hear what she has to say. There are a few things I'd like to say to her, too!"

A sneer spread across Monique's face, marring its beauty. She placed her hands on her hips. "You really think Jackson is happy with you? Well, he isn't. He's always calling me and telling me how much he misses me." The hateful smile was replaced with naked hatred. "He wanted a lady for a wife. I don't know what for. What does a lady know about making a man happy in bed? And that's all men are really interested in, you know. Sex. It makes their world go round. I should know. I make big money off the husbands of so-called ladies."

Brandeis glanced around to see if anyone had heard the shocking things Monique was saying.

"What's the matter, *Mrs. Gray*? Are you afraid I'll embarrass you?" Monique laughed harshly. "It's just like I figured. You high-and-mighty women are useless! A good woman would stand up and fight for her man."

"I don't lower myself to carry on verbal confrontations with whores," Brandeis replied. "And I don't have to fight for my man because there's *no* threat to our marriage."

Monique's voice lowered. "I loved Jackson!" she hissed. "I would have done anything for him. Anything! But he married *you.*"

Brandeis heard the pain in Monique's voice, saw it in her eyes, but she didn't care. "It was his choice, Monique," she said. *"Jackson wanted me and not you!* What you need to do now is get a life."

"Well, he doesn't love you anymore," Monique babbled. "He told me so. He's just staying with you because of his son. He doesn't—"

Brandeis held up her hand. "Don't waste your time lying to me, Monique. I don't want to hear it. I know you were the one telling Jackson all that crap about Martin and me. Anyway, it no longer matters, Monique. My husband and I love each other. There's nothing you can do or say to change that. The only person to lose in this game you're playing is you. You lost your self-respect a long time ago, but now, you've lost a really good friend in Jackson. I feel sorry for you."

"Oh, don't feel sorry for me," Monique said, trying desperately to salvage some pride. "Save it for yourself. You won't be able to hold on to him, either. He'll leave you just like he did me, when he tires of you. No woman can hang on to a man like Jackson. Mark my words, he'll get tired of you, sugar. Just you wait and see!"

"Even if he does leave me, *sugar*, it will not be because of you. It'll be because of something I've *really* done." Brandeis started to walk away, but turned to face Monique once more. "Oh, and, *sugar*, you may want to start thinking about a career change. You're getting a little flabby!" Brandeis took Carol's arm and walked away, leaving Monique standing in the parking lot, amazed, and tongue-tied.

"I guess you told her!" Carol said as she held the door to the restaurant open.

"What I really wanted to do was wring her neck!" Brandeis admitted.

"One fight at Applebees per family, please," Carol said under her breath as she scanned her menu.

Brandeis glanced up and laughed. "Okay, Carol."

"I heard the strangest rumor," Carol whispered. "That Carrie is marrying Martin. Is that true?"

"I'm afraid it is. I wish she could see what she's getting herself into," Brandeis said.

"Didn't you try to talk to her?"

"Yes. You know how she feels about me. She's too stubborn to listen."

"She's very young, Bran," Carol said sadly. "Some people have to learn the hard way."

The waitress brought their food. Brandeis was about to take a bite when she dropped her sandwich back on her plate. She could not believe her eyes. She felt her stomach churn. Seated at a corner table with a young woman Brandeis did not recognize, was Martin.

"What is it, Bran?" Carrie looked around until she, too, spotted Martin and his lunch companion. "Well, well, well. Looks like the groom-to-be is already bored. He's on to his next victim."

"I guess so." She sighed. "Poor Carrie. She really wants someone to love her."

"For that, she'll have to find herself a real man, and not some wannabe!"

"Carol!"

"Well?"

Brandeis laughed. "Hurry up and eat. I want to get out of here before he spots us."

"Looks like they're leaving. Good! They are. Now we can enjoy ourselves."

Martin was getting tired of all the talk of a wedding. He had to get out of here. He had no intention of ever marrying Carrie. She wanted to have a big wedding before she started to show.

Carrie was thumbing through various travel brochures and magazines. Travel literature was spread all over the dining room table. "Martin!"

"What?"

"You're not listening me. I was asking where we should go on our honeymoon."

He frowned. "I can't afford to take you on a honeymoon. I spent all my savings to get you that rock."

"I'll pay for our honeymoon."

"If you want a big fancy wedding, you'll have to pay for everything."

Carrie tried to ignore all the doubts creeping into her mind. Something was not quite right. As soon as she'd had the charges dropped, Martin had started acting sullen, like before.

Maybe she needed to give him a little reminder. "You know, my dad is still furious over my dropping the charges. He thinks I'm crazy for wanting to marry you."

That got Martin's attention. "Your dad just doesn't like me."

"Would you be crazy about someone who beats up your daughter?"

"No. I'd give the ba—"

"Exactly. Daddy says that as long as you treat me good, you'll be okay. He says the minute you lay another hand on me, he'll kill you."

"Your dad doesn't have to worry. I've changed, baby. I really have. Now, where are we going on our honeymoon?"

Carrie smiled and pointed to the Poconos Mountains brochure.

"I think we should go here. They have champagne-glass-shaped baths, heart-shaped Jacuzzis, and beds . . ."

How am I going to get the hell outta this? Martin wondered. He pushed his chair back from the table and stood up. He took the brochure from Carrie's hand and tossed it on the table. "I'm tired of talking, baby." He pulled her out of her chair.

Carrie moved into his arms. "What would you prefer to do, lover?"

He embraced her tightly. "I'm crazy 'bout you, girl. I can't keep my hands off you."

"Do you love me? You don't say it very often. Please tell me that you love me."

Martin bent his head and captured her mouth in a rapturous kiss. She clung to him as the touch of his lips sent pleasure pulsing through her. She returned his kiss passionately and from the depth of her heart.

Martin carried her into the bedroom. As he undressed, he thought, *This should take her mind off weddings for a while.*

Chapter 21

Brandeis got up from the vanity and turned down her bed. She switched on the lamp on her writing desk, then went to the armoire and withdrew a robe.

After belting the sash, Brandeis sat down to begin work on her admissions application to Howard University's School of Law. After a while, she turned off the desk lamp and walked over to the bed.

Jackson stood in the doorway, smiling. "Hi, honey. I'm home."

Brandeis turned to the sound of his voice. "I was wondering when you'd make it home."

"Why? Did you miss me?"

"Of course I missed you."

"I thought I'd find Brian with you. Has he gone to bed this early?"

"Yes. He played for a little while after we left Mom's house. I gave him a bath and a good rub down. He went right to sleep."

"Mmmm, a good rub down sounds good." Jackson pressed her lips to his.

She pulled away. "Take off your suit. I'll run a bath and join you. What do you think about that?"

"I think that's a brilliant idea."

Brandeis placed his jacket and tie on a hanger. "Oh, Jackson, you'll never believe who I ran into today."

"Who? Not Martin?"

"Well, yes. But not in the way you're thinking. He was at Applebees ... with another woman. Not Carrie. He didn't see me, but Carol and I saw him. We also ran into Monique."

"What?" Jackson cried.

"We saw Monique. She came over to talk to me in the parking lot. She tried to make me believe you weren't happy with me. That you wanted her."

"If I ever see that slut—"

"Jackson, just let it go," Brandeis pleaded. "We have each other. That's all that really matters. Isn't it? As long as we live, people are going to talk and tell lies. We can't do anything about that. However, we *can* choose not to give them a place in our lives. It's up to us who we believe. Who we trust."

"I guess you're right," Jackson whispered. He came to stand behind her.

She felt his hand gently stroke the tips of her breasts through the translucent material of her purple lace teddy. Desire began to flow throughout her veins. Her hand sought the hard, sinewy strength of his thigh and caressed it.

Jackson picked her up and carried her to the waiting bed. She watched as he stripped his clothes from his body. His evident arousal sent violent shivers of wanting through her. Strong, masculine hands cupped the soft mounds of her buttocks, pressing her to the powerful length of him. First he was on top, then she, in a dance of passion.

Later, as they lay in each other's arms, exhausted but satisfied, Jackson asked, "How about that bath?"

"Ready when you are. Only now, we have to run a new bath. The water's cold by now."

"Oh, I don't know. We can probably generate enough body heat to keep it hot." His mouth came down on hers hungrily.

"Mmmm, I think you're right." Brandeis climbed out of bed. She held her hand out to him and together they walked to the large roman tub. Jackson got in first and assisted Brandeis. Pulling her close, he placed himself into her. Skin against skin, two hearts beating in harmony, they soared higher and higher until, with mingled cries of fulfillment, they found their release.

"Ma'am, this is not a diamond."

"What?" Carrie could not believe her ears. "It's not eighteen-carat gold either?"

"The cubic zirconia sits in an eighteen-carat gold setting. It's a high-quality fake."

"That can't be true. It just can't be." Humiliation filled Carrie to the core. She stood there, shaking her head.

"Ma'am?"

"N-nothing. I'm sorry," she mumbled as she rushed out of the store. She was so embarrassed. *It's a high-quality fake! That bastard. He's done it again. He conned me again!* Tears threatened to spill. *Brandeis tried to warn me, but I wouldn't listen.*

Carrie stomped into her apartment and slammed the door. Martin walked out of the bedroom with a dazzling smile. She threw the ring at him, narrowly missing his eye. "I have tried to be good to you. All I ever asked in return was for you to love me. How could you be so cruel?"

His smile disappeared. "Girl, what's wrong with you?"

"That ring! It's not real. You gave me a cubic zirconia."

"Where in hell did you get that idea?" Martin knew he had to think fast. She could ruin everything for him.

"I took it to the jewelry store to get it appraised. I planned to have it insured. The clerk there said it was a high-quality fake. I felt like the world's biggest fool!"

"Look, I bought the ring from a friend," Martin said.

"From Mitch. I gave him all the money I had. He told me the ring was real. It looked real to me. I'm sorry. I guess I don't know much about diamonds. Please believe me when I say it wasn't intentional."

Carrie didn't know whether to believe Martin or not. Was this another lie? She wanted so much to believe he loved her. She needed to be loved by someone.

"I bet he's spread it all over town by now, how he fooled me," Martin said, getting into his lie. "He's nothing but a gossip. Why, he's worse than any woman I know. I'm so sorry, baby. I thought it was real. I really did. I'm going to hunt down that son of a b—"

Carrie ran to stop him from leaving. "Martin, no! You don't have to do something stupid. Don't worry about it. If it was an innocent mistake, fine. You can just get me another ring. A real diamond. I have a credit card from Freemans. We can go back there. That ought to stop Mitch from running his mouth."

"Sure, sure thing." Martin struggled to keep from laughing. She was so gullible! Desperate wench! He went to her and pulled her into his arms. "I love you, baby. I just wanted to show you how much. I didn't know I was getting ripped off. I wanted to get you a ring you'd be able to wear proudly." *There. That's a nice touch,* he thought.

"It's okay. I understand. You trusted someone and he betrayed you. I know what that feels like," Carrie said.

Martin was a little unnerved. Was Carrie referring to him? No, she was too desperate to marry him. He put his arms around her and held her tight. Then, he kissed her passionately. "Mmmm, I do love you so."

He really does love me. It wouldn't feel like this if he didn't, Carrie thought as she felt sensation after sensation. She didn't resist when he opened her white blouse, revealing a lacy bra. She unbuttoned his shirt as their tongues did a sensual dance. Soon, their clothes were strewn through the apartment, blazing a trail to the bedroom.

Afterward, Carrie sat up and reached for her robe. "I'm hungry, honey. You want something to eat?"

"Sure. I wish I could take you out . . ."

"Not tonight. I've got to go to an office function." She ran into the bathroom and took a quick shower.

Martin was still in bed when she came out. "What function?"

"Didn't I tell you?" Carrie pulled a fushia pantsuit from her closet. "Brandeis and Jackson are moving to D.C. They're leaving next weekend."

Martin wanted to bash her head in. Carrie knew damn well she hadn't told him. He knew she hadn't intended to say anything until the happy couple had left town.

"What were you gonna do? Try to keep it a secret from me?"

Carrie's eyes issued a challenge. "No. What concern is it of yours anyway? Do you still want her?"

"Hell, no!" Martin's mind was working furiously. He wasn't about to let Brandeis get away from him that easily. He had to move, now!

"Martin, why do you care what she does?" Carrie pressed.

"I'm not interested in her, baby. I'm just surprised, that's all." Martin watched Carrie dress, his mind busy. He could strangle her for trying to play games with him! Did Carrie really think she could keep him from getting what he wanted most? No damn way! He would just have to act sooner than he'd originally planned.

Brandeis cocked her head to one side, and listened. Out of the corner of her eye she could see the clock on the nightstand. It was after 11 A.M., too late for Jackson still to be home. He'd had to be in court by nine o'clock.

But there was the unmistakable sound of footsteps. Brandeis padded barefoot to the door. She fingered the belt on her jeans as she moved along the hallway to the baby's room. Below her, there was silence again. She waited, barely breathing. Just at the point where she began to believe she had imagined it, she heard the sounds again.

As Brandeis stealthily continued on to Brian's room, she realized she'd not considered a weapon. She glanced about the hallway, looking for something to use to protect herself and her son. She saw nothing and hurried to Brian's door.

There was silence again and Brandeis learned firsthand how it was possible for silence to be deafening. Blood rushed in her ears, her heart slammed in her chest, and her imagination marched ahead double time.

Outside her son's room, she pressed her ear to the door. He must still be sleeping. She carefully turned the handle.

It took a single step into the room to know she was not alone. She felt the presence of another person, the warmth of a body behind her, the tension of fear, the barely audible hum of controlled breathing.

Her first instinct was to rush to her baby. Almost immediately, something clamped over her mouth. It took her a moment to identify the thing over her mouth as a hand.

As she fought for breath, another hand captured her wrist and squeezed. The realization that no one could hear her made Brandeis redouble her efforts. She kicked backward, connecting twice in her struggles, but the hold on her never relented. She tried to bite before she sensed a creeping blackness at the edge of her vision. The pressure in her chest became enormous and she clawed at the hand over her mouth. The last thing she remembered was a familiar voice near her ear, the breath hot and damp, telling her to shut up.

She didn't imagine she was unconscious long. When she woke, she was on her bed.

"You're awake."

The voice came to her from across the room. It was only a husky whisper, but she had no problem making out the words.

Brandeis turned her head toward the voice. *It was Martin!* Finding her voice, she asked, "How did you get in here?"

"Don't worry 'bout that. Just pack a bag and let's get moving. I'm tired of playing games. You're mine and so is this kid."

"I don't belong to you, and neither does my child," she said.

"Look, we gotta go. Grab the baby and come on."

"I'm not going anywhere with you."

"If you don't, I'll just take the kid and split." Martin pulled out his gun. "What's it going to be? Are you going, or am I just taking the kid?"

"I'm not going to just let you walk out of here with my baby," Brandeis cried.

"You can't do too much about it if you're dead," Martin said coldly.

"I'll go with you." Brandeis sighed. Oh, how she wished Jackson was here.

"If you're hoping for your husband," Martin said, "he's in court, all day today."

"How do you know that?" Brandeis was startled.

"I called his office. I'm telling you this one last time. Come on, or I'll just shoot you here and take the kid. You belong to me. If I can't have you, I'll be damned if Jackson gets to keep you and live happily ever after."

Brandeis retrieved her sleeping son, diaper bag, and some extra clothes.

"You don't need to take all that stuff. I'll buy you whatever you need," Martin said, motioning with the gun for her to hurry.

"I need to pack some of his formula and bottles. He has to eat, Martin!"

"Fine. Just hurry, damn it!"

With Martin watching her, Brandeis glanced around her kitchen, chiding herself for already having packed away all of the knives.

"Come on, Brandeis. We need to get on the road. I want to be well on our way by noon."

"Where are you taking us?" she asked.

"You'll see when you get there. I'm not going to tell you in case you try to get away from me. I'm not stupid."

Brandeis thought otherwise, but with Martin standing

there, pointing a gun at her, she decided now was not the time to tell him so.

In a few minutes, they were in the car. They drove in silence. Brandeis looked back at her sleeping son.

"He's a beautiful child, Brandeis," Martin said.

"Yes, he is. Why are you doing this to us?"

"I love you," he said simply. "I love you and that baby is a part of you. I know how much you would miss him so I decided he would come with us. I want us to be a family."

"You don't get it! You just don't get it, Martin," Brandeis said, her voice husky with shock. "We can never be a family. I have a husband. Even if I weren't married, I wouldn't want you."

"Why not?" Martin asked. "You loved me in the beginning. Everything was fine 'til you got it in your head that I raped you."

"You *did* rape me."

"I'm tired of you telling this lie," Martin shouted. "I didn't rape you that night. You wanted me as much as I wanted you. I could see it in your eyes. You just got too much of that church talk in your head. I had some of those saintly women from your church and you know what? They're so freaky. No better than a whore, if you ask me."

"I don't care who you've been with," Brandeis replied. "I didn't want to take our relationship to that next step. I planned on waiting for my wedding night. You robbed me of that. The one gift I wanted to give my husband and you took it from me."

"If you'd married me, it would've been different. I took your virginity so I could marry you," Martin explained. "I knew that was the only way I could have you. I left town so that you had time to get over being angry with me. I was hoping you had gotten pregnant. That way, I knew I could come back any time I wanted. I told you I wanted to marry you. I meant that."

"Martin! I didn't want to marry *you*. I never wanted to marry you."

The car screeched to a sudden halt. Martin turned to

her. "Liar!" he shouted. "You just can't be honest with yourself. You were falling for me. I know you were. I treated you like a queen. Went to church, acted real proper toward you. I did all the things I know you'd like."

"Yes, you did, but it was all a lie, wasn't it? I had feelings for you but you didn't give me a chance to make my own choices. You wanted to rush me into giving you a commitment that I'd marry you."

"I wanted you from the first time I saw you, Brandeis," Martin went on. "I know you felt the same way. We—"

Brandeis didn't want to hear anymore. "Martin, please take me home. I want to go home to my husband."

"You can't go home," Martin said. *"I'm* gonna be your husband. We already have a son."

"He's *my* son. Mine and Jackson's."

"I know the boy is mine so stop your lying!"

Brandeis was scared. Martin had a crazed look on his face. She wondered if he really believed all the things he was saying. "Please, take us home."

"Shut up!" Martin glared at her as he started the car and slowly made his way back into traffic.

"Jackson's not going to let you get away with this," she said.

"Jackson can't do nothing 'bout this. Now, shut up!"

"Stop yelling at me. You're scaring my son!"

As if on cue the baby started to wail. Brandeis turned to try to comfort the child.

"Look, I'm sorry," Martin said. "I got a lot on my mind right now."

"I'll bet," she muttered.

"What'd you say?"

"Nothing."

"Where is Martin?" Jackson demanded as he stormed into Carrie's apartment.

"What the hell is your problem? You got some nerve coming in here like this." Carrie had no idea what was going on. She had been napping when she heard the knocking and yelling. As soon as she'd opened the door, Jackson blew in like a hurricane.

"He's taken Brandeis and the baby."

"*Who's* taken Brandeis and the baby?" Carrie feared she already knew the answer. She struggled for breath.

"Martin!"

"No, that not true! He wouldn't do this to me. He left a note saying he had some errands to run. He'll be back. You'll see." Carrie clutched her stomach. *He said he loved her. Could he do this to her?*

"I'm afraid he's not coming back," Jackson said grimly. "Look, Carrie. I'm sorry to be the one to tell you this, but he's been using you. Don't protect him anymore. Now, think. Where would he take them? Would he go back to Savannah?"

She dropped her lashes quickly to hide the hurt. "I-I d-don't know." Carrie wiped the back of her hand across her face to stop the flow of tears.

"Carrie, I'm so sorry to put you through this, but I really need your help. That bastard has my wife and son. Think!" Jackson was frantic with worry.

"He used to talk about this piece of property his grandfather left him in Villa Rica—"

"Where?"

"In Villa Rica. It's about twenty miles outside of Atlanta. He said that's where he wanted to settle down. He said that's where we were going to live."

"Did he tell you exactly *where* in Villa Rica?" Jackson pressed.

"No, but it shouldn't be hard to find. He said it was a really small town. Jackson," Carrie said, "what makes you think Martin took them?"

"Miss Mamie saw them getting into his car when she was leaving her sister's house. She said he had a gun pointed at Brandeis' back."

"Mamie's nothing but a blind bat!" Carrie cried. "A

nosy ol' bat. I don't believe it. Martin wouldn't do something so terrible!''

"She swears that's what she saw. She called the police and then had Mona call me. She wouldn't have made up something so horrible."

"Then the police should find them in no time. Martin left here in his Volvo. The one I was paying for," Carrie said dryly.

"They've changed cars. The police found the Volvo abandoned on Highway Three Forty-one.''

"I can't believe he did this to me," Carrie said. "He said he loved me. I believed him. That bastard!''

Martin ordered food from the drive through window at McDonald's.

Brandeis knew she had to think quickly before he left Brunswick too far behind. "Before we leave, I really need to go to the ladies' room," she said.

"If you go, I'll have to go with you."

"I'm not going to run away," Brandeis replied. "Where would I go with a baby?"

Martin was thoughtful. Finally, he pulled over into a parking space. "Okay, but I'll be right outside the bathroom door. Don't do somethin' stupid. And don't be thinkin' you gonna go in there and have a conversation. You'd better not talk to anybody. Do you hear me, girl?"

She glared at him but said nothing. They got out of the car and Martin locked the doors.

Before letting her into the ladies' room, he peeked inside. Not seeing anyone or hearing anything, he stepped aside to let her enter.

Brandeis searched her purse for a pen and piece of paper. She intended to leave a message for Jackson. A young, blonde-haired woman with the bluest eyes Brandeis had ever seen, came out of the last stall, giving her a start. She had thought the bathroom empty. Brandeis thanked God it wasn't.

She rushed over to the woman and quickly explained her circumstances. "I know this is going to sound crazy, but you've got to help me. I've been kidnapped. I need you to call my husband." She wrote down Jackson's pager number, cellular phone number and office number on a paper towel. She also included the roads they were traveling. "Stay here until I leave. You'll be safer."

She quickly changed the baby while the woman stood silently by, watching. Brandeis knew the woman was trying to discern if she was telling the truth. When Brian was in a new diaper, she once again pleaded for help.

Finally, the woman agreed. "Why won't you let me go get the manager?"

"Because Martin is standing right outside this door and he has a gun. I believe if he's cornered he'll use it, and I don't want anybody to get hurt."

Before Brandeis walked out, she looked back at the woman and mouthed a final thank-you.

She opened the door. Martin was there.

"I was 'bout to come looking for you." There was an suspicious edge to his voice.

"I had to change the baby. He was dirty," Brandeis replied, pleased at how nonchalant she sounded.

"Hmmm." He stopped and turned toward the bathroom. "Maybe I should go check to see if you left any messages for help." A satanic smile spread across his lips.

Brandeis wondered how she had ever thought him handsome. Trying not to show fear, she opened her purse. "See. I have nothing in here but my keys, a brush and my checkbook. I don't have a pen and I have no cosmetics. How on earth could I even attempt to leave a message? I thought I was the only woman you claim to trust. Apparently, you don't trust me, either," Brandeis said, trying to sound offended.

Martin seemed satisfied with her answer. "Sorry, but I have to be careful cause you're not thinking straight."

"I *would* have left a message if I'd had the means," she said. *Please, let that woman help me,* she prayed fervently.

"Com'on, we need to get a move on. I want to be miles away from here by sundown."

About fifteen minutes later, Brian started to cry. Brandeis tried everything she could think of to soothe him.

"Why is he crying like that?" The baby's wailing was beginning to get on Martin's nerves.

"Because he wants to be held. He's been in that car seat for a while. Pull over, so I can sit back there with him."

"Hell, no. I'm not a fool. You'll try to jump out, try to choke me or somethin' like that."

"Then I would only succeed in killing us all. If my son weren't in this car, I might try something. As long as my baby's here, I won't do anything to put him in danger."

"Aren't you mother of the year!" Martin sneered.

"I love my child." Brandeis smiled smoothly, betraying nothing of her true feelings. She hated Martin. She turned around and sang a lullaby. Brian quieted and after a few minutes, he fell to sleep.

"You're a good mother, Brandeis." Martin's expression suddenly turned sad. "He should have been mine."

"Why?"

"I love you, Brandeis. You're different from all the other women."

"Different in what way? Surely, I'm not the only one who didn't fall into bed with you."

Martin glanced at her as if she'd grown three heads. "What? Girl, you're the kind of woman a man marries. You're a good girl. Not the kind of girl who sleeps with every man she meets. I wanted me a virgin. My mom said I should only marry a virgin."

"And did your mother tell you to rape a woman if she refuses?" she asked quietly.

"I made love to you. I know you wanted me. I could tell from the looks you gave me. Plus, I treated you damn good. You know, women always complaining about not being able to find someone good and then when you do, you don't know how to act. I'm a real man, Brandeis. That's the kind a woman like you needs. When we made love—"

Brandeis could contain her fury no longer. "Martin, you raped me! You refuse to admit the truth but it was *rape.*"

"How in the hell can you say that?" he shouted. "We loved each other. We were going to be married."

Brandeis' rage mounted. She yelled as loudly as she could, ignoring the frightened sound of her son's crying. "You violated my rights. You damaged my feelings of self-worth. You damaged my marriage with your filthy lies. Furthermore, you never even had the guts to apologize for hurting me. You're a sick bastard and I hate you. Do you hear me, *I hate you!*"

Brian continued to scream and Brandeis turned to comfort her child. "I'm sorry, darling. Mommy didn't mean to scare you. Mommy loves you dearly," she cooed.

"No woman has ever told me no," he mumbled. "Oh, they start out saying it but they never mean it." He grabbed Brandeis by the arm, causing her to face him. "I don't owe you no apology. I loved you, hell, I still love you. Can't I make that clear to you?"

"Love? You don't know the meaning of the word. You want to control me, not love me. Sick bastard!" Brandeis' body shook with anger.

"Stop calling me that! I'm not sick," Martin said, "I thought you was a respectable girl. A man needs to find himself a wife he can trust. One he can be proud of."

"What about Carrie? Don't you care anything about her?"

"She was just a means to an end. I wanted to make sure you were okay—"

"Okay?" Brandeis forced herself to keep her voice even. "In what way?"

"I wanted to know whether or not you were carrying my child. I called and checked on you all the time. Then you up and married that son of a bi—"

"Whoa, I wouldn't go there, if I were you," Brandeis warned. "Jackson is the kindest, most decent man I've ever met. He loves me, really loves me."

"What I don't understand," Martin went on, as if Brandeis hadn't spoken, "is how you could get married and have sex if I supposedly raped you. Seems to me you'd still be scared of men."

Brandeis put her hands to her head. "Martin, there is a greater love than even the biggest sin. Only a few people are lucky enough to find it. I count myself among the fortunate."

"Yeah, well, we'll see what you say when we get to where we're going. I intend to have you again, Brandeis. I'll make you forget that uppity Negro." Martin leered at her.

Brandeis said nothing. She shivered despite the warmth of the car. It took her a moment to realize it wasn't the car's air-conditioning that set her teeth to chattering, but a frigid ache of fear.

She hardly noticed the wash of tears that began to stream down her cheeks. Brandeis felt as though she were dissolving with those tears.

"Oh, J-Jackson," she murmured, and with the words came a wave of grief and loss. The sobs that shook her left her shaking and weak. Finally, the flood slowed to a stream, and the stream to a trickle.

Martin reached over to put his arm around her, but she pushed it away.

"Don't touch me. D-don't you ever t-touch me again!"

"It'll be easier on you if you accept what's to be, Brandeis," he said. "I'm not trying to hurt you. I just want to love you. Damn! Why is everything so hard with you?"

"I don't love you, Martin. Any feelings I might have had for you died when you raped me," she stated flatly.

"Stop saying that!" Martin cried.

Brandeis could feel his eyes on her as she stared out the window. "Shouldn't you keep your eyes on the road? I'd hate for anything to happen to us," she said. Her mind raced with revenge fantasies.

Martin frowned, but turned his eyes to the road.

Brandeis prayed the woman in the ladies' room had called Jackson and the police. She prayed Jackson would find them soon.

Chapter 22

Jackson clicked on his cellular phone. He exited off the closest ramp and headed north. He had just spoken to the police and knew they had no idea which roads Martin was traveling. His hands tightened their grip on the steering wheel as he thought about his family in the hands of that crazed . . .

The ringing of his phone jarred him from his murderous thoughts. It was the police again, cautioning him not to do anything rash. They explained that they had everything under control.

Jackson could endure death and torture, but not the thought of his beautiful wife and son in Martin's hands. Jackson felt a rage well up within him. Then it ebbed, leaving him weak, as he realized his helplessness to aid his wife and child. The police had no idea what type of car Martin was driving. The thought made him physically ill as well as heartsick. The longer they went without finding his wife and son, the harder it was for him to retain hope. Yet, at that moment, without his realizing it, he determined to find his family. He would find them and get his revenge.

Although he'd agreed to head straight to the nearest

Highway Patrol Office, Jackson knew he wouldn't. He couldn't. His promise of protecting Brandeis wouldn't let him. Just as he was about to pull into a rest area, his phone rang.

"Yes?"

The voice on the other end was trembling. "H-hello. Is this Jackson Gray?"

"Yes it is. Who is this?"

"Look. I was just given a message for you in the ladies' bathroom at a McDonald's. It's from someone named Bran . . . Brandis . . ."

"Brandeis. She's my wife and she's been kidnapped." His voice was hoarse in his frustration.

"She told me that. The man's name is Martin. Martin St. Charles. She said they were traveling down Highway Eighty-two, heading to Waycross. I went to the bathroom right before she came in. I stayed in there until they left the restaurant so the man wouldn't know she talked to somebody. As soon as they got to the parking lot, I got the manager. We tried to see the license tag, but we couldn't. I did see what kind of car he was driving though. It's a ninety-one Nissan Maxima. Charcoal gray."

"Thank you so much for your help," Jackson said, hope flooding his body. "Have you called the police?"

"Yes, they're on their way here. I'm so sorry. I wish I could have done more to help your wife and son. She said the man had a gun."

"You've been a great help," Jackson said. "Please tell me your name."

"It's Joni. Joni Habersham. I'm praying that you find your wife and baby," she said.

"Thank you, Joni. I would like you to keep this number and call me in a week or so. My wife and I will want to thank you personally after all this is over."

"That's not necessary—"

"It is for me," Jackson said. "Please call me."

"I will. God be with you."

His body vibrated with new life as he thought about his

beautiful and intelligent wife. He didn't know how she was able to pull this off but what a brilliant idea. He reached once more for his phone, and placed calls to the highway patrol and to Mona.

"Martin, you look tired and you've been driving for hours. Why don't you let me drive for a while?"

"Hell, no! I'm okay. I know if I let you drive, we'll be on our way back to Brunswick."

"Then why don't we pull over? You can get some rest."

"I said, I'm fine." Martin was trying desperately to fight sleep. He was so tired but he wanted to be in Villa Rica by nightfall. Having the flat tire and no spare cost them precious hours. They had to sit and wait forty-five minutes before they could be towed to the nearest gas station. Then, they had to wait another thirty or forty minutes for the mechanic to return from his lunch.

Brandeis was tired, too, but she could not rest peacefully. She wanted to look behind them, but she didn't want to alarm Martin. She prayed the woman in the McDonald's restroom had called the police and Jackson.

Suddenly, Martin was alert. "What the hell!" He kept glancing into his rearview mirror. "I think we're being chased by the police."

Brandeis turned around. Her heart leaped with joy at what she saw. Several patrol cars flashing red and blue lights were racing toward them. Her happiness faded as they flew past them. A chill of apprehension slid down her spine as Martin grinned at her.

"I bet you thought they was coming to save you and that kid back there. Well, they ain't. I'm beginning to wonder if that husband of yours even wants you back."

She glared at him defiantly, hatred in her eyes. "If you expect me to admit defeat, you'll have a long wait. Jackson promised to protect me and he will."

"You are a fool," he growled.

Brandeis felt the lurch of Martin's car as he increased his speed. "What are you doing?"

"That car has been following us for a while now. It won't come close enough for me to see what kind it is and it won't pass me."

Brandeis turned around slowly. Her heart was hopeful. It was a Mercedes. She could tell from the headlights. Instinctively, she knew it was Jackson. He was here! He would save them.

"I'm not gonna take any chances," Martin said. He never saw the barest hint of a smile on her face.

"I'm gonna outrun this fool. I'm not gonna let them take my family from me." He pressed his foot down on the gas and sent the car shooting ahead.

Brandeis closed her eyes as they got dangerously close to a Ford Explorer. Martin looked as if he were going to force its driver right off the road. "Martin, please think of our safety. The baby's in the car. Besides, you don't really know for sure that car is following us."

Brandeis hoped with all her heart she and her son would be saved from this madman at the wheel. Up ahead, she could see the flashing lights of the police cars. They were coming back this way. *Oh Lord, please protect my innocent baby. He doesn't deserve this,* she prayed.

"Martin, the baby is in the car," Brandeis pleaded. "Please don't kill him. Stop the car and let us out. Please, let us go. I won't press charges. I promise. Please don't do this to my innocent child."

"The baby. Yeah, the baby," Martin muttered. "My son. He's my son."

Brandeis tried to think quickly. She didn't want her son to die. She didn't want to die. Maybe if she went along with this fool. "Yes, he's your son. Please slow down, please."

Martin turned to face her. "You lying bitch! You really think I'm crazy, don't you? I know that brat's not mine. I can add, ya know. You're nothing but a lying whore just like all the rest."

Brandeis shuddered. "Martin, please pay attention to

the road. I think there's some kind of accident up ahead. You're going to kill us all." No sooner had the words come out of her mouth than she realized that was exactly his intent. She closed her eyes and fervently prayed for divine intervention.

Martin pushed at the accelerator. At that instant, a truck roared around a curve toward them, its bright lights blinding Brandeis. Martin lost control of the car. She felt a tremendous lurch of springs and rubber. Gravel spattering. Then, a twisting of smashed metal.

Brandeis could hear someone screaming. She didn't realize it was her voice she was hearing. She fell forward. The last thing she heard was the frightened wail of her son.

Jackson rushed to the twisted, tangled mass of what was once the front end of the car. The pungent smell of gasoline assaulted him. His heart sank as he saw all the blood. So much blood. *"Oh, God, no . . . no,"* he cried. *"Please don't let her be dead."* In that moment he felt beaten, broken, exhausted to the very depths of his soul. He breathed a deep sigh of release when he felt a faint pulse at Brandeis' wrist.

Without too much trouble, Jackson was able to jar open the back door and safely retrieve his son. Quickly, he put Brian in his car, locked the doors, and returned to Brandeis. He found himself looking into the icy green eyes of Martin. In his hand was a match. He made several attempts before it finally ignited.

"If I can't . . . h-have her. Y-you . . . can't either. I'll b-blow up this here . . . car. She gonna die with me," he grunted.

Jackson thought hard about their situation. He would have to move Brandeis and move her quickly. He was hesitant. He didn't know the extent of her injuries. Quickly, he picked up a hand full of dirt and threw it at Martin.

"Wha—" Martin tried to rise up and dropped the burning match.

Jackson was frantic. He had hoped the dirt would put out the match. Without another thought, he grabbed Brandeis from the wreckage. He was halfway to his car when he felt the force of an explosion. He fell on top of his wife, covering her completely. She never made a sound. Suddenly, they were surrounded by dozens of police cars. In the distance, he could hear the blaring siren of an ambulance.

Jackson looked up, tears running down his cheeks. "Please help her," he cried. "Please save my wife. I had to get her out of that car. I h-had to. Please God, don't let her die . . ."

"Where is my wife?" Jackson demanded. "I need to be with her. Where is my son?"

"Sir, your wife is in surgery and your son is being examined as we speak. Why don't you have a seat over there. As soon as we know something, we'll let you know."

Jackson had been pacing the floor since arriving at the hospital. No amount of cajoling or direct orders could make him sit down. Finally, he decided to take a walk. He walked past the chapel, then backtracked. He paused for just a second before opening the door.

In the chapel, Jackson knelt down and prayed. *Oh, dear God, please let them be okay. Please don't take my family away from me. I had to save Bran. I had to. I couldn't bear to lose her.*

Jackson hoped he hadn't caused Bran more damage by moving her, but he couldn't let her burn in the car with that maniac.

Mona found him sitting with his face in his hands. She came in and sat beside him.

He looked up at Mona. "If Brandeis dies, it'll be my fault. I don't think I should have moved her like that. Then the explosion, the force of it . . . I . . ." Jackson could not finish.

"Jackson, you did exactly what you were supposed to

do," Mona whispered. "If you hadn't moved her, she would be dead for sure. She's still alive because of you. Remember that." Mona wiped away her tears. "Goodness, Jackson, where is our faith? Bran is a fighter. S-she's going to pull through. I have to believe that."

The doctor opened the chapel door. His eyes were full of compassion as he walked toward Jackson and Mona. "Mrs. Gray came through surgery okay. She's still in critical condition. We have no idea whether she'll pull through right now. We'll know more in a few hours."

Jackson could tell by the doctor's grim face that Brandeis was hovering near death. "When can I see her?" he asked quietly.

"You can see her now, if you'd like," the doctor replied.

Before he could ask about his son, a nurse joined them, carrying Brian. She handed him to Jackson. Except for a few cuts and bruises, Brian seemed fine. Scared, but fine.

Jackson kissed his son. "I pray that your mother lives. We need her," he whispered.

Mona reached for Brian. "I'll take him, Jackson. You go to Bran. She needs you now." She carried the baby to a chair where she sat and crooned to him, holding him tightly to her breast. "Oh, precious. How's my little precious sweetheart?" She whispered.

Jackson turned his attention back to the doctor. "You said I could see my wife now?"

"Yes, but remember, you can only stay for a few minutes."

Jackson ran to the emergency surgery recovery room and fell down into the chair beside Bran's bed. He stared at the mass of bandages that swathed her head, chest, and left leg. Her face was ashen and her breaths were scarcely more than whispers. He kissed her lips, which were winter cold.

"You can't die, honey," he whispered. "Brian and I need you. Please don't leave us." Hot tears flowed down his cheeks. "I love you." We've been through a lot and we've made it, baby. Don't give up now. We'll get through this, sweetheart."

Brandeis floated in and out of consciousness. She tried to fight her way out of the blackness that enveloped her, but the swirling mist held her in its grip. Her moan was soft and pained.

He smoothed the dark strands of hair from her cheeks.

She tried to talk. "J-Jack . . . son," she gasped. A numb floating sensation gave her body no boundaries. Her arms and legs seem detached. Brandeis ordered them to move, but they remained listless, connected to a body too exhausted and sore to move.

The pain reliever she had been given was doing little to ease her discomfort but was increasing her sense of disorientation. She felt as though her mind was staggering through a field of cotton balls. The pain did not go away, but receded into a corner of the nightmare and stayed there, mocking her with its persistence. And as it did so, she realized for the first time where its centers were. They were her abdomen and her face. From them radiated tendrils that fed pain into her spine, her hips, and her left leg. A wavery grayness soon drew her down in a restless sleep.

"I'm here, honey. I'm here." Jackson felt her squeeze his hand. She sighed but didn't open her eyes.

Time passed at an excruciatingly slow pace, but Jackson found much comfort in the knowledge that each minute Brandeis lived, she was growing stronger. Mona came in and sat with her. Every now and then, her lips moved but the words would not come. Her eyes didn't open.

Mona eased beside Jackson, massaging his shoulders. "Why don't you go home and get some rest. I'll stay with her tonight. Carol is going to take Brian back to the hotel with her."

Jackson shook his head. "No, Mom. I'm not leaving her. I am not going to leave, Bran. I intend to be here when she wakes up."

"I understand, dear. I'm going to ride with Carol to the hotel. Please call us if . . ."

"I will." Jackson stood up and walked Mona to the door. He placed a kiss on his son's cheek. "I love you, son."

Turning to Carol, he said, "Thank you for coming."

Carol smothered a sob. "I w-wouldn't be anywhere else."

He watched them until they disappeared down the long sterile corridor. He returned to the dimly lit hospital room.

Jackson remained by her bedside all night. He smoothed hair from her face. How pale she was! It was truly a miracle she had survived. She had lost so much blood.

When Brandeis awakened, the room was in a shadow. She could see it was daylight, for the streaks of light from the blinds hung on the ceiling. Weak as they were, they stabbed at her brain like knives.

"J-Jack—" Her voice sounded as if coming from a distance.

"Shhh, don't try to speak."

"J-Jack . . ."

"Shhh, sleep. You mustn't tire yourself out. Brian and I want you to get well. Your mother is here, too. We're all here, baby."

Just then a tall, slim man came in and greeted him. He was a bespectacled young man in his mid-thirties. He was the doctor that Jackson had talked to last night. After studying her medical chart, he approached the bed.

"Mrs. Gray, I'm Dr. Williams. I'm the surgical resident taking care of you this morning. You're in Waycross Memorial Hospital. Do you know why you're here? Do you remember what happened to you?"

Brandeis tried to shake her head, but immediately his hand reached to restrain her.

"No, Mrs. Gray. Don't try to move your head. Blink once for yes and twice for no. Can you hear me all right?"

Brandeis blinked.

"You had an automobile accident, Mrs. Gray. Do you remember?"

She blinked.

"That was twenty-eight hours ago," The doctor said. "Since then you've had some surgery to stop the internal bleeding. That explains the pain in your stomach. You have a special mask over your face to help us with your facial cuts and abrasions. Are you understanding me so far?"

Her eyelids fluttered closed, then opened with an effort.

"Your left leg is in a special brace, which will allow us to keep it immobile until we can perform some orthopedic surgery to correct your fractures. The most important thing for now is that we've got to keep you absolutely still. It's very, very important. Do you understand?"

Brandeis blinked.

As soon as the doctor left, Jackson was immediately by her side. He covered her hand with tiny kisses. "Carol and James will be here this afternoon. You must rest now."

"I-I hurt," she said between dry lips. "M-Martin . . ."

"He won't ever bother us again."

She settled down once again in a deep sleep.

All afternoon, Carol, James, Mona, and Jackson took turns sitting with her, talking to her. She would whimper every now and then, nothing more.

That evening, as Jackson was sitting with her, her eyes suddenly opened, and she looked as if she was trying to say something. He leaned closer to her.

"Yes, honey. What is it?"

"I-I I-love . . . you," she whispered.

Before he could respond, she had closed her eyes. The blackness returned like a balm. It seemed to understand her despair and beckoned her. She heard the taunting voice of Martin, telling her the world was a place she would be happy to leave. They could finally be happy. Be a family for eternity.

Jackson suddenly heard the drawn out humming on the heart monitor. She was gone!

"Noooo!" He screamed. *"You can't leave me!"*

Epilogue

Jackson stood by the gate as Mona departed from the plane. As soon as he spotted her he threw his hand up and waved to get her attention.

"Hi, Mom. It's good to see you. I've missed you dearly."

"I've missed you, too, Jackson. It's been hard these last few months . . . on all of us."

He was thoughtful for a few moments. A flicker of pain flashed in his eyes. "Yes, it has. But I'm glad you're here."

"Me, too."

Jackson led her through the airport in Washington, D.C., to the baggage claim area. They waited patiently for twenty minutes before they found all of her luggage.

They left Washington and headed for Arlington, Virginia. Mona looked around at the beautiful Georgian and colonial homes along the route. The scenery was picturesque.

They finally pulled up to a beautiful two-story colonial house. Red brick with white shutters.

"Oh, Jackson. This house is absolutely gorgeous! Those pictures you sent don't do it justice."

Jackson smiled. "I'm glad you like it. Come on, I'll show

you the inside. You're not going to believe how big Brian's gotten.''

"Oh, I miss him so much. I can't wait to see my grand-baby." Mona stopped Jackson as he was unloading the car, a silver Mercedes Benz. "I miss Bran so much, Jackson."

Jackson smiled and patted her hand. "I know."

They headed upstairs, to the room where Mona would be staying during her visit. He placed the luggage over in a corner and motioned for Mona to follow. They headed down the hallway to another bedroom.

Mona could tell from the decor that it was her grand-son's room. She grinned and rubbed her hands together. Jackson, leading the way, walked up to the door and peeked in. Looking back at Mona, he smiled.

Brandeis sat on the floor of her son's bedroom with her long shapely legs crossed. Brian played nearby as she went through book after book after book of wallpaper designs and accessories. "Oh, Brian, I'm not good at this decorating stuff! I wish Mom was here."

She never heard Jackson come up the stairs with a trailing Mona. They had arrived just in time to hear her comment. Jackson looked at Mona and smiled. He walked into the room.

"Hello, sweetheart. How was your day?" Jackson walked over and sat down beside her. Leaning over, he kissed her on the cheek.

She was irritable and looking for someone to take it out on. "Frustrating! And yours?"

"I've had an interesting day. I had to go out to the airport and I ran into someone . . ."

Brandeis glanced up at her husband impatiently. "Well, are you going to tell me who you ran into?"

"Testy aren't we?"

She was immediately ashamed of herself. "I'm sorry. It's just that I would like to have some idea how to make this beautiful house more beautiful, and I haven't a clue. Mom's good at stuff like this. Not me." She sighed loudly. "I wish she were here. Now who did you run into at the airport?'' Brandeis frowned. ''What were you doing at the airport anyway?''

''I went to the airport to pick up someone.''

''Okay, who?''

''Your mother.''

Brandeis pushed an errant curl out of her face. ''Jackson! Stop teasing me like this. You know how much I really miss her and—''

''You shouldn't fuss so, dear.'' Mona said as she eased into the room. ''You sound like a shrew.''

''Mom!'' Brandeis eased up, with Jackson's assistance and walked over to her mother, hugging her tight. ''I've missed you so much. How long are you going to stay? Can you please help me decorate?''

Jackson laughed. ''Slow down, honey. Your mother's going to be here for three weeks. I called her a couple of weeks ago and told her how upset and frustrated you were over decorating a five-bedroom house. She's going to help you and I'm paying her.''

''I told him that he didn't have to worry about paying me.'' Mona picked up Brian, who was fascinated with her gold earrings. His tiny fingers wrapped around the square and pulled. It slid off easily.

''No, Mom. Jackson's right. You should get paid for taking the time off to help us. I know sewing is how you make a living. Thanks so much for coming. I've got so much to tell you. As a matter of fact, I called you this morning to tell you my news. I wondered where you were.''

''What's your news, dear?'' She looked from Brandeis to Jackson.

Jackson looked as puzzled as she. He shrugged and said, ''I don't have any idea what she's talking about.''

''He's right, Mom. He doesn't know either. I found out right after he left home. I was so excited, I wanted to tell someone. Since neither of you could be found, I just told Brian.'' She couldn't keep the grin off her face.

''Honey, will you let us in on your little secret.'' Jackson was curious. Suddenly, he laughed and hugged her. "You got accepted, didn't you?"

Brandeis laughed. "Yes, I was accepted into Howard's Law School. I can start next fall."

Mona clapped her hands. "Oh, dear, that's wonderful news! I'm so happy for you. I know you're going to be one the best lawyers in Washington."

Jackson bent his head and kissed her deeply. "Congratulations, baby."

Brandeis looked at her mother and her husband, tears gleaming in her eyes. "I couldn't have made it without the two of you. I want you both to know how much I love you and appreciate what you've done for me. The rape, the car accident that almost killed me. Most people are not fortunate enough to have wonderful family members or friends such as yourselves in their lives. That's why I've decided to volunteer two days a week at a rape crisis center, to help others."

Mona smiled and gave her a thumbs up. "I think that's a wonderful way for you to provide closure to your pain. I'm very proud of you."

Jackson kissed his wife again. "I'm very proud of you, too."

Brandeis and Jackson left Mona and Brian upstairs, napping. They walked hand in hand, down the stairs. Jackson walked slowly as Brandeis walked with a slight limp.

During the first twelve weeks after her accident, she'd remained bedridden. The cast immobilizing her left side had been cut away after the twelfth week. Her rehabilitation had been slow and painful. Even so, her left leg was so badly injured from the crash that she would have a permanent limp. Brandeis had remained positive and cooperative with the doctors, nurses, and physical therapists.

After Jackson had her settled onto the plush sofa, he brought her a glass of wine. He stretched his lean body down the length of the chair, laying his head in her lap. He looked up at her and smiled.

Brandeis bent her head down, kissing him on the forehead. "Thank you so much, Jackson. You've been so good to me."

"You deserve it, baby. You've been through so much . . ."

She put a finger to his lips. "Look ahead, not back. That's what Mom used to tell me all the time. I admit, sometimes it is hard for me to do that. My life has changed so much because of Martin. Sometimes, when I look in the mirror and see the permanent scar on my forehead, when I look down at my leg and know that I'll never be able to wear high heels again, I feel so ugly and I hate him so damn much. But then, I look at you and see the love and adoration in your eyes. You make me feel beautiful. I realize that it could've been so much worse. I could have lost my entire leg or my life. As for my face, I think I look pretty good with bangs."

Jackson sat up and turned to face her. Putting her chin in his hands, he said, "You're beautiful with bangs and you still have exquisite legs. What's important is that we have each other, Bran. Throughout every pitfall, our love survived. That's all that matters. The physical attributes you possess are only window dressings. I married the person you are on the inside."

"I feel bad for Carrie," Brandeis said softly. "She really loved Martin. Now she has to deal with all the pain and humiliation Martin brought into her life, and raise her baby alone. That time she spent with me after Mom brought me home from the hospital . . . Well, she looked so heartbroken and sad. But she's very determined to have her baby and raise it by herself."

Brandeis ran her fingers across Jackson's chest. "I regret the way I used to treat her. I thought she was nothing but trouble. Carrie's not that way at all. Deep down, Carrie's a very sweet and loving person. Being the middle child in a family of nine was hard for her. She always felt left out. She says that was why she turned to men for attention. She just wants someone to love her. I really misjudged her."

"Don't be so hard on yourself, Bran," Jackson said. "I

think what Carrie's been through has changed her for the better. I believe Carrie is a very strong woman. She'll survive."

"I hope so, Jackson. Right now, she's saying she'll never trust another man. She's been hurt too many times."

"She just hasn't met the right man," Jackson said. "But she will."

"How can you be so sure?" Brandeis asked.

"It happened to us, didn't it? Mark my words, sweetheart, Carrie *will* find her knight in shining armor. Just wait and see."

Brandeis and Jackson spent time discussing the classes she should take during her first semester in law school, and how she would handle her studies and still be a wife and mother. Eventually, Brandeis drifted off to sleep. Smiling, Jackson left her on the sofa, sleeping. He went into the kitchen and prepared dinner.

An hour later, Jackson announced that dinner was ready.

At the dining table, Brandeis put her hand over her mother's. "Thank you so much for coming, Mom."

"It's a pleasure, dear. I think this is such a beautiful house. We are going to have so much fun decorating it."

"Yeah, right!" Brandeis wrinkled her nose at her mother.

From his high chair, Brian imitated his mother.

Jackson threw back his head and roared with laughter. "Mom, some things just never change, do they?"

AUTHOR'S NOTE

Acquaintance rape is commonly called date rape. Date rape is a misleading term which describes a serious crime that is misunderstood and underreported.

Rape is a violent act of aggression. It is one person overpowering and controlling another. It is horribly traumatic. Just because it happens on a date doesn't make it any less terrifying. In fact, a date rape may be even more terrifying because the rapist is someone the victim trusted, chose to be with, cared about, or even loved.

Date or acquaintance rape accounts for 60 to 80 percent of all reported rapes. But the true numbers are much higher than we know, since these victims are the least likely to report the crime to the police. They often feel a sense of responsibly for the attack.

Any victim of rape has a hard time with trust following an assault, but for the victim of date rape, this can be especially difficult. Dating after an assault requires courage, and it usually takes at least some recovery before a victim will even consider dating again.

Although it will take time, the victim's feelings of comfort, safety, and trust will return. Gentle encouragement from family and friends not only will help her to date again, but also will enable her to resume other normal activities.

If you are raped, report the crime to the police. Many victims delay for days or even weeks before reporting the attack. This makes it difficult to catch and successfully prosecute the offender. After reporting the crime to your local police, contact a rape crisis center.

Nationwide Sexual Violence Hotline:
call 1-800-656-HOPE

ABOUT THE AUTHOR

Jacquelin Thomas, a native of Brunswick, Georgia, now lives in Southern California with her family. She is currently at work on her next project. This is her first Arabesque romance.

COMING IN JULY . . .

HEAVEN SENT (0-7860-0530-0, $4.99/$6.50)
by Rochelle Alers
When Serena Morris-Vega returned to Costa Rica, corporate CEO David Cole showed up on the Vega estate, close to death. Serena soon discovers secrets about his true identity. David's gratitude towards Serena for saving his life turns into an all-consuming passion, and Serena finds him to be a dangerously seductive challenge.

LYRICS OF LOVE (0-7860-0531-9, $4.99/$6.50)
by Francine Craft
Gina Campbell was a famous singer married to police officer Joe Dauterive. When her brother turns up dead and Joe's name was ruined by the scandal, he asked for a divorce. Gina runs off to Lyric, her Pacific island hideaway . . . and when Joe followed her, he was set on rekindling their love and determined that nothing would keep them apart.

HEART'S DESIRE (0-7860-0532-7, $4.99/$6.50)
by Monica Jackson
Kara Kincaid has discovered that Senator Eastman is her father and that he abandoned her and her mother years ago to pursue his political ambitions. Now she wants revenge. Using everything in her power to get to the senator, she targets his right hand man, Brent Stevens. Their attraction to each other is sure to make a mess of her plans. It is not long before her scheme leads them both into a dangerous game and an uncontrollable passion.

EVERLASTING LOVE (0-7860-0533-5, $4.99/$6.50)
by Kayla Perrin
Two years ago, Whitney Jordan ran away from her husband, Javar, when a freak accident took the life of her small stepson. Guilt-ridden, she was returning to end the marriage when another accident leaves her in the hospital. When she finds Javar at her side they rekindle their love. Together, they fight to save their marriage . . . and Whitney's life from danger.

LOOK FOR THESE ARABESQUE ROMANCES

ENJOY THESE ARABESQUE FAVORITES!

FOREVER AFTER   (0-7860-0211-5, $4.99)
by Bette Ford

BODY AND SOUL   (0-7860-0160-7, $4.99)
by Felicia Mason

BETWEEN THE LINES   (0-7860-0267-0, $4.99)
by Angela Benson